# ADDISON

*By Leon Hale*

ADDISON
BONNEY'S PLACE
TURN SOUTH AT THE SECOND BRIDGE

# ADDISON

By Leon Hale

DOUBLEDAY & COMPANY, INC.
GARDEN CITY, NEW YORK
1979

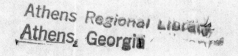

Library of Congress Cataloging in Publication Data
Hale, Leon.
Addison.
I. Title.
PZ4.H1635Ad [PS3558.A357] 813'.5'4
ISBN: 0-385-12911-4
Library of Congress Catalog Card Number 77–14892

Chapter 44 was published in *Vision* Magazine,
Dallas, Texas, November, 1978.

For Ellen Belle

# ADDISON

# ONE

EVERY DAY, he wrote a letter to Sarah.

He had a cheap writing kit with a cardboard flap and a brown lace to tie it down. When the sun got low he would take the kit and go outside and sit on the ground and put his back against the tent-shack, and write to Sarah.

The others would go out to be with him while he wrote. The three of them would sit together a little way apart from him, and try not to watch. They would talk among themselves, low, about birds and airplanes passing over, about the long shadows on the flat land, about the colors in the sunset.

But they weren't so interested in birds or planes or shadows or sunsets. They were interested in what he was saying in the letter, and wanted to be near when it was being said.

Because he might read them a sentence of what he wrote. He'd turn toward them grinning and say, "Hey, listen to this. How about this?" Then he'd feed them a funny line out of the letter, or maybe a thing he'd said about one of *them*. That's what they hoped for the most, that he'd tell Sarah something about them.

They didn't sit close to him because at letter-writing time, he was with Sarah so much. It was like he and Sarah were alone, and it was a personal and private time. If they sat close they could see the picture he was using, and it might be the one of Sarah naked from the waist up. That would be an embarrassment, to be caught staring at Sarah naked from the waist up.

Almost every week she sent him a new picture, a snapshot. He would choose one at letter-writing time and clip it to the writing pad and look at it while he wrote. The day she sent the bare-breasted picture he had shown it to them, quick, and just that once. He couldn't stand not to show it. He was too proud of her.

"All right, Troop." He called them Troop that way. "All right," waving the snapshot, "once and only once, for only five seconds, I'm gonna let you see what a real woman looks like. Just call it a part of your education." Then he turned the picture around and the heads of the three came together, jaw to jaw, because the picture was small and they had to crowd close to see. And so for those brief moments they feasted in wonder on Sarah naked from the waist up.

They had seen many pictures of Sarah, of her pretty face framed in gentle curls. Here in this photo was the soft sweetness in her eyes they had learned to look for, the same impressive dignity in the way she held her neck and shoulders.

Yet the snapshot stunned them. This was the most intimate photo they'd ever seen, because it was Sarah. All the nudity and sex they'd studied in porno magazines suddenly became cheap and uninteresting against the image of that sweet face smiling above the perfect breasts, in the picture of Sarah naked from the waist up.

And so at letter-writing time they kept apart from him, and thought of the picture, and took secret glances at his face. They learned to watch for the time that he'd depart.

His buttocks would scoot forward in the dirt and his shoulders would slide down the wall of the tent-shack a little way and his writing kit would fall forgotten on his stomach. The slight smile would come on his face. He'd stay that way for five minutes sometimes, gazing over the low-growing brush and cactus. He was gone, gone to be with Sarah, while the others sat and waited for him.

All four of them loved her. The younger ones—McKavett, Trinidad, and Booker—had never seen her except in pictures.

Then Addison. He was married to her.

# TWO

THEY WOULD GO into town at least once a week, seventeen miles on the bus, and almost always together. Addison was thirty then. When he was with the others he seemed much older.

Because The Troop looked even younger than they were. Booker was twenty-two, and Trinidad ten months older. McKavett was twenty-four but looked no older than the others and in most ways was less mature.

Then Addison was naturally a man who seemed older than he was. "I was born looking old," he'd say, "without any hair or teeth."

Something about the set of his eyes, and the loose skin around them, gave him the look of age. So often he kept a little combination frown and grin going, and it did curious things to the flesh at the outer corners of those hazel eyes. It produced a pattern of wrinkles that slanted at a forty-five-degree angle. If the wrinkle lines had extended they would have intersected high on his forehead, where his hair had been retreating since he was twenty-five. Even a few little children have these slanted wrinkles at their eye corners, and it makes their faces seem so mature.

Addison was a big man. Six-two, and strong. But he didn't look strong in the same way a weight lifter does. He didn't have the wide shoulders or the big biceps on the bull neck or the narrow hips. In fact, his butt was a little too broad to fit his shoulders. So his size wasn't impressive. He couldn't walk into a place, the way some large men can, and get immediate respect by being big.

He was dangerous, though. He could fight. He learned to box when he was eighteen, and he was good. Look what he did to that pipeliner in town, at The Puma. Trinidad and McKavett and Booker had lived with him in the tent-shack

3

a month when that happened. Until that night they hadn't suspected that Addison knew how to throw a punch. The pipeliner didn't suspect it either.

Because Addison seemed too agreeable to be a fighter, too congenial and obliging. He had a great interest in almost everything. He often walked with his head thrust a little way forward, as if what he was approaching was of special significance to him, as if he enjoyed seeing it and wanted to know more about it.

The night Booker moved into the tent-shack—he was the last of the four to come—he was sick. In town, waiting for the bus to bring him out, he had sat in a Mexican restaurant and drunk too much beer and then punished his insides with a great bait of enchiladas. When he walked in the tent-shack, his face was the color of a celery stalk.

In a few minutes he was back outside, spraying his dinner over the Great Southwest, and Addison crawled out of his blankets to help him. Held his head. Put wet towels to his throat. Told him he wasn't going to die. Told him there was a law in Texas against a man dying on Wednesday night. Finally got him back in his bunk.

The next morning when Addison was in the showers, Booker raised up on an elbow and rubbed his head carefully and asked McKavett, "Who is that old guy?"

"He ain't so old," McKavett said. "His name's Addison."

# THREE

AFTER BOOKER CAME, people in town began noticing the four of them together.

You can set two small young men following along behind an older and a bigger one and they won't draw much notice. But add a third small one and you have a group, a parade.

McKavett was five-seven, or so he claimed. Trinidad and Booker stair-stepped down from there. Booker's head barely topped Addison's shoulder.

4

Another thing that caused them to produce such a procession, they quickly got in the habit of walking about half a step behind Addison when they'd go about together. In the beginning it was a matter of trying to keep up with Addison's great stride. He refused to slow down for them or shorten his step, and they were forever hustling to keep up.

But being a short way behind had its reward. They didn't get flailed with his arms, when they stayed back. He was always talking to them, explaining, lecturing, telling benevolent lies, pointing out, waving, gesturing. So walking half a step back was better for them.

The first time they went to town after Booker came they went into The Puma for a beer. Jackson, the fat fellow who worked there, stood with his arms spread on the bar and studied them. They took stools four in a row, descending in height from Addison to McKavett to Trinidad to Booker.

"Give us four cold drafts, Mr. Jackson," Addison announced, "and all the news that's fit to tell."

Jackson looked down the line. "Well, by god, are they all yours?"

Addison laughed his great laugh. "Sure they are. They're not much, Mildred, but they're all mine. Of course now every one's got a different mother. This dark one here in the middle, his mama is a Comanche squaw, and the daughter of a great chief. If Trinidad ever gets what's rightfully his he'll inherit everything in Texas that's west of San Antonio. So you better serve him first, Mr. Jackson, and call him sir."

"Yeah, yeah." Jackson had heard Addison's speeches before.

But not Booker. He turned to Trinidad. "Who is your mother, anyhow?"

"Aw, don't pay any attention to all that crap," Trinidad said, grinning. "He's just talking."

Jackson was setting out the beer. "This last one down here," when he got to Booker, "don't look old enough to drink beer to me. But I'll serve him anyway, seeing he's with his daddy and all."

5

"Not old enough!" Addison roared. "Listen here, less than a week ago that little sawed-off fart downed a dozen cold ones and ate two orders of enchiladas at Lupe's, and lived to remember it."

Jackson almost grinned.

"Tell you something else about that kid," Addison said. "He hadn't been in this town two hours till he went over to The Shacks and made old Ella holler. Twice, what I hear. The reason he didn't grow any taller is, he went all to tool."

Jackson stared sleepy-eyed at the street. "Well, if he did make her holler he musta slipped up behind and poked her with a baseball bat."

Booker whispered to Trinidad, "Who's Ella?"

"Old redhead that runs a whorehouse. Call it The Shacks, the other side of town. She's got four-five gals over there."

"Well, I never have been there," Booker said. "What's Addison want to say all that for?"

Trinidad's Latin shrug. "He bullshits a lot. It's a kind of hobby with him."

"What's that Ella look like?" Booker asked.

Trinidad grinned and looked up the bar. "Hey, Add? Booker here wants to know what old Ella looks like."

"Well, she looks about like that bus we rode to town on," he said, "but she's got a lot more mileage on her."

# FOUR

ADDISON DIDN'T BULLSHIT, though, when he talked about Sarah.

Sometimes he'd get to missing her so bad the pain showed in his face. The nights they didn't go into town they liked to walk with him up to The Beer Garden at the front gate. The Bear, in his great benevolence, provided The Beer Garden. The men could spend their money there, and sing their songs and tell their jokes and swap their lies without going into town to get into fights with the pipeliners or bring back

6

gonorrhea from The Shacks. Addison wasn't really a drinker, and he would sit an hour or more sipping one beer, and if he didn't talk, they could tell—the misery of missing Sarah was on him. And he would rise up suddenly and go to the phone booths and call her, in violation of their rules.

Sarah was with her folks in Chicago, and she and Addison had a telephone rule—they talked only once a week. They had to limit the calls or go into bankruptcy from trying to make love by long distance. Addison broke the rule often. "But I don't do it except just when I can't help it."

After one of those calls he'd come back to the tent-shack humming and whistling and crawl in his bunk and The Troop would wait in silence.

Then he'd tell them.

"She had on her short nightgown, the peach-colored one with blue strings that tie at the top. But it leaves an opening, a kind of gap. It's my favorite gown. She had it on and she didn't even know I was gonna call . . ."

She would dress for him, in that silly-sweet way that people in love will do things. She was up there in Chicago and Addison was way the hell down in Texas with the coyotes and the tarantulas and the cactus, and if she knew he was going to call she'd have her hair done and her face all dolled up and be wearing something special, for the call. Just like he was going to walk in.

Because he would want to know exactly how she looked, so he could see her. He'd ask what she was wearing, or wasn't wearing. He'd want to know how she had herself positioned, and where. Was she sitting? Lying? On the bed? On the sofa? Were her legs crossed? Well, if they were, would she uncross them? Would she lie back, on the pillows? And lift one of her legs, the right one, just a little? Baby, baby . . .

It helped Addison's aching to come back to the tent-shack and tell them about it. And they became caught up in it almost the same as Addison was. How they did hunger to hear about Sarah.

7

". . . she was on the bed, and her gown was up over her knees. She's got the damnedest skin on her legs, on her thighs. So smooth. I put my hand there and . . ."

McKavett's head came up. "Really?"

An explosion from Trinidad. "OhgoddamnitMacyoudumb-asshutupandlisten!"

Then afterward, when he'd told them all he was going to tell, and they'd gotten quiet, and McKavett's swishing snore issued from his pillow, Trinidad spoke softly in the darkness.

"Addison?"

"Yeah?"

"I was just wondering . . . about her gown? Did she have anything . . . I mean was there anything else . . . you know . . . underneath?"

Addison took a great breath, and let it out slow.

"No, nothing underneath. Not a thing."

# FIVE

ADDISON HAD NO FEELING of wrongdoing about sharing Sarah with the others that way. Wasn't it harmless? It helped him survive without her, cut away some of the pain of not being with her, for them to know about her and be interested in her and to understand how it was to make love to her.

When a guy's in love, doesn't he want everybody on the planet to know about it? He wants them to envy him, that's it. Wants them to think, You lucky bastard, having a woman like that stuck on you, the kind of woman men everywhere will stop to watch when she walks down the street.

Writing Sarah about the Troop, he didn't tell her everything. He didn't tell her about showing them the picture of her naked from the waist up. But it didn't bother him that he had shown it.

It might have, if it had occurred to him that one day The Troop might meet Sarah, get to know her personally and not just through the letters and photographs. He didn't imagine that they ever would. Sarah would never see Spanish Wells, Texas. A few of the men had tried bringing their wives in, but it almost never worked. There was no decent place for them to stay, in town. The reason it didn't work, a guy would have to stay out there in the prickly pear and sleep in a tent while his warm young wife was seventeen miles away in some dreary rented room . . . and the streets of Spanish Wells were working alive with lonely, horny men far from their homes and their women. It just wasn't a situation a man wanted to put a warm young wife in.

So it didn't really matter what Addison told The Troop about Sarah, wasn't that right? She would never meet them and he wouldn't know them long himself. He had moved around the world a few years, and had learned about people like Booker and McKavett and Trinidad. He'd be suddenly thrown in with such guys, in some strange and lonely place, and they'd all grow so close, and it would happen quick, too, because they needed one another to endure.

Then one morning somebody would sit down at a desk and type off a flock of words and good-bye, he'd be gone, shipped out, to wherever the words said, and he'd never again see the people he was so close to and who were so important to him for that brief time.

Of course brief times, depending on the circumstances, can seem everlasting. Being seventeen miles south of Spanish Wells, Texas, and Sarah in Chicago was a circumstance that was creating fourteen-day weeks and sixty-day months for Addison. And he was facing a long, long summer. Soon after he arrived he had found out from Katherine that he was certain to be there a year.

Bowlegged, gum-chewing Katherine, the secretary who sat just outside The Bear's Nest in the headquarters building. She knew things that the men couldn't find out. "You'll be here a year," she said, "so just relax and enjoy it. Almost everybody stays a year. They don't keep anybody out here much longer than that, though."

9

After Booker came, in the tent-shack one night Addison told him about the year and quoted the source of his information, and McKavett said:

"Hey, Add, did you ask old Katherine if she's had any lately?"

"Come on, Mac," Trinidad said, "Addison's not gonna fool around with that stuff."

McKavett shrugged. "I didn't say he was. It wouldn't hurt to ask her if she'd had any lately."

"Just a friendly question, eh Mac?" Addison laughed.

"Will that Katherine screw?" Booker asked.

"They'll *all* screw," McKavett said.

"Listen to Great Lover," Trinidad said, and kicked the screen door open to spit outside.

"I'd say . . ." He paused, which was his signal that he was about to issue a Statement. When they got the signal The Troop always turned to him and listened. "I'd have to say it's just not so that they'll all screw because all of 'em won't. Some of 'em save it at least till they're in love. Some save it till they get married. Some save it till they see they're not *gonna* get married. And some save it all their lives, and take it with 'em to the cemetery and bury it."

They sat hushed and still, while they considered the Statement, just as if it had been read to them out of some great book of wisdom and truth and could not be questioned.

Then McKavett muttered, almost too low for them to hear, "Anyhow, I bet you that Katherine's not one of 'em savin' it to bury in no graveyard."

Which got a grin out of Addison. He said, "I expect you're right, Mac. Judging from the signs I've seen, and unless I'm just getting old and dirty-minded, I'd guess that Katherine is taking her britches off for The Bear Himself, with his wife in LA so much and all."

He went out to do his letter-writing. McKavett followed close behind, ahead of the others. "Did you get a letter today from Sarah?"

"You bet, sure did."
"What'd she say?"
"Said tell you hello."
"Really?"
"Yeah, really."
"I'll be damn."

# SIX

SO IT WAS McKavett that began the exchange of greetings
and notes between Sarah and The Troop.

Addison had finished his letter, and Booker and Trinidad
had gone to see a movie they had already seen twice.
McKavett was watching Addison put his letter in the envelope. He pretended to be using the last of the day's light to
read a grimy paperback. He'd been reading on that little
book a month.

"Add?" Trying to sound casual. "You happen to have any
room left in that envelope, maybe you could put this in." He
held out a sheet of stationery with a few scribbled lines on
it. "It's for Sarah. From me."

"Oh? Well, OK, sure. Let's have it."

"You better read it first. See if it's all right."

"I don't need to read it."

But McKavett insisted. "Be better."

So Addison read what McKavett had written: "Dear Sara,
how are you, fine I hope. How is that Chicago weather. Its
hot here in the day and cool at night. I sleep across from
Addison. Well I must close. Yours truely, Melvin S. McKavett."

Addison nodded. "She'll like that."

A little embarrassed, McKavett walked away toward the
latrine in that sloppy, foot-dragging way he traveled. Addison stood and watched him go. McKavett always looked
like he needed repair and maintenance. By a barber. Or a
tailor. Or a tough DI who'd make him stand straight and

quit dragging his feet and pull up his pants and put his shirttail in.

The note to Sarah surprised Addison. He'd never seen McKavett write a letter. Well, for that matter he'd never seen the others write one either. Trinidad talked about hearing from home. Booker spoke of a girl in Pennsylvania, so evidently he wrote to her. But so far as Addison knew, McKavett didn't write to anybody.

He hadn't really learned much about The Troop. He had used them mainly for selfish purposes, wasn't that so? Used them to help fight the misery of being separated from Sarah.

He entertained himself with them—making up those ridiculous tales about Trinidad's mother being the daughter of a famous Indian chief . . . about Booker being that same famous Cannonball Booker of the University of Pennsylvania, who at age nineteen and standing five feet and four inches tall and weighing one hundred and forty-five pounds bulled his way through the Alabama line for two hundred yards and three touchdowns that time in the Sugar Bowl . . . and then over here on your left we've got Melvin Sims McKavett that his daddy owns so much land in Georgia—god oh mighty General Lee!—he's got title to all of Crocker County and won't recognize the Emancipation Proclamation and owns ninety-seven slaves, not counting young ones under three feet tall . . .

Addison enjoyed the diversion of that, and The Troop learned to love the attention he paid them in this way. But he didn't really know anything about them. McKavett was coming back from the latrine now, his scrawny frame silhouetted in the dusk by the latrine light. What an improbable circumstance, Addison thought, that this skinny, spindle-assed kid from Georgia would be here with him in this place, writing a childish how-are-you-fine-I-hope letter to Sarah. God but he's a homely little bastard. Buck-toothed. Eyes too close-set. One shoulder higher than the other. Corn-shuck hair. Angry red skin. Well, what the hell, weren't the others homely as well? Just ugly as Sunday sins.

Trinidad with his pockmarks and scarred face and clipped ear. Booker with those deep-sunken eyes and the Frankenstein monster brows and that strange protruding lower jaw that seemed to wobble at times on loose hinges. He almost laughed aloud, adding up their looks that way.

Before he sealed Sarah's envelope he added a couple of lines and suggested she answer McKavett's note separately. He told her, "It might mean a lot to him."

## SEVEN

SATURDAY NIGHT IN TOWN. They went to Lupe's for Mexican food and ended up at The Puma, drinking beer and watching the girls. Practically all the unattached girls in Spanish Wells, and they didn't amount to a large flock, showed up Friday and Saturday nights at The Puma to dance. Addison led them to a table in the back and sat there with that little inquisitive grin. Just like he was seeing everything for the first time, and liking it fine, and needing to ask a few friendly questions. The Troop was about to learn something about Addison that they didn't imagine could be so.

"Add?" Booker, leaning across the table and talking low. "You suppose any of these old gals in here are whores?"

"Shoot fire no," Addison said brightly. "All the whores in Spanish Wells are over at The Shacks, busy as ants. They wouldn't waste any time sitting around here on a Saturday night when the whole damn world's horny. I've seen old Ella in here, but not on Saturday night."

"Hey, Mac," Trinidad said, grinning sort of crooked. He was into his second beer already. When he drank, Trinidad tended to become brash. He'd drink three or four beers and suddenly he was bold, pushy. "You see that black-headed girl with that big old boy in the white shirt? He's not dancing with her. Why don't you go ask her to dance?"

"What are you talkin' about? I can't dance."

"She looks pretty good from here," Trinidad said.

"You so interested in her," McKavett said, "why don't *you* go ask her to dance?"

"All right, by god I will." And he did, as soon as he drained his beer bottle. They watched him go to the table, have a brief exchange with the girl. He returned, shrugging. "She says the music's too fast."

Booker brought up one of his guttural laughs, a kind of grunt-laugh. "I don't think that old boy was too pleased, you asking her to dance."

Addison had noticed that too. The guy may be a Mexican hater. "Expect it'd be a good idea, when you want to dance with a gal in here and she's with a guy, to ask the guy first."

But Trinidad was charging away, chesty and bold. "Hell, it's the *girl* I want to *dance* with." He ordered another beer. "I'm gonna ask her again, when I get a slower song."

"OK, do it your own way then," Addison said, still pleasant and smiling. When the fellow in the white shirt got up to use the phone, Addison studied his walk. Pretty good-sized fellow. About as tall as Addison and heavier. A pipeliner, probably.

Before White Shirt returned, Trinidad went again to the girl's table. The others could see her shake her head, but Trinidad didn't leave. He sat down to talk to her and he was still sitting there when White Shirt returned. He tapped Trinidad on the shoulder and jerked a thumb. Get going, the thumb said.

White Shirt walked back with Trinidad and asked Addison, "Is this kid here your friend?"

"Why yes, he sure is," Addison said, so bright and pleasant. "His name's Trinidad, and this is McKavett here, and Booker, and my name's Addison, and it's good to meet you. Could we get your name?"

"My name's Bates, but this kid here is beginning to get on my nerves. Is he drunk or something?"

"I don't think so. Are you drunk, Trinidad?"

"No." He wasn't too chesty now, either.

Addison kept his pleasant face. "Mr. Bates, if Trinidad has bothered you, why, he may want to beg your pardon. How about it, Trinidad, would you beg Mr. Bates' pardon?"

"OK. I didn't mean anything. Just wanted to dance."

"Well, just keep him away from my table," Bates said. "I don't know why he's in here anyhow. Ain't no Mexican girls in here for him."

Addison's little smile faded a bit. "Mr. Bates, Trinidad dances with any girl that wants to dance with him. Whites. Blacks. I've seen him dance with yellow ones. Red ones. Brown ones." Which wasn't true, but in tense situations Addison sometimes got creative that way.

Bates kept boring in. "I don't want any pock-faced greaser messing around my table."

Which almost finished off Addison's grin. "Now Mr. Bates, that's sure not very nice. I doubt you really meant to say that. Would you like to tell Trinidad that you didn't mean to say it?"

"No. I damn sure wouldn't."

Addison nodded. "Well then, just to keep us from having trouble, I'll apologize for you." He turned to Trinidad. "Mr. Bates wants to say he's sorry for what he said. Do you accept?"

Trinidad twisted in his seat but didn't say anything.

Addison looked back to Bates. "He accepts."

Bates seemed close to taking a swing at Addison. Instead he stuck his jaw out and said, "Listen, you stay away from me."

Addison's grin was back now, bright as ever. "Why, I don't remember ever seeking out your company, Mr. Bates. Seems to me like you came over here seeking out mine."

Bates evidently had trouble deciding what to do. Finally he turned away and went back to his table.

"You guys ready to get out of here?" Booker suggested.

"All right with me," McKavett said.

And Trinidad nodded agreement.

But not Addison. "Wait awhile. I'm gonna get me a beer.

15

This one's got hot on me." Beers were always getting hot on him, and left half consumed. He couldn't get the waitress' attention so he got up and went to the bar. Trinidad went to the restroom. Bates went in there behind him. And came out before Trinidad did.

"You reckon anything's happened to him?" McKavett asked when Addison came back.

"We'll sure see." Addison went in the restroom to find Trinidad mopping at the front of his clothes with a handkerchief, and holding his throat with his other hand.

"Son of a bitch peed on me," he said.

"Bates did?"

"Pinned me in the corner and hauled out and peed all over my pants."

Addison didn't ask anything more. He helped Trinidad clean up the best they could. Before they went out he fished a mop bucket from under the washbasin and ran about half a gallon of water in it. And carried it out.

"You guys wait here," he told The Troop, and walked over and stood grinning by Bates' table.

"What's that?" Bates asked, looking at the bucket. He stood up slowly.

"It's a bucket with three or four secondhand beers in it," Addison told him, and dashed the water on Bates' shirt just above his belt. It wet him pretty well, from the waist to the knees.

"Oh-oh! Shoot fire!" Addison exclaimed. "My hand slipped, Mr. Bates. Seems like my aim's not too good, same as yours in the crapper while ago."

Getting wet down with what he thought was urine put Bates into a shivering rage. "All right, you son of a bitch, you get outside unless you want me to whip your ass in here."

"I don't like to fight, Mr. Bates."

"Get on out there." Bates shoved Addison toward the front, and so he went on, protesting all the way that he didn't want to fight. The Puma's customers streamed into the parking lot to watch.

16

It was really an odd kind of fight. Bates started to throw a punch and Addison said, "Wait a minute! Wait a minute now!" And fished his sun glasses out of his shirt pocket and tossed them to Booker. Bates moved in again and Addison backed off a step. "Hold it! Hold it! Hold it!" And peeled his wristwatch and flipped it to Trinidad. Then his pen and pencil and his billfold went to McKavett, and finally Bates let out a sort of animal roar and lunged at Addison, and then —suddenly it was all over, and Bates was lying still in the gravel of the parking lot.

Addison hit him twice, a left that caught him at the side of the mouth and then a straight right that made the aw-fullest noise when it struck his jaw. The crowd was stunned, silent, and stood looking down at Bates, and Addison was turned away and bent at the waist and holding his hands in his stomach, they hurt so bad from the hitting.

The Troop would tell about that short fight as long as they lived and the part they liked to talk about the most was what happened afterward.

Addison went back in The Puma and got the black-haired girl. She located a fellow who would say he was a friend of Bates', and they all got in somebody's car—the girl, the friend, Bates, Addison, The Troop, everybody—and they rounded up a doctor, because Bates wasn't really doing very well. At 1:30 A.M. they were all in the X-ray room of the Morelia County Hospital and Clinic. A tired-eyed young doctor was telling them, "He's got one hell of a jaw fracture. It's just as well he lost these teeth, because the spaces will give him somewhere to stick the straws. He's going to be on liquids while his jaw's wired, at least six weeks."

It was almost two o'clock when Addison walked with The Troop along the deserted main drag of Spanish Wells, hur-rying to catch the last bus. Booker and McKavett were recovering from the shock of seeing Addison perform, and were getting excited. Addison was now more than just a big fellow they liked. They looked at him with pride and awe and wonder. He was a giant, and he was their friend.

"Man!" Booker's voice was almost a shriek, he was so

17

high. "I thought I'd seen a guy get hit! But gee-sus! Busted his jaw!"

"Well, I sure didn't mean to," Addison said quietly. "I sure didn't intend to hit him that hard. I pretty near ruined my hand." He walked with his right hand against his ribs, tucked gently under his left arm.

Trinidad stayed close to Addison, his skinny legs churning to keep up. He was a little subdued because of his part in the trouble. But McKavett and Booker were drunk on the delight of Addison's victory. They were a couple of kids, reliving a scene from a Saturday afternoon Western.

McKavett, giggling, ran ahead of the others and found himself a stage, in the light of a street lamp. "Hey, Book, lookit this! Here it is!" He assumed a fighting stance and tried to mimick Addison's voice. "I don't really want to fight, Mr. Bates." Then throwing a fast left and following through with the right. "Pow! Pow!" And Booker, getting in on the act, playing Bates, falling, quivering on the sidewalk. Then leaping up and running a little way, laughing with McKavett, the two of them turning to look back at Addison to see if he was grinning at their performance.

On the bus, Addison and The Troop sat in the back in a close huddle and talked about the night.

"Add, how come you never said you were a fighter like that?"

"Well, I'm not, really. I mean I don't *like* to fight on beer-joint parking lots. I can't say I enjoy fighting anywhere, even in the ring. But I learned a good deal about boxing, a long time ago. Took a bunch of lessons."

"How come you took lessons if you don't like to fight?"

"Because I found out that sooner or later a man's just got to fight, and he won't have a choice."

"You mean because some old boy like Bates needs his butt whipped?"

Addison shook his head. "Not that at all. But at some time or other, you're gonna have to defend yourself. That's the main reason for learning how to fight. Defense. Then other times, well, you have to fight just because you're a man, I guess you'd say. Like you're out with a girl, and some smartass insults her. You can't just tell him he's a bad boy, can you? Hell no, you got to do something about it, or else find a new way to shave without a mirror so you won't have to look at yourself. But defense, that's the thing. The reason I got interested in boxing, one time I got the pure-dee whey beat out of me by a kid who wasn't much bigger than any one of you."

"Aw. How could he do that?"

"By knowing how to fight. After he wrecked my wagon I went and took lessons. Off and on I stayed with it two, three years, till I got so I could handle myself pretty well. Just knowing the basic stuff makes a lot of difference. You take a fellow like Bates. He's big, and strong, and tough, and he might even have a reputation for being a fighter. If he does it's because he's been fighting with guys that don't know any more about it than he does. He's just a swinger. All these brawlers, they can hit hard, but they don't know their ass about defending themselves. So when they come across somebody that knows boxing, they get in bad trouble. But listen here . . ."

They all bent closer, in response to the signal that he was about to let go of a Message. "There's a responsibility in knowing how to fight. It's almost like you're carrying around a weapon, a gun, and if you use it right, to protect yourself, that's fine. But you go to getting mad, or drunk, and start blasting away in public, bad things begin happening. *Really* bad sometimes. Just like tonight, I'm sure not proud of that. It ought not to have happened. I got mad at Bates, and I baited him. He did a crappy thing and maybe he deserves the jaw, I don't know, but it could have been handled some other way. Been better, really. Because now he's laid up, and you can bet that one way or the other before we hear the last of it, I'll have myself some grief over what happened tonight."

It was three-thirty before they all got in bed, and Trinidad asked, "Add, you think a guy my size could learn to box and do any good at it?"

"Sure."

"Would you teach me?"

Addison laughed softly. "I could show you a few things."

"Hey," from Booker, "I'd like to get in on that."

"Me too." From McKavett.

And so, three times a week in the gymnasium behind the headquarters building, he gave them boxing lessons.

# EIGHT

TWO WEEKS after the fight Trinidad drew cleaning detail at the headquarters building. He was up front sweeping when Katherine reported for work.

She wore a shiny brown skirt that was too tight. But the way it stretched across her behind was tempting to Trinidad. The men joked about Katherine's bowlegs. Trinidad considered them outstanding. He watched Katherine go down the hall in the long-legged stride she had. He felt a surge in his loins, and wondered what kind of underwear she had on.

Within a couple of minutes she had returned to the front, and startled Trinidad with a sudden question. "Where's your big buddy?"

Katherine had developed a keen interest in Addison's activities. But where Addison was at the moment was a delicate matter, and Trinidad tried to play dumb. "Who you mean?"

She grinned. "I mean your big buddy. Addison."

Trinidad didn't want to look at her and pretended to be interested in his sweeping. "He's sick."

"In his bunk?"

"No, he's got the flu, I guess. He's in the hospital."

"What hospital?"

"Why, here on the base."

Her grin got wider. "Nope. No he's not. I checked. The report says he is, but he's not."

Trinidad kept sweeping, not looking at her.

"I don't suppose," she said, "he'd be on that cargo flight with Charley Biggs."

She knew, then. It was true. Addison *was* on that cargo flight. The Troop and several other of Addison's buddies were trying to cover for him. But here was Katherine, grinning and knowing. That could be trouble.

The trip for Addison became possible—well, tracing it back all the way, it became possible because of a toy pistol.

One night in town, before The Troop came, Addison was strolling along in front of Spanish Wells' principal liquor store, owned and operated by a little prune-faced gent named Deke Fowler. It was almost closing time and the street was deserted.

Not many people will survey the interior of a liquor store they just happen to be walking past. But Addison did, the same way he surveyed everything, and through the window he saw Deke Fowler being robbed by a fellow with a toy pistol.

He stepped inside. Fowler was trembling before the cash register. Addison called to him, laughter in his voice. "Hey, mister? You know this guy hasn't got anything but a toy pistol?" He laughed aloud then. "I had one just like it when I was about four years old. Shoot fire. Little old toy pistol like that's not any good for robbing liquor stores."

He came then, all smiling and friendly, and stood up close to the fellow with the toy pistol. And the fellow gave up. Didn't say anything. Just slumped, all loose and head-bowed. Finally Fowler recovered from his astonishment long enough to call the police, who came and took the guy away.

After they'd shaken hands and swapped names and Addison was ready to leave, Fowler said to him, "Listen here, if I can ever do anything for you, you sing out, all right?"

The only thing Fowler ever did for Addison, he sold him

good scotch by the case at wholesale prices. Which wasn't any sacrifice but it was the closest to it that anybody in Spanish Wells had ever known Deke Fowler to come.

Addison seldom drank whisky so he had little personal use for good scotch even at wholesale. But he knew two people who did have use for it.

One was Captain Charley Biggs. Another was Lieutenant Colonel Sanford Brookfield. Captain Biggs, on an irregular schedule, drove a large and roomy airplane out of Spanish Wells to many faraway places, including the state of Illinois. Colonel Brookfield, a medical doctor in civilian life, sat in charge of the base hospital, sipping constantly on a heavy brown coffee mug. Not long after he came to Spanish Wells, without really trying Addison acquired some mildly interesting facts pertaining to these fine officers.

From Katherine he learned that every Friday, if he didn't have to pilot his large airplane to some faraway place, Captain Biggs drove forty-two miles west to Mercury City. There he stayed until Sunday afternoon with a dark-haired schoolteacher who had a calico cat, a garage apartment, and a deep reverence for good scotch.

With regard to Colonel Brookfield, Addison noticed when his duties took him briefly into the colonel's office, that the good doctor's person gave off a peculiar aroma. Out of curiosity Addison traced it to that big coffee mug on the colonel's desk. One secret sniff said the mug had enjoyed a long acquaintanceship with something in addition to coffee. Scotch.

"What do you want out of me?" asked Captain Biggs when Addison came humming into his quarters one night with a little gift—six bottles of excellent scotch.

"The first time you take one of those airplane trips anywhere near Chicago, let me ride along."

"What do you want out of me?" said Colonel Brookfield, in turn, when Addison presented him with the other half of the scotch.

"I'd like to be sick for three days, and listed on the daily report as a hospital case under your special care."

And so that's how he went to see Sarah, on Captain Biggs' large airplane, with Colonel Brookfield personally entering on the record that Addison had dysentery and was excused from duty.

# NINE

THE SECOND NIGHT he was in Chicago, The Troop sat in the tent-shack and worried about Katherine squealing on him.

"She might not tell," Trinidad said. "She's got the hots for old Add. Maybe she'll keep quiet."

They didn't even go up to The Beer Garden. They kept in their bunks and thought about Sarah and Addison together, picturing them, watching them make love, seeing them in bed, just as Addison had talked about so often.

"What if they can't do it?" Booker suggested.

"How come they couldn't do it?" McKavett said.

"Well, like maybe her folks are there all the time, or they got company all over the house, and they can't do it."

Trinidad let fly his expression of disgust. "For cripe's sake, they're married, aren't they? It ain't like they've got to get permission. They can go in the bedroom and lock the door and screw forty times, they want to. Hell, they want to, they can go out and do it in the front yard."

That brought McKavett up. "You think the front yard? You think they'd do it in the front yard?"

"Godamighty, Mac, you dumb-ass. I was just making an example."

"Well, Add said they done it on the stair steps that time, and on second base at the ball park, too."

"That's damn sure right," Booker confirmed. "On second damn base, at the *ball* park."

"All right," Trinidad said, "but that was one o'clock in the morning and wasn't anybody else inside of two blocks. It's just one of them funny things that horny people do when nobody's looking."

But McKavett wanted to stick to the front yard. The front yard appealed to him. "Well, if it was dark and nobody was watchin', then maybe they *would* do it in the front yard. That's what *I'm* saying."

"All right, all right," Trinidad conceded. "Let 'em do it in the front yard."

They were quiet then a few minutes, and each watched his own private picture show, coming direct from Chicago to Spanish Wells.

Then, "They might be goin' at it right now, hot and heavy."

"I don't know. What time is it?"

"About nine o'clock."

"Be too early, maybe."

"Shoot."

"Well, wait now. What time is it in Chicago?" That was McKavett.

Trinidad's snort. "It's the same time in Chicago as it is here."

"What you talkin' about, man? Chicago's fifteen hundred and somethin' miles from here. I heard Add say how far it is."

"Don't make no difference. It's still the same time as here."

"Well now wait." McKavett tried to organize his argument. "Awright, on the way here I come through El Paso. And the clocks there are an hour different from what they are here, and that's about two hundred and fifty miles away, they said. Now, here you try to tell me that the clocks stay an hour different between here and El Paso, just two hundred and fifty miles away, and yonder's Chicago fifteen hundred miles up there, and there ain't no difference between their clocks and ours?"

"That's exactly right," Trinidad said.

"Ain't no way that can be right."

Here came Trinidad's tone of strained patience. "McKavett. Look. Time here and in Chicago is the same because

Chicago is north. El Paso is west. Time changes east and west but not north and south."

McKavett visualized a map of the country, the best he could. "You mean the time don't change goin' up and down? Only sideways?"

"That's right."

"That don't add up."

"Well, it's a fact."

"Why? How *come* clocks don't change between here and Chicago, when they do between here and El Paso?"

"McKavett," Trinidad said, "that's the dumbest damn question I ever heard anybody ask. Gee-sus!" He pulled a sheet over his head and wondered what the answer to the question might be.

Defeated as always, McKavett lay quiet. He debated whether this would be the right time. He had meant to wait till Addison came back. He wanted so much for Addison to witness his victory. But he needed the moment now, immediately, before Trinidad and Booker went to sleep. He cleared his throat and said:

"I had a letter from Sarah today."

A bored groan from Trinidad.

"Horseshit," from Booker.

"No horseshit," McKavett said. "Show it to you." He switched on a light and fished in his pillow case and found his billfold. He wasn't able to suppress a little grin. He pulled from the wallet a carefully folded pink envelope that drew stares from Booker and Trinidad. It was the size and color of the envelopes from Sarah they'd watched Addison open so many times. McKavett handed over the note. They read it without speaking.

It was short. It said Sarah was pleased to hear from McKavett. It said she felt as if she knew him already, since Addison spoke of him so often in his letters. It said she hoped that someday they would all be able to get together and have good times. At the end she called him Melvin, and said she thought of him as a special friend.

Finally Trinidad said, a little croaky, "You wrote to Sarah?"

"Yeah, sure. Addison sent it for me."

"I'll be damn," Trinidad said quietly.

"I'll be damn," said Booker.

Trinidad put out the light and said no more. McKavett stared into the darkness and saw his moving pictures there. He saw Addison and Sarah on a bed. They were naked. Addison lay between those smooth legs, his face against her large breasts. McKavett closed his eyes and began the changing of the picture, as he did every night.

The face at Sarah's breast was distorted at first. Slowly it came up, and when it focused it was not the face of Addison any longer. It was McKavett's face there, buried between those breasts that he had come to know so well from the picture Addison had shown. Sarah smiled down at him, and tonight for the first time since the pictures began coming, she spoke to him. Never before had anyone spoken to him anything so beautiful and so intimate. She said, "Melvin, I think of you as my special friend."

# TEN

CAPTAIN CHARLEY BIGGS' great airplane returned to Spanish Wells at four o'clock on a Friday afternoon.

Addison held his bag up under his arm. Anybody watching him come off the plane might think the bag was a package, that he'd met the plane and taken it off. He hustled across the ramp and wished for darkness. Walked with his head down, as if not seeing anyone would keep anyone from seeing him. He cut through a hangar and avoided the front gate by leaping over a low hedge, part of The Bear's Base Beautification Program.

But she caught him anyway.

"Hey, Addison!" She was waiting out front in that dirty maroon station wagon. Katherine, who knew all things, even

26

the ETA of Captain Biggs' airplane. "That's a pretty good leap for somebody's been in the hospital. How's your dysentery?"

He was nailed, so he walked to the station wagon. Find out how much she knows. Everything, probably.

Before he reached the car, Katherine turned quickly away and unbuttoned the two top buttons on her blouse.

"How's things in The Bear's Nest?" he asked, standing at the window.

"Slow. Bear's gone. Seems like a lot of people are traveling now. Does the wind really blow, all the time, in Chicago?"

He grinned and looked down and made little patterns with his finger on the car door. She knows.

"You wouldn't tell bad things about me, would you, to The Bear?" This gal could make trouble for him.

"I might. I'm the Base Bitch. Didn't you know that?"

"Naw. Come on now."

"Get in," she said. "Let's go up to The Garden. Buy me a beer. Friday afternoon."

Addison judged he would be wise to go.

She didn't talk, driving to The Beer Garden. Addison thought of Sarah, and became uncomfortable. For a second he imagined she could see him, being met and picked up by this Katherine person, when it hadn't been five hours since they'd made love in Chicago.

They drove past the base theater, and Addison turned away from Katherine and pretended to study the marquee. He scratched at his ear and let his hand pass across his face. And there it was still, Sarah's girl-smell on his hand. While they waited for Captain Biggs' airplane, he had led her to a bench in a corner, away from everybody. They sat close and spread their coats over their legs, as if they were cold. They weren't cold. He put his hand up her skirt and went a little way inside her, feeling her, so soft and silky and moist, and until he had to leave they sat just that way. Not moving, for they were both exhausted from lovemaking. Just being close, and feeling. Then all the way home he lay on a pile of

GI comforters with his head on his hand and the faint smell of inside-Sarah in his nostrils.

But he was uncomfortable now, being here in Katherine's station wagon with Sarah's scent still on him.

The crowd at The Garden was thin and he was glad of that. Over the beer she said to him, "You need to be nice to me, Addison. I might save you a lot of trouble."

"By not telling The Bear about my trip?"

"Not just that. Your little fight in town, too. That Ramos, that Spanish Wells police detective, he was out here again Wednesday. Talked to The Bear himself, this time."

"I've seen Major Burke about that fight. We got it all straightened out."

"Then you better go tell that guy's wife, that guy you put in the hospital, you better go tell *her* it's straightened out because she's sure not acting like it is."

He studied the foam dying in his beer and didn't respond.

"It sure wasn't too smart of you, with this fight thing hanging over you, to go flying off to Chicago for three days like you're on some kind of vacation trip."

"I couldn't help it," he said. "I *had* to go."

She stared at him until he looked away.

"Addison, you need to be nice to me."

He nodded.


# ELEVEN

SOMETIMES, in the tent-shack, he talked to The Troop about his family, about his growing up. It pleased him that they were so interested. They seemed to have a deep hunger for it, almost as intense as their yearning to hear about Sarah.

To The Troop, his life at home had been a fairy tale, so entirely different from anything they had experienced or even imagined.

"Rich!" he roared when Booker asked. "Shoot fire no!"

"Well, I always heard people in Texas were rich and lived on ranches and had oil wells."

"Yeah"—Addison nodded—"and I always heard everybody in Pennsylvania was a coal miner. Hell, Book, you're in Texas now, look around. When you go into town you don't see any oil wells spouting out Cadillacs and Continentals in Spanish Wells, do you? And half the damn ranchers in this state aren't even making a living, without they work in town. Then those boys clodding up and down the streets wearing those cowboy boots, they're not ranchers anyhow, and don't know a barn door from a bull's ass about cattle. Like as not they're clerking in grocery stores somewhere.

"But my folks being rich, my Old Man would sure howl if he heard that. He's principal of the high school there at Pandoval, in that little old poor-mouth district hadn't got enough money to buy blackboards. He didn't even get to be a principal till he was fifty-five. Stayed a teacher for thirty years, in one little half-ass town after another. And you know why? Because he wouldn't sell out. Because he's got the fool notion that reading and writing and arithmetic are more important than a damned football game, and that's not really a very popular notion with school trustees in this state. He's still hanging in there, arguing that when a kid gets out of high school he ought to know how to make change and know the difference between the courthouse and the city hall.

"The Old Man's notions on education didn't rub off much on me, but that wasn't his fault. I was always too busy chasing tail to pay him attention or see how smart he was. But I tell you what, Mildred, that old rascal is the most man I ever knew. *Big* old dude, bigger than I am, and still strong as a red barn and he's nearly sixty-four. His old belly flat as that footlocker and just as hard. Right now, if I got backed into a corner and they gave me the choice of who to call for help, that's who I'd call, my Old Man."

He stopped awhile and swallowed, and cleared his throat, and his eyes were moist. Then he grinned. "I tell you something else. If I did call him, he'd come, too."

The Troop listened in great wonder to all that, to a man speaking of his own father with such respect, and admiration, and love. How did such a thing come to exist?

But look here, he was that way about his entire blinking family. He wrote to his mother once a week, and she to him. He had two older sisters and *they* wrote to him, sent him homemade cookies, comic valentines, birthday cakes. He had uncles and aunts and cousins that wrote to him, and buddies from all over the planet, and four or five old girl friends that didn't know he was married yet.

"From your *sister?*" exclaimed Booker when Addison passed around homemade cookies. "Really? I got a sister. I haven't even heard from her since I left home."

"I got three," McKavett said, cookie crumbs falling from his mouth, "and they don't even know where I am."

"I got five sisters and two brothers," Trinidad said, reaching for the cookie box. "Last time I was home, one of my sisters gave me this." He put a finger to a small scar by the side of his nose and grinned. "Hit me with a beer can. A full beer can."

Addison shook his head and smiled the sad little smile he used to comment on things like that.

"Man, I used to fight with my sisters," Trinidad said. "You ever fight with your sisters, Add?"

"Hell no, shoot fire no. I always got along all right with them. They were good to me. Well, still are." Holding up a cookie. "They're a couple of great gals. They're tall, big, like the Old Man. You ought to see them walking down the street with their mother. Mama's a little bitty old thing, wouldn't weigh a hundred and ten wrapped in a wet sheet. Just cute as hell.

"Every kid she had was damn near big as she was when it came out of her. When I was about seven or eight years old, there'd be a gang of neighborhood kids playing in the yard and Mama would be right out there playing with us, just like she was one of us. She *was* one of us. Victoria, that's my oldest sister, she was bigger than Mama time she was eleven years old. But listen, you know something about my mother and the Old Man?"

"No, what?" The response came in unison that way, from Trinidad and Booker, and it startled McKavett a little. But all three leaned forward to hear, just as if he was about to tell a dirty joke they didn't want to miss.

"Mama and the Old Man are so stuck on one another, still, it's a kind of joke. The night after I graduated from high school, my sisters and I were sitting out in the car, waiting on the folks to come out and go with us to eat. Every time one of his kids graduated from high school, the Old Man got the family together and took us all out to eat Mexican food. That was his idea of a big celebration. Both my sisters were already married then, and had a crop of kids coming on. I think three or four of the older ones were there in the car with us, I don't know.

"Anyhow, we waited, and Mama and the Old Man didn't come, and they didn't come, and finally Victoria said, 'Go tell 'em we're gonna starve if they don't come on.' So I went in, back to the back, and you know what they were doing? By god they were in there *gettin' it!* They had the door closed but I knew the sounds. Hell, I knew their sounds time I was old enough to cuss. There they were, they had three grown children out in the car waiting for them, and a handful of grandkids, and they're in the house just bangin' away, like they couldn't stand it if they didn't do it right that minute.

"Well, I went back out to the car and told 'em what was going on, the best I could in front of the children, and Victoria said, 'My word, that's obscene!' But it tickled her. And Kat too. I heard 'em laughing about it later on.

"Kat. Kathleen, really. Mama always called her Kat. She's two years younger than Victoria. Mama wasn't but eighteen when she had Victoria. Victoria's twelve years older than I

31

am, so that'd make her forty-two now. You ought to see her. Really a classy dame, I tell you.

"Well, Kat too, same way. Kat and Victoria, they're somebody, that pair. They're not exactly movie-star pretty but they've got these beautiful eyes, and just perfect skin, and small waists, and big fine tits. Real *women*. When they were still at home we always had boys by the covey hanging around the house, following along behind Victoria and Kat, drooling at the mouth and looking down their dresses."

He passed around the box of Victoria's cookies again and said, "That family of mine, they're a crowd of characters. We have a hell of a lot of fun when we get together. Christmas, I guess, is the best. We get us a multitude together, at Christmas.

"Doesn't make much difference where we meet, long as Mama and the Old Man are there. Moving around so much, we never did get stuck on one particular house, the way most people do. To me, wherever the folks were, that was home to me.

"Even on moving day, Mama could dig out her big old skillet and fry up a bunch of stuff, and make cornbread, and we might eat on the damn floor at the new place but it was already home, the first night, just quick as Mama unpacked her skillet.

"And when Victoria played the piano, too. The Old Man always made the movers load the piano last, so it'd come off the truck first at the new place, and he'd make Victoria sit down, first thing, and play something bright and bouncy. It was like he thought a house wasn't fit to move into till Victoria had played there. Neighbors used to tell us, later on, after we'd got acquainted, about hearing that music on the day we moved in. They'd say, 'Listen to that bunch of damn fools. Haven't even got the cookstove unloaded yet and they're in yonder playing the piano.'

"But at Christmas, when that gang of aunts and uncles comes, and nieces, and nephews, and cousins, some of 'em come in there from so far away they look like foreigners.

"What am I talking about, shoot fire, some of 'em *are* foreigners. You take Kat's bunch. She married a Greek. I don't mean some Greek runs a restaurant in Fort Worth. I mean a genuine *Greek*, from Greece. Kat had half a dozen old boys sitting on the front porch begging her to run off with 'em, and she gets on an airplane and flies across the ocean and runs into this Greek and wham, they get married on the spot. They been laying around loving up babies ever since. Got six, I think it is, and I'm not sure they're finished yet. So when Kat's bunch comes, we have an international damn convention.

"We'll have lawyers in that bunch, nurses, sergeants, majors, we'll have janitors, café cooks, preachers—hell, we even got one ex-convict. It's true. Mama's younger sister May married an old boy did seven years in state prison for going around writing checks when he didn't have any money in the bank. Well, he did his time and came out and got him a job at a lumberyard and he's just the best old boy you'd want to have around. Tell you what, too, that rascal can sing. Tenor? Make you want to cry. Always a lot of singing at those get-togethers. Louann plays the piano now, and she's better than Victoria, I guess. Louann, that's Victoria's oldest girl. Got two children of her own now. So Victoria's a dang grandmother already, twice, at forty-two. How about that?"

He blinked. "Now that's something to think about, there. My own sister, a grandmother. What would that make me?"

# TWELVE

HE AND BOOKER were in the gym, having a boxing lesson. Booker had been quiet ever since Addison talked so much about his family. He was preoccupied, not doing much good at the boxing.

"Let's knock it off for tonight," Addison said.

They put up the gear and showered and walked toward

the tent-shack. Booker walked with his hands jammed in his pockets. A stocky little gnome, his head way too big for his body. Pimply face. Flat features. Lower jaw protruding. Addison sneaked a glance at him. In profile a bulge of fat showed above Booker's belt. Little guy'll have a pot gut to carry around before he's thirty, he doesn't watch out. Something's chewing on him tonight, though.

"Say, Add, you know what I said about my sister?"

"That you hadn't heard from her since you left home."

He nodded. "Well, that's true."

Addison waited, thinking he'd have more to say. But it didn't come. "But you hear from your mother, you said. And your girl? Where is she? In Allentown?"

Booker reached down—it was such a short reach for him to the ground—and picked up a little rock and flipped it into the darkness. "I haven't heard from my mother, either, since I was eighteen. I don't have a girl that writes to me, either."

"Oh?"

"I just made that up." He looked at Addison quickly and showed a crooked smile but there was no mirth in it.

"I see."

"I got a dad, somewhere, I guess. I just barely remember him. He left when I was about four."

Maybe he wants to talk about his dad. "Why don't you try to find him?"

"I wouldn't know how. Anyhow he might not want me to find him."

"I bet he would. You could talk to Major Burke. He might help on something like that. Burke's a pretty decent guy."

"Maybe. Couldn't hurt, I guess."

"Want me to speak to him about it?"

"Yeah. That'd be good."

"All right. Tomorrow."

Booker went down for another rock, and whipped it into one of The Bear's neat-trimmed hedges. "McKavett said he wrote to Sarah."

"That's right."

"And she answered him."

"That's right too. She did."

Down for more rocks. He threw two in quick succession, and in the amber light of a street lamp they hopped crazily on the asphalt. "You think I could write to her?"

"Why sure."

"And she'd answer?"

"Sure. Guarantee it."

When they were under the street lamp Booker stopped and looked up at Addison's face. He rubbed the rock dust off his hands on the seat of his pants. "Before we go back to the tent, will you walk up to The Garden with me and get a beer?"

"Not unless you buy."

"I'll buy." He giggled a little.

You pitiful little bastard, Addison thought.

# THIRTEEN

"THE PROBLEM," Major Burke said to Addison, "so far, is the guy's wife. Turns out she and Bates are separated, or used to be. Weren't living together at the time you flattened him. But when you put him in the hospital she came rolling in here all full of righteous indignation."

Burke leaned back in his office chair and locked his hands behind his neck and look worried. His natural look. All the knotty little headaches that came to The Bear's Nest filtered through to him, and each one seemed to etch another crease in Major Burke's face.

"They're not gonna file charges, are they?" asked Addison.

"She keeps saying they are," Burke told him, "but they haven't. She seems to be just making waves, mostly. Bothering The Bear, talking to the police, going to see the prosecuting attorney. I don't know, she may have the idea she can get the government to pay her a pile of money on this thing somehow.

"Anyhow, until something definite happens, best thing for you to do is just keep your head down. Stay out of tight places, for god's sake. Be better if you didn't go to town but I know you will, so when you do, don't get into any scrapes. If you even get close to anything that smells like a fight, do an about-face and head the other way and don't look back."

## FOURTEEN

A MONTH after Addison's trip to Chicago, Sarah's letter-writing duties had surely increased.

That McKavett had written to Sarah and gotten an answer was a shocker to the others. Trinidad, especially. He was mortified that McKavett, that dumb-ass McKavett, had been the one who thought of writing. It pained him to follow McKavett's lead but he had no choice. Because now here was Booker writing too, and if Trinidad didn't write she might think he didn't want to.

And so the envelope mailed daily to Chicago became thicker and thicker, often carrying four letters instead of one. When the sun got low and Addison went out to lean against the tent-shack and write to Sarah, The Troop went out too, the same as always. Except now they didn't sit apart and try not to watch him. They all leaned against the tent-shack and wrote to Sarah together.

On successive days—Booker first, then McKavett, then Trinidad—they had trudged to the PX and bought letter-writing kits exactly like Addison's, with the cardboard flap and the brown lace to tie it down.

Each would sit for an hour, or as long as Addison wrote, and sometimes produce no more than three or four awkward sentences. Addison would write pages and pages, while they watched in disbelief. How was he able to write without a pause for a solid hour? What did he write about?

A part of what he wrote was this:

"Letting them write to you may have been a mistake. I'm

afraid it's gotten out of control. All three want to write every day now. They're just so hungry to get mail. After you wrote McKavett, I thought the other two were going to pass away. Trinidad, especially. He takes everything so hard."

"I'm beginning to think not a one of them has ever had a date, or anything much to do with girls. Maybe you'd understand why if you could see them. They're awful homely little outfits.

"Trinidad says he keeps in touch with his family in Arizona and sometimes he makes big talk about girls, and friends, and dances back home. But I don't know, I suspect he is bluffing, the way Booker did so long about his mother and his girl in Pennsylvania.

"I need to ask you to do one more thing for them. They want you to send them each a picture of yourself. Just one of the snapshots will do, something they can carry in their billfolds. And be sure and sign it. How does it feel, having four guys in love with you at once?

"This morning I took Major Burke's car to the Spanish Wells Airport to pick up a big shot civilian. (Airport: A grass strip and a wind sock.) While I was waiting I watched a lady pilot go out to her little airplane and she walked a lot like you. But her legs were too short and her butt wasn't as nice as yours. Someday if they ever have a butt contest I will enter yours, and it will win World's Nicest Behind, because you have the only one on the planet that's not too skinny and not too fat and sticks out just exactly far enough and wiggles precisely the right way when you walk . . ."

Every day when he finished writing, The Troop would hand in their contributions to the envelope, almost like students turning in assignments. They would wait, watching his face, while he read what they'd written.

When this mass-write-to-Sarah campaign began, he had told them they could write whatever they wished and there was no need for him to check it. But he changed his mind on about the third day.

"Hey, Add?" It was Booker asking. "How do you spell that guy's name? That Bates."

Which got Addison's attention. "Why do you need to know that? You're not telling Sarah about that trouble we had at The Puma, are you?"

"I can't think of nothing else to say."

"Tell you what, let's just leave it out," Addison suggested. "Sarah's not too happy about me fighting. It'd just bother her."

McKavett said, "You mean she don't even know how you laid out ol' Bates that way? Man, if I'd done that I'd be tellin' everybody I know, just how I done it."

"Anyhow," Addison said, "let's leave it out of the letters."

When he finished, and sealed the envelope, the four of them walked together to the base post office, to watch the letter to Sarah disappear into the slot.


# FIFTEEN

CAPTAIN CHARLEY BIGGS, wearing his cocky baseball cap and chewing on a long cigar, swaggered around a corner of the ready room and almost stepped on Addison's feet.

Addison was on a bench near the front door. He had a parachute in his lap. He had snapped open the little inspection flap, which revealed the chute pin and about two square inches of packed nylon. He sat gazing out at the flight line, rubbing his index finger back and forth, back and forth, slowly across that tiny rectangle of nylon.

Captain Charley Biggs stared. "Addison? What the hell you doing there?"

Gradually Addison acknowledged the presence of Captain Biggs. He tapped the nylon showing in the inspection window and said, "It feels like Sarah's behind."

"Like what?"

"It feels like my wife Sarah's behind. There's not anything

else on this whole damn base that feels anything like Sarah's behind, except this little patch of parachute nylon. So I come down here and Abner lets me have a chute for a little while, so I can feel this patch of nylon like this."

"And does that help you?"

"Why sure. It sure does."

Captain Biggs looked thoughtful a few seconds, nodded, and swaggered on. "That's a damn good idea, Addison," he said.

# SIXTEEN

HERE WAS TRINIDAD in a most unusual circumstance— on the bus, going into town, without the others.

He chose the five-thirty bus, which was always crowded. Only four seats were not taken when he got aboard at The Beer Garden by the front gate. Quickly he surveyed the faces and picked a heavyset buck private with slick black hair and horn-rim glasses. Trinidad slipped in the seat beside him.

"Hey. How's it go?"

A vague smile from Horn-rims, in answer to the greeting, and a shrug. "Same old crap."

"Yeah. Same old crap."

Trinidad let a couple of miles slide by before he opened up. "Been here long?"

"Six months," said Horn-rims. "Too damn long."

Trinidad waited another couple of miles and tried again. "Where you from?"

"Ohio. Akron. You?"

Ah, a question. Maybe he'd talk, after all.

"Arizona," Trinidad answered. "You been there?"

Shake of the head. "Nah. Seen pictures. Desert, mostly, isn't it? About like this stuff here?" Waved a hand at West Texas going by.

"Not all of it. Arizona's got some pretty country, in places."

"That's what they keep telling me about Texas but I damn sure haven't seen any of it."

"Tell you one thing"—Trinidad tried to sound like he was just making talk, not steering the conversation—"about Arizona. It's sure got pretty girls."

"That right?"

"I mean." Be cool now. Lead him along gently. "You married?"

"Nah. You?"

Trinidad shook no. "Engaged, though," he said. "Gonna get married Christmas, if I can get home."

For a few seconds then he weakened. Stunned, by his own words. He turned and shot a quick look behind, as if he expected Addison or McKavett or Booker to be there, hearing him.

"Arizona girl?"

"Huh?"

"You engaged to an Arizona girl?"

"Oh." Recovering now. "Yeah, sure. Lives in Bisbee."

He let it ride another mile. Two miles. Then he said, "She's coming in, tonight. That's why I'm going in, to meet her. She's coming in tonight on the bus, from Bisbee."

"Long ride," Horn-rims said.

"Yeah, that's what I told her, but she wanted to come."

Silence again, and Trinidad wasn't sure he was going to bring it off. Go ahead, try.

"She's going to stay a week."

That did turn Horn-rims' head, away from the Desert Southwest a minute. "A week, huh?" He grinned. "Good times, right?"

"You bet." Trinidad nodded. Maybe it would work now, to bring out the picture. "I got a picture of her here somewhere." He made a bad show of patting pockets. "Here it is." He drew it out of the top left pocket of his khaki shirt. "Her name's Sarah."

It was the snapshot she had sent to them all, to Trinidad and McKavett and Booker, after Addison asked her to do it. She sent the same picture to each one, and signed them in the lower left-hand corner in exactly the same way. "Love, Sarah." She had begun signing the little notes she wrote to them the same way, "Love, Sarah," without realizing what it meant to them. Love! From Sarah!

In the snapshot Sarah wore jeans and a checkered shirt, but they failed to hide her curvy beauty. Horn-rims took the picture and studied it closely, holding it near his face. "This is *your* girl?" He looked then at Trinidad, at the too-sharp features and the scarred and pockmarked face and the narrow, humped little shoulders. And this was Trinidad's moment of glory, seeing the stranger stare at his ugliness and then look back down at the picture of Sarah.

"Godamighty she's sure built," Horn-rims said.

"Yeah, she sure is."

"How long will she be here?"

"A week. Six days and seven nights."

"What you gonna do, show her the town?" Horn-rims laughed, for there was little to show anybody in Spanish Wells.

"We'll think of something." A sly little grin.

"Gee-sus!" Horn-rims seemed reluctant to hand back the snapshot. "Seven nights." He held the picture a long while. He would look out the bus window a mile or so but then return to Sarah's snapshot, and Trinidad sat silent and watched his face. He didn't give the picture back until the bus had slowed for its first stop in Spanish Wells.

With Sarah safely back in his shirt pocket at last, Trinidad swung off the bus and walked quickly around the corner, walked with long steps, arms swinging in a military manner, head high. Before he took the bus back to the base he walked several blocks. And for a little while, he felt very good.

# SEVENTEEN

AFTER THE EXCHANGE of notes began, The Troop's yearning to hear about Sarah deepened. Now they began probing, asking for information Addison had never given out. How much did Sarah weigh? Did she like baseball? Didn't she used to have a lot of boyfriends, before Addison? Did she like to dance? Could she swim? Did she ever cuss, say hell and damn? Did she have sisters? Did she ever get mad at Addison?

Some details they couldn't hear enough, no matter how many times Addison repeated them.

"Tell how you met her, that first time."

"I've told that."

"Tell it again."

Sometimes he pretended it was a bother, but there was nothing he enjoyed more, there in Spanish Wells, than talking about a Sarah-connected event or circumstance.

He met her at what promised to be, before he went, one of the world's most ordinary company parties. It was held in the banquet room of a Chicago restaurant. A friend of his was going round with a girl who worked for the company. A big construction outfit. Hickam Construction.

Anyhow the friend—Robinson Nash, crazy old boy from West Virginia, everybody called him Crusoe—he got Addison to go with him to the party. "Lot of good chow and free booze and plenty of women."

The food and booze didn't interest Addison but the women did. "Let me tell you, Robinson Crusoe, I've had me a long drouth on women."

For three weeks he'd been laid up in the hospital with some kind of strange virus they couldn't hang a name on. Feeling really tough. Even too tough to hustle the nurses, and for Addison that was *tough*-tough. He came out looking gaunt, not his best.

She was dressed in red. Red sweater. Red skirt. Red shoes. When he first saw her she was in a group and Crusoe's girl was struggling through one of those mass introductions, just as if everybody was going to remember all the names and keep them hooked up to the right people.

". . . and this is Lillian, and this is Sarah, and this is . . ."

He did stay with her face a few seconds and got behind, while he made an assessment. Addison thought of himself as a plenty capable assessor. He had assessed women, by then, in about half the states and four foreign nations and it was his devout hope to assess them the world over before he was through, and he wasn't able to imagine a more worthwhile goal.

She had a sweet face, that Sarah person. Such calm and gentle eyes. A lot of the finest storms blew up out of calms like this. Her hair special, wavy and light brown. He liked the way it kept itself close to her face in soft curls, so natural-looking. Something in her eyes bothered him an instant. A reserved look. Standoffish? He didn't need any reserved women, not tonight.

Then Anna-something, one of those double first names. Somewhat older. A loud talker and jumpy and twisty and flare-hipped. One of those women, by Addison's rules of assessment, that when you stick it in her she just explodes, by god. Her face was attractive in a hard, experienced way, and to Addison in his drouthy condition she looked incredibly sexy. His condition led him to imagine that Anna-something was very, very horny and that a reasonable effort on his part would surely get her into the back seat of a car, right there in the restaurant parking lot. Addison was in such a great hurry.

And so he set out to make a project of Anna-something, and was encouraged right away when she happily belly-rubbed with him on the dance floor.

During the third belly-rubbing session, Addison's eyes caught the calm face of that Sarah girl. And she was staring at him. Addison wasn't a stranger to being looked at by

43

women but it did interest him that when he returned the stare, she didn't look away. So he smiled at her. She didn't return the smile. Her expression didn't even change. She wasn't flirting with him, then, she was studying him. Now that wasn't usual, in Addison's experience. What could it mean?

Then Anna-something went to the restroom. "Don't go away, Texas. You stir me up." Addison eased back around to the bar and the crowded table where Sarah sat. He stood near the wall and watched from the side, where she couldn't see him.

She wasn't talking much. She just sat, and yet she wasn't vacant. She was so organized somehow, so in control, evidently feeling no need whatever to contribute to the chatter going on around her.

Addison discovered that he had missed some vital factors in his earlier assessment. One was, she looked so great in that red sweater. It puzzled him that he hadn't noticed that at first, since it was of immense importance. Had he spent all that time looking at her face?

He wished he could watch her walk. His system assigned great weight to how a girl looked when she walked across a crowded room, going away. He liked to check what happened to her bearing, the swing of her hips, the set of her shoulders, when she knew people were watching her.

She sat with her back to the dance floor. Addison drifted past the bar, holding his warm beer, and stood almost directly behind her. He watched the dancers and heard her order a drink from the waiter. "Just ginger ale, please." The waiter said, "Nothing in it?" And she said, "Nothing, thank you." She wasn't drinking, there in a crowd that was pouring down free booze. This girl might be special. One thing sure, she wasn't any back-seat-in-the-parking-lot. He could tell that by the look of her, so composed and complete. Addison imagined he could look at most girls and tell whether they were in need, and even what they were in need *of*. But this girl showed no such sign. For a moment Addison considered not being in a hurry tonight. Then:

"Hey, Texas." Anna-something was back. She came up behind him and stood close, touching. He could feel her shoulder on his back and a small hard breast pressing against his upper arm, and that put him in a great hurry again.

He shouldn't have drunk the whiskey. Addison and hard liquor had a bad history. But she wanted him to drink, urged it on him, said she didn't want to drink alone, and so he drank. Carefully, at first. Because he was just out of the hospital, and not up to par.

But after a while, sipping and belly-rubbing with Anna-something, he saw there was no longer any need to be cautious with the whiskey, and he drank freely. Even gulped it down. Because it was now clear to him that he could drink the stuff all night, and he wondered why he had ever held back. All it was doing, it was just helping him do everything exactly right.

So he said to her, "Let's go outside and get some fresh air." She went right along outside with him. He grinned and gave himself congratulations for coming up with that foxy notion—to go out for fresh air that way. How was that, gang, for guile?

He didn't seem able to do or say anything that wasn't right. They walked among the cars in the parking lot. It was time for him to make his move. He let himself be guided, on what to do and say, by what seemed natural and right, since he was doing everything so well now.

He turned to her and put one hand on her behind and the other on the small hard breast he had felt inside and he said to her, "Ever since I came here tonight and saw you, I've been wanting to get in your pants."

She drew away from him. He stood before her, grinning a fool's grin, weaving a little. She grasped her right wrist and drew it around almost behind her. She set her feet. She was

45

a tennis player, about to let go a two-fisted backhand. And she raked him across the mouth with a most extraordinary slap, a rear-handed blow, loaded with an emerald and a blue diamond on her rings.

So she hurt him. He spun, and whimpered a little, and held his mouth and jaw where the rings hit. And she said to him, quietly, "Why you rural son of a bitch, who do you think you're talking to?" Then she went back inside.

After that he was sick. Partly from the blow, partly from the rebuke, but mostly from the booze. He ended up sitting, a long time, holding his head, on the parking lot curb under a light pole. When his offended stomach demanded it, he would creep into the shrubbery and vomit, and creep back. How long he was there he did not know. Or care.

In a vague way he was aware at one point that the red shoes were in front of him, and he was being spoken to by a voice at a very great altitude. He didn't respond. A surge of nausea was on him then, and when the red shoes went away he crept into the shrubbery again.

When the red shoes returned he was back on the curb. The voice, not at such a great height now, was saying things he could understand.

"Listen, this place is closing. Everybody's leaving. Did you come with anyone?"

"Crusoe," he managed.

"Who?"

"Rob'son Crusoe."

"Brother." She bent down, closer to him. "Do you have a car?"

"Yeah. A Merc. Blue Merc."

She looked around the parking lot, almost deserted now. "Where is it?"

"Pandoval."

"Where?"

"Pandoval. Texas. Old Man's drivin' it." He hadn't even looked up at her yet. Just sat there on the curb with his jaws in his hands, staring at the red shoes in the dim light.

"Pretty shoes." He let one snaky finger come forward, to touch the toe of her shoe.

"Can you walk?"

"Damn right. Do it ever' day."

"Well, see if you can do it to my car. You can't stay out here. It's not safe."

She found an all-night restaurant and got him into a booth and put two cups of coffee down him. They sat without talking during the coffee. Addison worked on getting his eyes to focus better. Made some progress.

"Did you ever eat anything?"

Shook his head. And she ordered him soft-scrambled eggs.

"Do you have any money?"

"Sure." Working on the eggs.

"Let me see."

He handed over his billfold. Without hesitation, just as if she was accustomed to taking men's billfolds, she opened it and looked. Thirty-five dollars. Then she got up and walked the length of the restaurant to a pay phone. Addison was seeing a lot better now and he studied her walk, and finally everything connected up—why, look here, this is that pretty girl from the party, the one with soft curls and big dark eyes and the calm face. Hey, look at how that skirt swings when she walks. Isn't that just right?

Coming back from the phone she saw he was making his return, to be among the living again, and she gave him just a clue of a smile, mostly with those eyes. Even before she sat down again she started talking.

"Why don't you go wash your face? You're a disaster."

He grunted, and nodded, and went. And she checked, to see that he was walking all right now. When he came back, she was gone.

She'd left a note on the table: "There's a motel just across the street. I called, and they're saving a room for you. I got your name from your billfold. In case you're wondering what hit you at the party, her name is Anna Sue Hickam, child bride of our company president, the man who bought

47

all that whiskey you drank. Mr. Hickam lets Anna Sue run and play that way at parties, but it is dangerous to take her outside."

She didn't sign the note and he couldn't remember her name. Walking over to the motel, feeling a lot better, he indulged in an exciting thought: that when he got to the room she reserved, she would be there, in bed, waiting for him. Wouldn't *that* be something. He tried to visualize the way she would look when he unlocked the door. Tried to see her sitting up in the bed, her shoulders bare, with the sheet around her. But he didn't really have any confidence that she'd be there. Not *this* gal. And she wasn't.

But that was the beginning of it, between Sarah and Addison.

# EIGHTEEN

HIS PHONE CALL to Hickam Construction the next morning was answered by a gruff security guard who said it was Sunday and nobody was working. He stayed in the room all day, thinking she might call. She didn't call. He tried desperately to remember the name of Crusoe's girl. He could not.

No way to find Crusoe on a Sunday. He'd be holed up in a hotel or motel somewhere. He even played with the idea of calling Hickam's residence and pretending an emergency and asking Hickam—well, asking what? For the name of one of his employees who wore red shoes to the party and had a beautiful walk? He stayed in the motel till dark, and the clerk charged him for two full nights. He argued, and lost, and the bill cleaned him out.

He didn't even locate Crusoe until Monday night, to get the name of his girl. Phyllis Bradley. "But you stay away from that stuff, you hear? I'm not through with it, quite yet."

Addison talked to Phyllis at work Tuesday afternoon.

"Her name is Sarah. Sarah Allen. She works in Personnel. But she's not here today. She's in a meeting somewhere."

It was Thursday before he got her on the phone.

"Who, please?" she asked when he spoke his name.

"Addison!" he said impatiently. He wasn't accustomed to being forgotten in five days. But she laughed then, and Addison relaxed. She'd been kidding, maybe, about not remembering.

She was busy Friday night, though. Saturday, too. In fact, she would be away for the weekend. Something about that "away for the weekend" troubled him, tugged at his insides.

"I could come in next Tuesday night," he said. "How about that?"

"I'm sorry. Tuesday is my night out . . . with the girls."

"Let me go with you. I *like* girls."

Here came the pretty laugh again. "I noticed that at the party."

Now that was a zinger. "No, look, let me tell you something. That deal at the party, that's not my style. That liquor had me wiped out. That was the first I'd had in a long time, and it did me in. I don't get along too well with liquor. I don't even drink it, as a rule. Listen, that's the truth."

She didn't respond to that little speech. He pressed on:

"Thing is, I need to talk to you, even if it's just for a little while. There's something I've got to find out. I could come before you go out, on Tuesday. Or meet you after you get through with whatever you're going to do." There was a tone in his voice that was foreign to Addison. What it was, he was pleading. Addison had never before pled with a girl, for a date or for anything. "The problem is, if I don't come Tuesday I can't make it for another week. *Seven more days!*"

Finally she said, "Got a pencil?"

"You bet. Shoot."

She gave him a street address. "That's where I'll be Tuesday night. I'll be there until around nine-thirty."

"But what time will you *get* there?"

"At seven-thirty. But I'll be busy those two hours."

"Are you saying don't come early?"

"No, but if you do, you might not enjoy it."

It was obvious she had a reason for not telling him what kind of place it was, a residence or a theater or a club or whatever. So he didn't ask.

He went early, though. At eight o'clock he was standing in the middle of the street, looking around, double-checking the address. He was at the right place, and it was a church. With singing inside. Sounded like young voices.

He looked in. Nobody was in the pews. A choir of young girls was practicing. Sarah was at the piano. He sat on a back seat and listened until there was a short break. She came smiling up the aisle to sit with him a few minutes.

"Your night out with the girls, huh?" he teased.

"That's right. Thirty-six of them. Well, thirty-five, tonight. We have one out with the measles."

"You're here every Tuesday night?"

"Wednesday night too, for the midweek service. I'm the resident piano gal around here. Also Thursday night, for adult choir. Then Sunday morning, and Sunday night again, and all the other nights when anything special goes on."

"Hoo wee. That's a lot of piano playing."

"Well, it's a job. I get paid. A little, anyway."

"But do you like it? Enjoy it?"

She put one of those deep looks of hers on Addison and let it stay a second or two before she answered. As if what she said might be very, very important. "Yes, I do enjoy it. My music, and these kids, and this church, they mean a great deal to me."

He nodded. "Then that's good that you're here so much."

She had to go back to her piano then. She was a few steps down the aisle and he called to her softly. "Sarah?" The first time he'd ever spoken her name, except on the phone. She turned quickly, and answered with her eyes and arched brows and at that instant she was just beautiful.

He said quietly, almost whispered, "You're even prettier than I remembered."

That night, while he sat in the back pew of an empty church, watching her, hearing her play for those little girls—that's when Sarah happened to Addison. After that hour, he would never again be the same person.

For the next three months he sat in that church many nights, up close to her. Studying her. Trying to follow the movement of her fingers on the keys. Waiting for the swell of her breasts beneath her blouse when she breathed. Tracing the path of her eyes, moving from the music to the keyboard to the director. And sometimes to Addison, and he would search for the small soft jerk of muscle at the corner of her mouth that said things to him.

Oh, he had some grand arguments with himself about what had happened. He wasn't really ready to accept it. And so some nights he would force himself to stay away from the church. He would walk, along dark residential streets, and try to understand this frightening thing that had come to pass. He even tried to talk himself into believing that she wasn't so much different from any of the others. Look, it just happens this one is going to be one extra-special piece of delicious tail, and it takes extra effort this time, isn't that right? Then maybe he'd turn a corner and there he'd be at the church, without even realizing he was so near. Why, one night he ended up at the church and she wasn't even there, because she was out of town, gone to drive her folks up to her brother's place in Wisconsin.

It just can't be, Addison argued. Having this happen, it just didn't fit his plans. The last time he was home, he'd talked about that to the Old Man.

The Old Man had driven him three miles outside town where he was paying installments on five acres of bald prairie, bald except for the young trees he'd planted on it. "Maybe in a few years," he told Addison, "when you get your tomcattin' done and get ready to settle in, you might

51

220739    Athens Regional Library
Athens, Georgia

want to come back, you can't tell. Won't be long till these elms'll be throwing shade. Be a good place for kids."

Addison laughed at that notion. "I don't know, Pop. I don't really think I'll ever get married. Seems to me that'd spoil the fun. I'd rather love 'em all, every one I can get to, and it's gonna take me a terrible long time to make it around. Shoot fire, I never have been to China yet, to see if that stuff really runs crossways, like they say. What am I talking about, I never even been to France, for god's sake, to see if the girls wear pants."

The Old Man nodded, and tried to keep from grinning too wide. "Yeah, well, I've known men with less lofty ambitions. The only thing, don't let it shock you too deep when you run across one you're not able to walk away from."

Had that really happened, then, so quick, so soon after the Old Man said it? He tested. He imagined for a minute that the next day they shipped him out, maybe overseas again, and he wouldn't see Sarah for months, for a year. It made an actual pain, inside him, to think about it.

Why, he was even having trouble walking away from her for two days. Every night he saw her, it took longer to leave. They would stand, wrapped up in each other, saying it was late and they had to get up early, and then just keep standing. Addison couldn't get enough of the feel of her; of her arms around his neck; her fingers on his face; the curve of her hip beneath his hand; the press of her breasts and loins; the taste of her in his mouth. Each time, it took him longer and longer to walk away.

Even so, he fought it for almost three months before he surrendered.

They were downtown shopping, walking along a crowded street, and suddenly the time came for him to talk about it.

They were waiting for a traffic light, but when it changed he didn't step off the curb. He pulled her back and turned her, a hand on each of her shoulders, and faced her squarely and said in the most solemn way, "Listen, do you understand what's happened?"

Of course she knew exactly what he meant. "Yes. I understand."

"Everything is different now. The whole damn world's different."

"Yes, I know."

"*I'm* different."

"Yes, so am I."

"Do you like it?" he asked.

"Yes. Do you?"

"Yes. But it scares me. It means so much. I didn't know it would change everything this way."

"I didn't know either. But it's happened."

"Yes. Boy, it sure has."

Then he kissed her gently and the light changed and they put their arms around one another and stood a long time, feeling the awesome power of this mysterious and beautiful and frightening thing that had come to pass, and the people on the street walked around them.

# NINETEEN

SUNDAY AFTERNOON, in the tent-shack. Addison rose out of his bunk and tossed aside the book he'd been reading and snapped to mock attention, a signal that he was about to let loose one of his Military Announcements.

"All right, Troop? Front and center! Fall in! Tench-*hut!* Listen here, men, and specially you *noo* men, this here's gonna be picture-makin' day. She wants pictures of us all, together and separate, and she wants us shaved, shined, showered, shampooed, reamed, steamed, and dry-cleaned. So by the numbers, now, check armpits!"

While he had them listening and laughing he raised an elbow and made a pretense of sniffing under his arm, and he reeled, and caught himself on a bunk post, and turned cross-eyed and said, "Hoo-o-o-o wee! I smell like two feet down-wind from a billy goat. You know what my mama used to say? She'd say, 'Add, if you can smell yourself, it means you been stinkin' already for three days.' All right, all the rest of you sweethearts that haven't had a bath for a month, let's hit the showers. That Sarah girl would smell me in the picture, by god, if I don't upgrade my fragrance some."

He took a towel and his shaving gear and headed toward the showers, and here they came, filing along behind him.

They *needed* to follow him. Sometimes Addison studied them when they weren't watching, as he studied so many things, and he thought, All right, sure, they're all three ugly as hell but they'd look a hundred per cent better if they'd keep themselves policed up a little bit. Shoot fire, anybody can keep clean.

When Sarah sent the pictures to The Troop she demanded, in return, pictures of them. They were a long time getting sent, though. Not a one of The Troop was eager to send her a picture of himself. They all avoided cameras. Once when they were in town, killing time, horsing around the streets, Addison stopped them at one of those curtained, coin-operated photo booths and said, "Hey, come on, let's all bunch in here and make a gang picture of ourselves. We could hang it in the post office and collect the reward."

But they didn't want to pose. If Addison had said let's go rob a liquor store, or go jump in a deep lake somewhere, most likely they'd have considered it a fine idea. They balked, though, on the pictures.

Still, given enough time, he could cajole and bluff and tease them into almost anything. It often meant treating them like babies, playing games, cracking bad jokes.

"OK, you dirty little bastards," he said in the showers that Sunday afternoon, "scrub your butts. I don't want any dirty butts showing up in pictures sent to *my* best girl." And they'd laugh, and they'd scrub, too, and that was good because they didn't bathe often enough, for god's sake, and that bothered Addison.

He was brought up in a home where he wasn't allowed to poke his feet between his mother's sheets unless they'd been scrubbed with a stiff brush. Sometimes he talked to The Troop about that, and they listened, and absorbed, with as much interest as if he'd been talking about sex, or about whipping somebody's tail in a boxing match.

"Before I was big enough to mow grass my mama used to call me in every morning before I left for school and make me stand inspection. She'd say, 'My law, look at those hands. I wish you'd solve me the mystery of how a boy can take a bath and never get his hands wet.' She'd say, 'Listen here, your daddy makes our livin' at that school, and I won't have any of those high-nosed trustees hearin' about a kid of his goin' to school with dirty hands.'

"Then I'd be on up there fifteen, sixteen years old, and I'd start out somewhere and she'd yell at me, she'd holler, 'You come on back here and let me smella you.' And she'd sniff around on me like an old mama wolf and she'd say, 'Phew! You make me think of a cesspool we had in Lampasas one time. Get in yonder and hose yourself down or I'll take your britches off and do it myself.'

"Then she'd lecture me some. She'd say, 'Listen here, I know you're off chasing girls now, after dark. All right, the best thing you can be when you catch one is *clean*. You go to stinkin' yourself up with stale sweat and onions and cigarettes and whiskey, you're apt to end up a hermit.' And I used to tell her, 'Well, shoot fire, Mama, I don't want to smell like Victoria and Kat. I want to smell like a man.' And she'd say, 'All right, you just be damn sure you smell like a clean one. That's the main thing that melted me,' she'd say, 'when your daddy came along and made me follow him off into everlasting poverty this way—he smelled like a *clean man*.'"

Which was so strange, such a marvel to The Troop, to learn that there were families like that, that there were sons and mothers who could talk to each other, and care, even about the way one another smelled.

So when he got them tuned in and listening, he laid it on heavy. "OK, Troop, it's toothbrush time," he said in the

55

showers. "Let's all shine 'em up." And they dug into their kits and fished out toothbrushes, for maybe the first time in ten days. And Addison uncovered a remarkable fact—that Booker didn't even *have* a toothbrush.

"Whatever in the hell happened to it?"

"Beats me," Booker said, laughing, trying to pass it off as a joke. "It just disappeared."

"I expect," Addison said, "we ought to advertise in that Spanish Wells wipe, in the lost and found, see if anybody's found ol' Book's toothbrush."

Then the picture-taking session in front of the tent-shack. He had them lined up, reluctant, but agreeing to undergo the torture to fulfill a request from Sarah.

"McKavett, pull your pants up a little," Addison said, looking at them through the camera's viewfinder. "Now you got 'em all crooked in front. Mac, the trouble with those pants," letting his camera down now, "they're too damn big for you. You haven't got enough ass to hold 'em up. Turn around a second, and let me see. Why hell, Mac, you haven't got *any* ass. Folks, this here's the famous Assless McKavett, who was behind the door when they passed out the rear ends in the state of Georgia. Mac, what you oughta do is take those pants up yonder to Jonsey and get him to cut 'em down to your size. My god, looks like I've got to tell you buzzards *every*thing to do, just like I've taken you to raise." And how happily they grinned at that good-natured complaint.

"Trinidad? Stand up straight, dammit. You're gonna be humpbacked, you don't straighten up. Didn't you birds ever go through basic? Looka there, Trinidad, you're two inches taller when you stand up and get the kinks out. Booker? Pull in your gut and move over to your left a little. God dang, here I been tellin' Sarah I'm livin' with three soldiers. Shoot. Yawl look like something the flies wouldn't light on . . ."

They liked it. And it worked:

The next night Booker came in showing off three toothbrushes he'd bought. McKavett carried his khakis to the base tailor shop to be altered. And when the snapshots came back, Trinidad proposed another picture-taking session before the photos were sent to Sarah. "I wasn't standing up quite straight," he told Addison, "in these."

Addison said, "You're getting mighty damn particular."

# TWENTY

THEY WERE AT THE BEER GARDEN near the front gate, Addison and The Troop, sitting with a gang of others, telling stories about what they would do when they left Spanish Wells behind and went back where they'd rather be.

Master Sergeant Runge came, all full of importance and beer, and sat across from Addison and said, "Hear you're a fighter."

"Naw, not really. I used to box some."

"How much you weigh?"

"Two, two ten. Haven't weighed lately."

"We're making up a card," Runge said, "for the second of next month, in the gym. Gonna have eight, ten matches. I could put you down. Maybe put you in with that Grover boy, from Oklahoma. He's about your size. You know him?"

Addison nodded. "I know him. But I'm not interested. Thanks anyway, Sergeant."

"We're gonna have some pretty nice trophies, even for the losers," Runge said.

"He wouldn't lose," Booker blurted. He couldn't stand not to say it. "He damn sure wouldn't lose."

"Well, that's hard to say. If he doesn't fight, we won't ever know, will we?" The sergeant was answering Booker's comment but he was looking at Addison.

"That's right," Addison said, "we won't ever know."

"He wouldn't lose." That was Trinidad, casting his vote with Booker.

"We're having the fights for the men, for morale," Runge said. "It's not like we're promoting, for money."

Addison said, "Well, I'll do my part on that. I'll help set up the ring, or sweep the gym. Whatever. Except fight."

"Hell"—Runge let the disgust show—"I thought they told me you were a fighter. Doesn't sound to me like you got the stomach for it."

McKavett wouldn't sit still for that. "By god you oughta seen 'im in town that night at The Puma when . . ."

Addison put a hand on McKavett's wrist. "We don't need to get into that. Sergeant, you're not going to shame me into fighting on that card."

"Afraid you might get that face cut up a little, huh?"

Addison smiled, and stared at Runge hard.

"Shit," said Runge, and got up and left.

"I wish you could fight *him*," Booker said when Runge was out of range.

They walked slowly toward the tent-shack. The Troop was quiet, disappointed that Addison didn't want to fight. How they would love to see him in the ring. Addison sensed their disappointment.

"You know something funny about fighting?" he said. "It's a little like the Old West, in gunslinging times. Take you guys, all three of you. You've been learning a little about boxing. If you get pretty good at it, and go out and have yourself a fight, and win, why a lot of people are gonna think you're going around looking for more fights all the time.

"Now a lot of these beer-joint brawlers, they really *are* that way. They get to feeling strutty on Saturday night, and they got to prove something, try to whip somebody, especially somebody who's supposed to be a good fighter. That Oklahoma fellow. Grover? That's the way he is. He was at The Puma that night and saw me hit Bates and he's been picking at me ever since, trying to get me to take a punch at him. I expect it was him that put the sergeant onto me. Guys like Grover are always going around looking for ways

58

to build a reputation. He'll hear about a guy somewhere who's been whipping tails, so he goes and looks him up and tries him out.

"I had a little old fight in Long Beach one night. I was stationed at Santa Ana then. I was out in front of a place called the Circle Bar and this damn sailor came up and started hitting on me, and hell, I didn't have any choice but to hit him back.

"Wasn't much to it, really. He was ready to quit pretty soon, and I forgot all about it. Well, I guess it was two weeks later, I was back in Long Beach, moseying along The Pike there, looking at the girls, and I went back by that Circle Bar place. And there was a great big old snaggletooth fellow collared me in there and wanted to know if I wasn't the one that had whipped that sailor two weeks before. I'll just be damned if he hadn't heard about it and come all the way from San Diego, looking for me."

"Wanting to whip you?"

"Yeah, sure."

"Did he try?"

"Yeah, sure."

"Did he do it?"

"Naw."

# TWENTY-ONE

McKAVETT had been in a dark mood the entire day.

Addison sat with him at noon chow and he didn't eat much, just stirred his food around on the tray and wouldn't talk. Then that evening, at letter-writing time, he didn't go out and sit with the others. Kept in his bunk and looked at the ceiling.

It was his turn to go to the gym with Addison but he told Booker to go, that he didn't much feel like going. Addison got Trinidad aside. "See if you can find out what his trouble is. He's got his dauber down about something."

59

When Addison and Booker left, Trinidad switched on his radio. "How about a little music?"

McKavett turned on his side and raised up on an elbow, his face all full of concern, and he said, "I been thinkin'."

"What about?"

"About Sarah."

"What about her?"

"Somethin's wrong. It just come to me, last night."

"What came to you?"

"Well, you know that picture of her Addison's got, where she's half nekkid with her tits showin' and all?"

"Yeah."

"Well, what I want to know is, who *took* that picture, by god."

## TWENTY-TWO

WHEN McKAVETT WAS SIXTEEN, his father took him fishing on the Altasilo River not far from their home in Georgia. It surprised him to be taken along. Billy McKavett was forever disappearing for two and three days at a time, hunting or fishing or whatever, but never before had he taken his only son.

Billy McKavett was a wiry little carpenter, with dark eyes and smooth brown skin and curly, greasy black hair. In his young times he was considered by some, including himself, to be good with the girls.

"You're sixteen," he said to McKavett the day they went to the river. "Have you got your wick dipped yet?"

He was consumed by that expression, dip your wick. Used it constantly in various forms. Get my wick dipped. Dip the old wick. Something to dip my wick in. McKavett remembered his father using the expression even before he understood what it meant.

"No." McKavett looked away, out the window of the pickup truck. He was not comfortable with his father. And now to be suddenly struck with the question about getting his wick dipped, that was painful and embarrassing.

"Well, hell," Billy McKavett said to his only son, his homely, skinny son with the red skin and the white brows, "maybe we ought to see about it on this trip. A fella oughtn't to get seventeen without he gets his wick dipped. I got mine when I was twelve."

So that's what the fishing trip was about, a maiden wick-dipping voyage for Billy McKavett's son.

The two of them had a curious habit of never looking at one another square in the face. It wasn't that way in the beginning, at least not for McKavett, because in the beginning he thought of his father as handsome and smart. He loved to watch him work, drive nails, saw boards so beautiful and even. He loved the way Billy McKavett would look away from his work now and then, and pull his lips back tight, and squirt spit through his front teeth.

But the time came early to McKavett when he knew that his father didn't like him. Days would pass and Billy McKavett would not speak to his son. Then when he did, he seemed to focus his eyes not on McKavett's face but on the wall above his head, or on a piece of furniture off to one side.

There was the day McKavett rode to the post office with his father and a huge friend came to the window of the truck to talk and he said, "So this is that boy. I was afraid he was gonna get grown before I ever saw him." And Billy McKavett answered, "Yeah, that's him. Ain't he the ugliest little fart you ever run across?" He laughed then, but McKavett would remember, always, those words coming out of his father. The huge friend chuckled in a nervous way and reached out and rubbed McKavett's head and said something like, "Well, he's a real boy. Boys ain't supposed to be pretty." Then Billy McKavett, not willing to let the matter drop, spit out the window and said, "You notice he favors his old lady a whole lot. Hell, I ain't even sure he's mine. If he is I damn sure didn't mark him." The big friend couldn't be sure Billy McKavett was joking, but the conversation made him uncomfortable and he said he had to be getting on.

"I ain't even sure he's mine."

McKavett would repeat those words to himself so many hundreds of times. He would stand before the dirty mirror in the bathroom when his skin was pimpling and search the face before him, search for signs of his father's face that he admired. But not a clue of Billy McKavett was there, not the smooth tan skin or the dark level eyes. "I sure didn't mark him." The face in the bathroom mirror was Emma McKavett's. "You notice he favors his old lady." Billy McKavett was sure right about that. Emma had given her son those close-set eyes and the gash for a mouth that looked a little like a scar.

After he left the Altasillo Valley, when McKavett thought of his mother he was able to see her in only two scenes.

In one she was in the kitchen. In his bunk at Spanish Wells, lying there hearing Addison talk about those happy times playing ball with his mother back home, McKavett would drift back to that dreary kitchen in Georgia. There was Emma McKavett at her sink.

He would be sitting at the kitchen table where they ate. So her back was to him, and her house dress always hung crooked and her reddish hair was frizzy in the glare from the window that had no curtain.

She would seem to hang there, over that sink, never speaking, never humming, never looking up. Sometimes he wanted to yell at her, "Look out the window!" It was like she was a prisoner at that sink and she accepted that she'd be there always and wasn't allowed even to look outside.

So that was one of the ways he could see her. The other way was when they were at the picnic, on the creek in Fuller's pasture and all the Fullers were there, and the Tankersleys, and the Spurgers, all that bunch, five or six families of them, on the Fourth of July.

Billy McKavett had a quart of cheap vodka out there.

62

Some of them had never tasted vodka, and Billy was pouring tastes of it for those who wanted to try it. Most of the women were drinking lemonade, and Billy would dribble a shot of the vodka in their glasses and they would sip at it and say what they thought. "It takes like coal oil to me." And, "To me it tastes like hell." And Emma McKavett: "It don't taste like nothin' to me. I can't even taste it."

"Well then," Billy said, "seein' you can't taste it you might as well have another shot." And he kept pouring the vodka into the glass of his skinny little homely wife. Every now and then he'd look in her glass and if she'd drunk it down a little way he'd fill it back up. Emma was pleased that her husband was paying attention to her in a crowd, because usually in crowds he acted as if she hadn't even come.

Well, she got drunk.

Really staggering, reeling drunk on that vodka, and there was a lot of laughing about it, and Billy seemed to enjoy it. He had this sort of nasty, leering smile that he'd wear when he was up to mischief. He'd turn that smile on the crowd—well, on Lorene Fuller, mainly, and wink at her—and pour a little more vodka in Emma's glass, and it got pretty bad. There in front of the children and all.

Emma started acting crazy. Trying to tell jokes that she couldn't tell. Using words like shit and fart, and it was so strange, Emma McKavett doing that, because she always just sat back and kept quiet.

Just before they were ready to eat she took a couple of steps backward, to catch herself when she staggered, and she fell. Fell over a hunk of hickory that Arlis Fuller had brought up there to barbecue with. She went straight backward and landed hard on her butt and her legs spraddled and her dress came up and she had on that loose-legged underwear.

To McKavett it was an eternity that she sat there in that spraddled way, while everybody stared at her crotch. There was ugly laughter from the men. High-pitched cackles from the women. Children nudged one another with their elbows,

63

and crowded together to get a better look, and some that were down on the creek came running to see what the ruckus was about.

Billy made no move to get his wife up. He leaned against a tree and sucked on a cigarette. Held the near-empty vodka bottle down along his leg. Blew smoke out his nostrils and grinned his vicious grin. While Emma sat down there in the dirt with her legs apart, her arms back and her palms on the ground for support, her eyes all hazy-drunk. And she looked down at herself and grinned in a wet and crooked way, as if she was looking at something that belonged to somebody else.

McKavett ran.

Ran sobbing, in great gulping sobs. Ran to the creek and into a heavy thicket, through briars and vines, his eyes all tear-blurred so that he bounced off trees and straddled saplings but felt nothing. The loose leg of his mother's underwear covered only half the dark hair and McKavett couldn't bear it, looking with all the others at that private place he had come out of, all slick and red and ugly, fourteen years before.

He stayed in Fuller's woods two nights before the men found him. And Billy McKavett said, "Sometimes I think something's the matter with that kid."

## TWENTY-THREE

IT WAS A POINT OF HONOR with Flora Ward that she was a most particular kind of a prostitute.

She was a businesswoman. She operated a combination beer joint and filling station on the west bank of the Altasillo in the south part of Georgia, and she did all right.

At the start, she was associated in this enterprise with her husky husband Frank. But Frank had an itching foot and soon tired of pumping gas and staying put. He took a job driving a truck.

So three weeks out of most months Frank was herding his rig across Arizona or Tennessee or Pennsylvania, while Flora pumped gas and popped caps there on the Altasillo. Where she stayed almost constantly horny.

When Frank drove away in that big truck Flora was in her mid-thirties and quite healthy, and she needed a great lot of attention after dark to keep her calm. She began accepting the necessary amount from certain of her customers. She had a loose, good-natured sexiness that appealed to most men. Her body was soft and rounded and its movements promised abundant pleasures. And so there was no shortage of customers willing to see Flora didn't suffer while her husband was off somewhere in that big truck.

One night a highway construction foreman spent a rewarding four hours in Flora's bed and when he departed he left her a ten-dollar bill, as a token of his friendship and appreciation. Was Flora insulted? No indeed. She thought it was sweet, and used the ten to buy perfume.

Then Frank came home, on a night when he was supposed to be in Kansas. He found Flora in bed, but not asleep. She was entertaining a fellow Frank had never even met. So he became upset, and shouted about it a great deal, and finally left and didn't come back.

Flora missed him. She missed his paychecks as well. So after that the little tokens of friendship and appreciation from the customers became more important. Instead of buying perfume, Flora used them to pay bills.

In this way she gradually became, as she thought of herself, a part-time and exceptional whore. She had rules and values. She wouldn't go to bed with anybody unless she thought he would give her pleasure. She wouldn't take money for going unless she needed it. And in this way Flora Ward got by, and kept in a good humor.

At three o'clock in the afternoon on the day Billy McKavett took his only son to the river, Flora was dozing. She was slouched in one of her own beer-drinking booths. Not a customer was in the place. Billy's truck woke her.

She looked out, saw who it was, and gave a little grunt. A corner of her mouth turned down a moment. But she stepped behind the bar, checked her face, and patted her hair. She was having a slow month. Sometimes, during slow months, she was able to anticipate pleasure out of going to bed with customers she didn't even like. Such as Billy McKavett.

"Hey, Billy."

"Flora. How's business?"

"Full house. Listen to 'em roar. I may not be able to find you a seat. Whatta you gents up to?"

"Aw, me and this boy's down on the river a little way. We got a bunch of throw lines out, and a camp pitched, and while we're waitin' for them ol' cats to get hooked we thought we'd ease up here and get us a few beers, and maybe talk a little business." Billy had a few beers in him already.

"What kind of business you want to talk? Monkey?" She grinned, and McKavett looked at her and tried to grin back but he wasn't able to. He was all nerves, and wished desperately he was somewhere else.

"What we got on our mind, Flora," said Billy McKavett—he was using his leer—"is pussy. This boy here's pushin' on toward seventeen and hadn't ever had his wick dipped. I thought maybe today'd be a good time to get it done."

Flora seemed to notice McKavett for the first time, studied him with her eyes smiling. He just couldn't bear to be inspected that way. He ducked off the stool and went to the restroom.

"I'm not sure that boy's interested," she said.

"He's interested. Anyhow you let me worry about that."

Flora was still doubtful. "Why don't you let 'im go out and hustle it up himself? Girl closer to his own age maybe."

Billy shook his head. "Naw. Look at him. Not any girls his own age gonna take 'em off for an ugly little fart like that."

"He ain't no prize on looks, that's for sure. Seems like a pretty nice kid though."

"How much?" Billy said flatly.

66

"For me to take the boy to the back?"

Billy nodded. "That's what we come for, to get his wick dipped."

"Twelve, then."

Billy whooped. "Twelve my ass!"

"No, twelve *my* ass."

"Hell's afire, Flo, you ain't no college girl, for cry sake."

"I'll be the best *he's* ever had."

Billy considered. Then the leer came to his face. "Tell you what. Deal. I pay ten, but I get to watch."

Flora's head was wagging before he got it out. "No. None of that kooky stuff. I don't like third parties. It'll have to be between me and the boy." She looked at the clock behind the bar. "You lookin' for a deal, OK. I got no help this time of day. You stay out here and watch the front and I take the boy back and perform the operation and the price is ten."

Billy pointed to the icebox. "And I get two free beers," he bargained.

"My god," she sighed. "OK, two free beers."

"And if he can't cut it, or if he fires before he sees the enemy—you know what I mean?—I get to come in and do the job myself."

Flo's head was wagging again. "Billy McKavett, you better quit messin' around with me. You haven't ever been one of my favorite people and this afternoon I specially don't like you."

McKavett was back from the restroom.

"You go with Flora," his father told him.

Flora made no move. She stood crooked with a hand on her hip and her head to one side, pretending impatience, and looked at Billy until he took his wallet out. He gave her the ten and pointed to the icebox, and she pulled him a beer and said to McKavett, "What's your name, Billy Junior?"

"Melvin."

"Well, come on, Melvin."

"Go on," his father said again. Billy was looking at him now, straight in the eye, for the first time in so long.

She took his hand lightly. They went through a door at

the end of the bar and along a short hall into connecting quarters where Flora lived. A fat little slick-haired brown dog met them, all full of wags and squeaks, and its claws went tick-tick-tick on the linoleum. Flora picked the dog up and petted it and talked baby talk to it. Which was strange to McKavett, and yet in a curious way reassuring, that a woman about to go to bed with a stranger would do that, pet a little dog that way, and care about it.

She led him to a square bedroom with fluffy curtains and a yellow chenille spread on the bed. She sat on the edge of the bed and looked at the floor a while, staring, as if her mind was somewhere else. Then she began taking her shoes off.

McKavett stood in the middle of the room and thought of his mother.

Flora was about his mother's age. But her opposite, in almost all ways. Her hair was jet black from dyeing. Her body soft and full. And bulging some. She had the beginning of a pot belly. Her blouse was too small, so that it gapped between buttons at the top and McKavett could see a strap of her brassiere and the white skin of one breast. He thought of what she wore under her skirt. Would she take her skirt off? He hoped she wouldn't be wearing loose-legged underwear. To McKavett, Flora Ward was a thoroughly attractive woman.

"Well, come on, Melvin, let's have your pants off. It's better with your pants off."

She got up and reached for his belt buckle and, because he couldn't help doing it, he drew back from her, shrunk from her, and said, "Wait a minute! Wait a minute!" His voice was broken and high.

Silence, for a long moment, while Flo studied his face. "Sit down there, Melvin." She waved at a small bench with a yellow skirt around it, in front of a mirrored dresser across the room. McKavett sat, and released a great breath, and she saw him shudder as the air came out of him.

"Do you want to do this, or not?" she asked.

He got his breath back and cleared his throat. "I don't know," he croaked.

"I don't think you do."

"But my dad, he . . . well . . ."

"Tell you what, let's just don't tell him any different. I'll keep his money and we'll stay in here another few minutes and then we'll go out lookin' just as screwed as we can look. And when he asks you—he'll ask you how it was, just as soon as you drive away. And you tell him it was a damn good piece, OK?"

"OK."

She went out to fool with the little slick-haired dog again. She stayed about ten minutes and stuck her head back in and grinned and asked, "Are you through?" She started on toward the front.

"Miz Ward?" He couldn't get the croak out of his voice. But he had to tell her before they went back, and finally here it came. "I think you're a real pretty lady."

She laughed but she gave him a light thump on his red cheek and said, "You come back to see me, later on. Without your dad."

McKavett felt uplifted when they walked in together. His father misread the flush on his face and laughed out loud. Billy McKavett bought a case of beer and said to Flora before they left, "I got another free one comin'. That was the deal."

Flo pulled him another beer and said, "I know damn well you drank two at least while we were in the back."

Billy laughed again. "Well, I need a little tip, seein' I'm bringin' you business this way."

"Well, you drive a mighty hard bargain, Billy." She caught McKavett's eye, and they both smiled, and she winked at him.

They weren't a hundred yards down the road when he asked, just as Flora said he would, "Well, how was it?"

"It was a damn good piece," McKavett answered.

"Shit. How would *you* know?" But the leer was on his mouth. Billy McKavett had loved that little adventure.

McKavett felt good, riding back to their camp. He blurted out the thought that was in him. "That Miz Ward, she's a nice lady, you know?"

His father almost missed a turn, yelling and whooping and laughing. "Flora? A nice lady? Gees cries, boy, she ain't nothin' but a damned old whore!"

"Well, even if she is, maybe she could still be a nice lady."

Billy McKavett shook his head, took a long pull from his beer bottle, belched, and said this to his only son:

"Somethin' you better remember, boy, about women. The only things they're worth a damn for in this world is to fuck and fry bacon."

# TWENTY-FOUR

WHEN HE WAS EIGHTEEN, McKavett had been passed along in school to the tenth grade. He was an embarrassment to his teachers, a joke to his classmates. He made no trouble, he just didn't do his schoolwork.

Then there was the day he sat in the principal's office and the principal was looking at a spot on the office wall above and to the right of McKavett's head, just the way his father always did. ". . . and we do find that not all of us are suited to formal schooling . . . it's certainly no disgrace . . . there are other ways, other paths to take . . . learn a trade, perhaps . . . or the military . . ."

McKavett's home life had fallen apart. His father, fortified with six beers and a pint of whiskey, had carefully driven his pickup through a bridge railing on the Altasillo and into seventeen feet of water. Emma McKavett left at last the place of her imprisonment there at the sink in that dreary kitchen. She moved in with an older sister. McKavett got in the habit of not showing up for meals at his aunt's house. When he didn't show, when he slept somewhere else, nobody went forth to look for him, nor asked where he'd been when he did show.

And so he went in the Army.

On his first furlough he returned to the Altasillo Valley. He could find no trace of his family. He went then to Flora Ward's. "Come back to see me." Not many people had ever said that to him.

He had to tell Flora who he was. "Oh, yeah. Billy McKavett's boy. Well, you haven't done a hell of a lot of growin', have you." He hung around Flora's for two days, drinking beer, watching Flora work. She was fatter but still a pretty lady.

"Look, soldier," she said to him when he showed up at her place at ten o'clock for the third straight morning, "you haven't lost anything around here. Why don't you get on down the road? You sittin' around here, starin' at me, it's gettin' on my nerves."

After that day he never went back to the Altasillo. His home was the Army. He got along all right. He did as he was told and made no trouble. It suited him that in the Army he was not required to progress, as in school. On furloughs he wandered, mainly in the city nearest where he was stationed, and sat through dozens of bad Western movies. He was not unhappy. He was not anything.

Everything he owned he carried with him when he walked across the base at Spanish Wells, looking for the tent-shack he'd been assigned. He pulled on the screen door and there was a big guy grinning at him and holding out a hand and saying, "Howdy. My name's Addison. You like a top bunk, or a bottom?"

## TWENTY-FIVE

"TRINIDAD," he said, laughing from the pitcher's mound, "you swing a bat like my sister Victoria. Shoot fire, man, you're not sweepin' down cobwebs, you're supposed to be swingin' at the ball. Now look here a minute."

He had them all three out on one of The Bear's softball diamonds. Marched them out there in a military manner after they had astonished him by confessing they never had played ball, of any kind. Not baseball, not football, not basketball.

"Just take a nice, relaxed, comfortable stance here at the plate," he said, demonstrating now for Trinidad. Booker and McKavett stood in the outfield, waiting to run down whatever Trinidad might hit. "Spread your feet a little. And be loose. You're all tensed up. Use your wrists, see? You got good quick wrists, now use 'em. Just keep your eye on the ball, and when it comes over just take a nice easy level swing. Don't try to kill it. OK, here she comes. Just meet it solid.

"Oh well, hell, Trinidad, you got to stride, step into the pitch. Looka here, now watch this. You want to get your arms out, away from your body some. Look at my back elbow here, about parallel to the ground, see? That way, when you swing, you're more apt to come through level and meet the ball solid. When your pitch gets close, step forward this way when you swing, to get your weight behind it. You can stand flat-footed like that and you won't ever hit it past second base.

"Now come on, try it again. Here she comes . . . All right, that's a little better. Least it looks more like you've got hold of a bat instead of a broom. Arms out, now, like I said. Level swing. Here we go. Hey! Lookit that! Screamin' base hit, fans! (Talking like a play-by-play announcer now.) It's in the hole in left-center! All the way to the fence! One run scores! *Two* runs score! Here's Trinidad rounding second! Goin' for three! Here's the throw! Gonna be close! Headfirst slide! He's *in* there! (Faster now, and higher-pitched.) So - it's - all - tied - up - two - to - two - in - the - bottom - of - the - ninth - with - one - out - and - the - winning - run - sitting - on - third - base - in - the - person - of - Big - Chief - Trinidad - the - pride - of - Arizona! Listen to that crowd. GOIN' WILD! . . ."

The Troop stood stone-still, listening to his performance,

marveling at it. Then he motioned them in closer to him, like a manager calling a conference before the next pitch.

"Listen here, you think it's not important for a guy to know how to hit a ball, or sink a basket, or catch a pass? It *feels* good, is why it's important. It fills a guy up inside, feeds his spirit you might say. One of the finest feelings in this world is to hit a ball out here on the meat end of the bat, in just the right spot, so it's all solid and comfortable and you know, when you hit it, that it won't even think of comin' down till it flies over the fence. I can't think of anything going, next to pussy, that feels that good. All right, who's next in the batter's box? Booker? Get your dusty butt in there. Hustle! You think I'm out here in this hot sun tryin' to get a friggin' tan?"

They were happiest at such times, when he was teaching them things.

# TWENTY-SIX

MEN WERE RUNNING. Holding their heads high, looking at whatever they were running toward. All running to the same place. Shouting. Excited.

Addison knew it meant a fight. Men always ran to a fight, in a way that they ran to nothing else. The only thing that surprised him, when he came closer, was that the men were running to his own tent-shack. He pushed through, to the little clearing at the center of the crowd. His face sagged when he saw.

Booker and Trinidad were there in the sand, rolling and straining and beating at one another.

He let them get up once. Both were so tired they could scarcely lift an arm. Trinidad swung a wide right, *slung* it, really, and it missed by a foot and Booker ducked and lowered his head and charged awkwardly. He put his shoulder in Trinidad's middle and they went rolling and spitting in the sand again.

Then Addison stepped in and grabbed them by an arm and yanked them up and stood between them. The men shouted their objections, as for some mysterious reason men do everywhere when two of their kind are restrained from beating on one another. "Keep out of it, Add! Come on, let 'em go! Let 'em fight!"

Addison marched them through the crowd to the tent-shack door and pushed them through and announced, "OK, you birds, the show's over. If this fight starts up again I'll have 'em announce it in advance and maybe I'll sell tickets. That's all you'll see, for free."

They growled, and began to disperse.

He sat them on their footlockers and waited while they finished spitting sand and inspecting themselves for damages.

Then, "What the hell was that all about?"

Trinidad cut his dark eyes at Booker and said, "You tell him what it was about."

"He called me a son of a bitch," Booker charged.

"Tell him why!"

Addison looked to Booker. Booker looked away.

"He stole Sarah's picture," Trinidad said, with his darkest Indian look. "The one where she hasn't got anything on her top."

Back to Booker. "I *didn't* steal it!"

"He was jerkin' off with it!" Trinidad's voice was shrill, so high it broke. "He had it under the damn sheet and he was jerkin' off with Sarah's picture!"

"That's not true!"

"All right, all right, hold it down," Addison said quietly. "Let's try to keep this in the family. Where's the picture now?"

They found it on the floor, behind Booker's bunk. It was torn at one corner and creased across the middle. Addison opened his footlocker and put the picture in his writing kit where he kept them all. He stepped to the door.

"Come on, Trinidad. Come out here a second."

74

They walked toward the latrine. "Look," he told Trinidad, "let's just let this thing ride. Forget it. Don't say anything else about it."

"But my god, Add, he took Sarah's picture, and he was beatin' his meat with it. I caught him at it! Damn, Add."

"He ought not to have taken the picture, that's sure right. But it's partly my fault. I guess I shouldn't have shown it, to begin with. But aside from that, well, I just can't much blame him for doing the same thing I've done myself, a good many times."

It took a while for that to sink in on Trinidad. He walked, in quick little short steps, the way he did when he was surprised or perplexed. He walked a tight circle around Addison and came to a stop in front of him and looked up and asked, "Really?"

Addison nodded. "You go on to the latrine, anywhere, for a couple minutes. Let me talk to Booker."

Booker was still there on his footlocker.

"Add, listen, takin' that picture, that was bad. I don't know why I did that."

"Well, you won't do it again."

"No. Add, I . . ." He needed to talk about why he took the picture but he couldn't, and suddenly he was crying, his face down on his knees and his arms wrapped around his head, and he stayed that way a long while, crying softly, and Addison kept quiet and let him get it all out.

"You know something, Book?" he said finally. "One of these days we're gonna look back at Spanish Wells and it's gonna be like a crazy damn dream, a weird kind of time, everything about it. Being out here in a creeping desert, for god's sake, living in a tent, when there's so many pretty places to be, and better things to do. It's not real easy, I know. And we do—well, we do whatever it takes, to stand it, and get by, because sometimes it's awful lonesome. I've done a few pretty peculiar things myself out here.

"So how about let's just forget it, about the picture. If you're trying to apologize for going in my footlocker, why

OK, I accept. And my picture has been messed up. Sarah's got the negative and she can get me another print. Won't cost much, but it'll be some trouble to get. Say a buck, to cover the print and the bother. You got a buck?"

"Sure, sure."

"Then fork it over, and we call it even."

When Trinidad came back, Addison told them, "All right, we're forgetting what caused that argument, or whatever it was. But I have to say this—by god I was embarrassed. Here I been workin' my tail off how many weeks in that gym, givin' you birds boxing lessons, and when you get in a scrap you forget everything I've taught you. If ever you have another fight and anybody asks where you learned, I sure hope you won't say it was me taught you. You looked like a couple of junior high school girls, gruntin' and rollin' in the dirt. Shoot fire, I looked any minute for you to start pullin' hair."

So there they were grinning at each other. And when McKavett came in, from watching a cowboy show at The Bear's movie house, he said, "Somebody in the latrine said yawl had a fight. Yawl really have a fight?"

"Naw," Addison said, "they were just fartin' around."

"We were just fartin' around," Trinidad said.

It was sundown. Addison took out his writing kit. So did Booker, and McKavett, and Trinidad. They all went out and sat in the sand, and wrote to Sarah.

# TWENTY-SEVEN

"TELL ABOUT THE FIRST NIGHT you and her did it," they said.

"Naw, come on, I told that two three times already. Anyhow I've been telling too much. Sarah knew I was talking about all that stuff she'd skin me and stretch my hide on an ironin' board."

"She won't ever know."

"We won't ever tell her."

76

"Tell again, about the first time."

So he told them again. He loved to tell it. He told it to himself, over and over so many times, to make it happen again, to relive the exquisite experience of making love to Sarah the first time. The first *times*—oh, those first five weeks.

Addison was a long, long way from a virgin when his trail ended that night at the company party in Chicago. He grew up with a large number of affectionate and generous-hearted neighbor girls and female cousins, and to Addison they were every one so mysterious and such a delight to touch and to smell. From his very beginning Addison loved girls. And why shouldn't he? The first day he looked around him with any awareness at all he was surrounded by smiling females, who patted him, spoke sweet words to him, fed him, kept him comfortable.

When he reached the stage where most young boys were avoiding girls, Addison was already chasing them. He grew up loving girls. And girls, in that way they have of understanding what's not said out loud or written down, knew he loved them, and loved him in return.

Addison never had any trouble understanding this. He was thankful for it. How nice it was to live among beauty and tenderness. His family understood as well. But some of their friends did not, and bothered about it. One who bothered about it was a high school coach and a fellow faculty member of Addison's father.

"It may not be any of my business, A.L.," the coach said when Addison wasn't quite sixteen, "but I've been wondering if you've noticed something about that boy."

"I've tried to notice everything about him I could," Addison's father said, "ever since we've had him. Am I missing something?"

"Well, I don't know. What I mean is, he fools around with girls so much. If he was mine, that'd worry me."

"Why?"

The coach shrugged. "It just doesn't seem quite normal to

me. Just for instance, yesterday I came by the field on the way home and there was a big touch football game going on. Twenty-five or thirty of our boys mixed up in it. Your boy was out there but he wasn't in the football game. The reason I noticed, I've been watching him. He's got a deep chest and he's gonna be a big boy, and coordinated too. I'd like to try to make a tackle out of him. I bet time he's seventeen he's gonna be weighin' one-eighty, maybe one-ninety. He might be a real hoss, if he doesn't mind gettin' hit. Does he like to get hit?"

Addison's father pretended not to understand what that meant. "I don't expect he does. *I* sure don't like to get hit."

"No, I mean does he like to mix it up. Body contact, you know. Because at the field yesterday when the football game was going on, he was over there behind the gym playing volley ball with a bunch of girls."

"Volley ball's a good game. Used to play it myself some."

"Sure it's a good game. But playing it with girls, that's what bothers me. And I sure can't make a tackle out of him if he's gonna spend his time playing with girls."

Addison's father nodded. "I see. Well, I tell you what, Coach. Let's just don't worry about it. Liking girls that way, that may be something the kid inherited and can't help. Got it from my side, I expect. My Old Man was the same way. Used to tell me, he'd say, 'A.L., unless I'm goin' out to fight wars or skin mules, if you give me the choice I'll take women over men every time. They're twice as dependable, and they *feel* so much better.'"

The coach grinned doubtfully about that.

The year Addison was a junior, that same coach took his football team to the semi-finals in the state championship playoffs. One of the principal reasons was Addison. Not a tackle but a fierce, raging, laughing linebacker and defensive captain. At the close of the season he was named to the Texas all-state team, chosen from players in the biggest schoolboy football system in all of creation. And college athletic departments were already sending him Christmas cards.

It was also that same coach whose blood pressure leaped forty points the day Addison came by his office to announce that he wouldn't be playing football his senior year. He'd gotten interested in boxing, and didn't want to play football any longer.

The coach grieved so deeply about that. He had been kept comfortable over a long hot Texas summer by the lovely thought that with Addison leading his defense next season, he had a solid shot at the state title. And all the professional benefits that accompany such an achievement in a football-crazy state. He appealed to Addison's father.

"He's making an awful mistake, A.L. With a good senior year, and putting on ten more pounds, he could have his pick of any college in the country and write his own ticket. My godamighty, A.L., it'd be worth money! Maybe even a pro career."

"But he's gotten interested in this boxing, and he's serious about it."

"Boxing! Shit!" That coach was so anguished. "Goddamn, A.L., he's not gonna go out and win the goddamn heavyweight *title!*"

Addison's father kept so calm. "Well, I don't know, Coach. Not two years ago you were saying yourself that he wouldn't make a football player because he fooled around so much with girls. Maybe you could be wrong about the boxing, too."

"Shit, A.L., come on. You know boxing's not going to do a damn thing for him. It's not gonna get him through college."

"Well, I don't think he's interested in college right now. Says he wants to travel."

"Travel where? Where's he gonna go?"

"Oh, all around, I guess. Told me the other day he wanted to go to China and see if Oriental vaginas really run crossways. I told him I'd go with him if I could get away."

So the coach gave up. That fall, while the football team won six and lost four, Addison worked weekends in a gymnasium sixty miles away in Fort Worth, where he found somebody who agreed to teach him boxing.

# TWENTY-EIGHT

THE REWARDS of loving girls became evident to Addison when he was very young. He was nine, and large for his age, when his twin cousins Cora and Alma, smiling and overweight and thirteen, pushed him up the ladder of their father's hayloft. There they happily stripped him naked and explored every inch of him.

They opened their clothing and took turns holding him to their soft warm skin. And they said sweet things to him. "You're nice. Here. Put your hand here."

Addison thought that was lovely. How much better it was than wrestling in the dirt with boys.

With that early beginning, then, Addison had made love to a great many girls indeed by the time he got to Sarah, for he was twenty-eight and he had kept on the move.

But Sarah was a shock to him. Loving girls was not the same as loving Sarah. The vast difference intimidated him. Frightened him a little. For the first time he knew the awful fear that he would love and not be loved in return. It didn't seem quite possible to him that Sarah could love him as he loved her. Or maybe she would stop loving him because of what she would learn about his past, or because of something he might do that would repulse her.

Be careful, he said. Don't screw this up. Be honest with her. Play it straight.

"I never have been any Little White Jesus," he told her. "I guess you know that."

She nodded and gave him the soft calm smile that caused such a storm to rise inside him. "You've known a lot of girls, you mean."

"Well, yeah, some."

"And you've been to bed with a lot of them, I expect."

"Well . . ."

"Do you want to know about me? Whether I'm a virgin?"

"No-no!" He held his hands out, palms toward her, as if he

wanted to keep that information away from him. "I'm not asking you that, and I never will."

The sweet smile, still there, so full of love. "Well, if you do ask me, I'll tell you."

"I'm not asking."

They planned to be married there in her church. "Right there by your piano, so I can hold onto it, keep from falling on my face." They set a date two months from the day they stood in the street and talked about what had happened to them. That was the soonest they could get the church, the soonest Addison's folks could come up from Texas, the soonest they could accomplish all the arranging.

"Listen," he told her, "if you need more time, take it. I want everything to be just right for you, just exactly right. Because, girl, this is the only time you're ever gonna be doing this. Fifty years from now I want you to remember all this, your wedding, your engagement and all, and say, 'Well, it was done just right, just the way it ought to have been done.' And if that's old-fashioned, if it's cornball, that's fine with me."

"Are you saying you intend two months from now to carry me across the threshold pure and sweet and unmolested?"

"That's what I'm saying if that's the way you want it."

She laughed then, her breath warm and minty on his face. "If that's how you intend to do it, love, you had better get your hand out of my blouse."

He didn't take it out, though. "I said I could do it. I didn't say it would be easy for me."

And it wasn't easy, for either of them. In fact, it was so hard for them that it didn't work at all. The trouble was, they weren't able to maintain an interest in anything except each other. They did try. "Maybe if we go to a movie." But in the theater they would end up in a corner of the balcony, necking and whispering and fumbling at one another's underwear, and when they came out they'd have to look at the marquee to see the name of the picture they were supposed to have watched.

They tried going swimming a few times. But they

wouldn't get good and wet before they'd be wrapped around one another, clawing at shoulder straps and trunks. "We're going to get arrested," she said, and they stopped going swimming.

He loved to go shopping with her, and stand before show windows and admire their reflection. "Look there. A hell of a good-looking pair."

"Beautiful," she'd say. And then, "Your hand is on my behind."

"I know. That's because it feels so good. All smooth, and curvy."

"But you shouldn't have your hand there in public."

"Are we in public?" He looked around, surprised. "I'll be damned."

They would take long walks at night in parks. He would pull her to a secluded picnic table and go to work on her buttons and unhook her brassiere and drive her to desperation with long wet kisses. He would seat her just so, in the moonlight, and arrange her open blouse in just the right way to display her breasts. Then he'd step back, cautioning her not to move, and he'd stand there admiring her, and make crazy little speeches about the National Buh-zoom Contest being held this year in Long Beach, California, and how she could win it without even showing up, all she'd have to do would be send a picture of 'em. "What am I talking about, shoot fire. You wouldn't have to send but a picture of just *one* of 'em."

She would laugh and call him an idiot, but she loved the little speeches, he could tell.

Once she said, "I may as well stop wearing a bra if you're going to take it off every time you come near me."

He shook his head. "No, keep wearing it. I like for you to have it on because I like to take it off. If you're going to stop wearing something, stop wearing pants."

Which was the beginning of the end of their abstinence program. A week later they were in one another's arms on a blanket in Sarah's back yard, on a little patch of lawn beside her mother's flower garden. Her parents had gone up to Wisconsin for the weekend. Sarah had cooked for him. A soft warm night. They lay together and explored and felt and tasted and talked of the most intimate matters. Both almost undressed. Both actually hurting from the deep physical need of one another.

Then Sarah, sweet-faced Sarah who played the piano at the church and wore the soft curls that framed her face, whispering desperately: "Addison! I love you! Please! *Put it in!*"

And so the honeymoon began, five weeks early.

## TWENTY-NINE

"TELL ABOUT where you did it," they demanded.

"Just everywhere. A lot of places."

"Like in hotels, and motels?"

"Yeah, sure."

"In the car? Ever in the car?"

"Oh hell yeah. Lot of times in the car."

"Not in her house, I don't guess. You couldn't do it in her house, with her folks there and all."

"Well, her folks went out sometimes. Anyhow we did it plenty of times with them there in the house, upstairs, you know, and gone to bed. One time we did it on the stairs, and her folks sleeping I don't guess twenty feet away. I *hope* they were sleeping. But shoot fire, what am I talking about, one time we did it on second base, in a damn ball park."

Which brought McKavett rising out of his blankets. "You mean with people there, in the stands?"

Addison laughed, and Trinidad said, "McKavett, you got to be the dumbest ass in the United States Army."

"Tell us about it on second base."

"No, tell about on the stairs, first."

"No, second base, second base."

83

It was true enough about second base, and about the stairway as well. When Addison told The Troop tales to make them laugh, his imagination often ran wild and free. But about making love to Sarah, he kept to the truth. The very fact was a wonder to him, and he felt no need to color it.

When they began the early honeymoon it was soon after the first of the month and both of them had just been paid. Within two weeks they were both broke. They spent themselves penniless renting motel and hotel rooms. On a procession of squeaky beds they frantically worked the edge off the craving they had developed for one another. They held absolute marathons of lovemaking, charging each other again and again, scarcely talking, until at last they couldn't continue and they would lie naked and panting and look at one another until checkout time.

Saturdays and Sundays and once during the week Addison could make it into Chicago, with the permission of his superiors. Between times, he made it to Chicago without permission. The nights he couldn't make it, they spent on the telephone. They began developing a technique of making love over the phone, a system that would help Addison endure the months he spent at Spanish Wells.

"We're gonna have to stay away from those damn motels," he'd tell her on the phone. "They're breaking us. Hell, we won't have enough cash to get out of town on a honeymoon."

"I don't care," she'd say. "We'll sleep in the park, or on the beach. I like you in the sand. You're something, in the sand."

So they would think of places to make love, places that didn't cost anything.

"On park benches," he'd suggest. "You could sit on my lap, and I'd cover your legs with my jacket or something and if anybody came along they wouldn't even know what we were doing."

"How about behind bushes, on the grass?" she'd say. "I love you on the grass. On the grass you're something, just like in the sand."

"In the car, on the front seat."

"We could do it in the lake, in the water."

"Then standing up, in a dark place somewhere, like Sunday night. Did you like it standing up?"

"I loved it standing up. You're something, standing up. How about on the sofa, here at home, after Mother and Dad have gone to bed?"

"A fine idea. The stairs, too, I think the stairs. You know that place that's flat, there where the stairs turn, halfway up to the second floor?"

"The landing."

"The first time I was ever in that house, you sat there on that landing for a while. I don't remember why."

She laughed. "I was threatening to go up and go to bed and leave you. It was three o'clock and I couldn't get you to go home."

"Anyhow, you sat on the landing and you were so damned pretty there, looking down at me. Once in a while you let your legs open a little and I could see your thigh, just for a second, and I thought, my god, if I could ever put my hand there on that place on your leg, just one time, it would feel so good I'd just faint dead away. Did you do that on purpose—open your legs that way?"

"No. I didn't even know I was doing it. You ought to be ashamed, looking up my dress the very first time you came in the house."

"Well, I did, and I'm glad."

"You want to hear something that will surprise you about that night?"

"You bet. I love surprises."

"I wanted to go to bed with you even then. I thought about it even before then. I thought about it even at that crazy party, the first time I saw you."

"Sarah, listen here, I love you so damn bad I don't feel normal any longer. When I'm not with you, I feel like I'm partly absent, like somebody has cut something off me and I'm not all together. And I do silly things now that I didn't used to do, and I think dumb thoughts. There's some things about being this bad in love that I don't really like. You know what I did last night? I dreamed about your belly button."

She giggled. "Really? Well, that's not silly. I think it's sweet."

"Of course it's silly. Of all the damn things I could dream about I pick a belly button, for god's sake. The thing is, it's a beautiful belly button. I'm crazy about the damn thing just because it happens to be on your belly. You see what I'm talking about? Here I am in love with a belly button. I didn't understand *anything* about being in love."

"Addison, baby . . ."

"I love all your other parts, too. Elbows, kneecaps. Whoever in hell or on earth would think of being in love with a kneecap? Well, me, *I* would. A *kneecap!* What am I talking about, I even love that little old wart or whatever it is on your rib, down there below your right arm. That little old wart is just as important to me as that furry warm business between your legs."

He seemed to catch himself then, and said, "Well, now wait a minute. I take that back. A wart couldn't be that important. But I love everything on you, like that funny little wrinkle at the left corner of your mouth that twitches just before you smile at me . . ."

"Oh, Addison!"

"I love your insides, too. Your stomach, and your liver, and your collarbones, and your gizzard."

The giggle again. "I haven't got a gizzard."

"Of course you've got a gizzard. All God's chillun got gizzards. They're down there by your spleen, and just a little bit east."

"My heaven, I've fallen in love with a crazy person."

"Sarah."

"Yes."

"Let's do it in the church."

"The church! We can't do it in the church."

"On the stair landing, then. It's important to me."

"All right, love, the stair landing. Maybe tomorrow night if you can get here."

"There's somewhere else I'd like to do it."

"Where?"

"In Wrigley Field, on second base."

"Addison!"

"Sure, Wrigley Field, with forty thousand fans on hand. Just before the bottom of the seventh, say, and I lead you out there and I've got the mike to the PA system, see, and I make this announcement, I say, 'Ladies and Gentlemen, introducing, on my right, not wearing any pants, my beautiful and best girl Sarah Allen, winner of the Best Boobs Contest held recently on the West Coast. Miss Allen plays the piano at the church, and made pretty near straight A's in school, and has long straight legs and a nice round behind that wiggles just right when she walks. And now next on the program, we're gonna make love for you here at second base before we start play in the bottom of the seventh.'

"And the crowd would cheer, and our names would go up on the scoreboard, and when we did it the whole damn continent would shake, and out yonder on the Coast I expect they'd register it anyway a six on that Richter Scale. Then people would know how it is. They'd understand, and they'd be talking about it pretty soon everywhere. Right now they don't even know anything's happened. They're just going along acting like the world's the same as it was before I ever met you . . ."

"Addison!"

"Listen, do you know what I'm trying to tell you? This thing that's happened to me, to us, it's almost more than I can stand. I can't hold it all inside me. I want to rent airplanes and write it in the sky, and take out ads about it in the paper, and yell about it from monuments and towers and tall places like that. I want people to *know* about it. I want 'em to notice you when you walk around outside. I want 'em to say, 'Hey, look there, at that pretty girl with the long straight legs. That's Sarah. That's old Addison's girl. Why, she *loves* that crazy bird!' "

"Oh, Addison!"

# THIRTY

A WEEK BEFORE THE WEDDING. They were walking, late at night, in the park. They came to a softball field. Deserted at that hour. The light poles and the low bleachers were dim shapes in the darkness.

She stopped and pulled at his arm.

"What is it?"

"Look," she said. "Wrigley Field."

He stared a moment at the bleachers. "Well, I'll be damned. It sure is Wrigley. I didn't recognize it at first."

Without any further words they walked slowly, arms about one another, through the entranceway between the bleachers. They went around the heavy wire backstop and onto the diamond.

They stepped across home plate, and over the pitcher's mound, and stood a while at second base before they began.

Then quickly they attended to one another's buttons and zippers. By then they were expert in the matter of buttons and zippers. He spread his khaki shirt there on the base, and put her down and kissed her everywhere, and made swift and thorough love to her in the darkness.

When they finished they allowed themselves to lie there only a few moments. Just long enough for him to turn and look at the empty bleachers silhouetted against the park lights a block away.

"Did you hear the crowd?" he asked her.

"I heard bells. Do they ring bells?"

"Yes, sometimes they do." He kissed her, as gently and tenderly as he could. "Must have been forty thousand people in the stands. Now they'll know how it is, and spread the news. That's good."

"Yes," she said, "that's good."

They got up and fixed their clothes and walked out slowly, just the way they came in. Over the pitcher's mound. Around the heavy wire backstop. Between the low-slung bleachers.

"I feel so good," he said. "I liked that."

She walked pressed against him, her arms around his middle. "I liked it too. You're an excellent second baseman."

## THIRTY-ONE

ADDISON WATCHED FROM A DISTANCE. Sergeant Runge had backed Booker against the wall of the gymnasium and was giving him hell about something. His appearance, most likely. When Runge walked off he left Booker stuffing his shirttail in.

"The worst thing about it, he calls me Tub of Guts. Always Tub of Guts." Following the encounter, Booker walked with Addison toward the mess hall. Even after making the adjustments the sergeant demanded, he still looked like a sack of dirty laundry. "I don't know why he's got to give me hell like that all the time."

"Well," Addison said, "maybe he'd leave you alone if you tried looking a little sharper."

Addison himself always kept sharp. Even seventeen miles out there in the wilderness where nobody but Old Regulars like Sergeant Runge worried about proper dress, Addison kept sharp. When he reported for duty at the headquarters building, he was just right. Khakis clean and creased. Shoes shined. Shirt fitted, so it wouldn't blouse and balloon around his middle. Always fresh-shaved, and smelling the way the women he was raised with thought he ought to smell.

Victoria and Kat and his mother were forever tugging and

pulling and straightening and combing and brushing on him when he was growing up. Making him change socks because the color didn't match what he wore. Sitting him down and manicuring him. Telling him to stand up straight. Gently fussing at him.

He enjoyed the memory of that. Talked about it now to Booker, since the subject had been brought around again by the sergeant.

"Victoria used to ride my tail about like Runge does you, on how I looked. She'd tell me—lord, I heard it a hundred times—she'd say, 'When you go out in public you owe it to yourself and to people who care about you to look the best you can.' I remember one day I was getting on my bicycle to go across town to my aunt's house for something, and Victoria yelled out the window at me about some dirty old pants I had on. I told her, well, shoot fire, I wasn't gonna see anybody but just Aunt Gloria, and she said, 'But Aunt Gloria loves you, and you need to look nice for her.' And damn if she didn't make me go back in the house and change clothes.

"Then she used to say, 'When you're *with* somebody, maybe just a friend walking along the street, you owe it to that person to look right. Because then you're a part of a pair, and one of you reflects on the other.' She got all that stuff from Mama. I used to hear Mama preaching to her about it. I guess she was right, though."

Booker twisted that protruding lower jaw of his and cut those sad eyes up at Addison and gave him the mirthless grin and said, "At my house didn't anybody ever talk about how anybody looked. Nobody gave a damn."

"Well, somebody gives a damn now."

"Yeah. Sergeant Runge."

"No, I mean your friends. Hell, Book, even way out here on this old prairie, you've got friends. Me, I'm one *of* 'em. *I* give a damn."

Booker looked down and hitched up his pants a little.

# THIRTY-TWO

WHEN ADDISON RETURNED from the trip to Chicago, he left Sarah sitting on the nest.

She didn't tell him until she'd been to the doctor twice and was certain. Then she broke the news on the fourth page of a six-page letter while writing about the adventures of the family pets. A dachshund named Fräulein, and a cat called Black Cat.

"Fräulein is pregnant. She had a long and embarrassing date in the front yard with a spotted dog from across the street. Black Cat is in the same condition. She went out romancing and didn't come home all night. Dad says she has taken seriously what was poked at her in fun. He says that every time it happens. In my own case, I trace my condition to that last night you were here, when the moonlight was so bright on the bed. Ever since you left I've been feeling pregnant. This morning when I went to see Dr. Graves he said I am pregnant indeed and that I will continue being pregnant until the middle of December."

# THIRTY-THREE

"I HATE TO TELL YOU THIS," she said, "but you've got a new problem." Katherine, leaning across his desk, grinning her lop-sided grin that said she didn't really hate to tell him at all.

"What's my new problem?" Addison asked.

"Charley Biggs is in mucho trouble."

"What kind?"

"He's been misbehaving. Turns out he's been hauling things in that airplane that he's not supposed to haul, and he's been taking little favors for it."

"What kind of favors?"

"Like money. He's been hauling freight that doesn't belong to Uncle Sam. Hauling it for private parties, and taking a lot of money for doing it."

"Captain Biggs would do that?" That was hard for Addison to believe. Charley Biggs was a free spirit but he seemed a good officer. He had flown a lot of combat. Addison liked him.

"He's been doing it a long time," Katherine said.

"How do you know about it?" He knew how, but let her go ahead and say it.

"Oh, it's all written down. It's in one of those big baskets on The Bear's desk right now. The Bear sure is in a bad humor about it, too."

She straightened up, pushed away from the desk, and stood with her hands at her waist and her shoulders back and she looked really all right in that blouse, standing behind the desk so her bowlegs didn't show. In times before Sarah, Addison would have perished, if necessary, doing whatever it took to get inside that blouse. Out there among the cactus, bowlegs or straight, Katherine would have been an immediate project. Even now he couldn't help wondering how far everything would descend, along her front, if her bra was unhooked.

"What's all this got to do with me?" he asked.

"Because of what happened last March 16th."

Addison turned to the calendar behind him. March 16th was the day he had ridden to Chicago with Biggs. "Wasn't anything funny going on that day on that airplane."

"Not unless you call ten pounds of Mexican heroin funny," Katherine said quietly.

"Really? Captain Biggs was running dope?"

"A tidy little ten-pound package, delivered in Chicago."

Package. When she said that word, Addison's heart surged. A ten-pound package. He could see it, riding on the back seat of Sarah's car. Instantly he was back in Chicago on March 16th, looking into Captain Biggs' grinning face while they stood under the wing. Hearing the conversation again. Hearing it so clearly.

He was about to hurry away to meet Sarah, and Biggs had called to him. "Oh say, Add?" Sounding as if he'd just happened to think of something. "Are you going to have a car while you're here?"

"Yes sir. Sarah's. Need a lift?"

"No, but I have a little parcel I need delivered. How about dropping it off for me?"

"Sure, Captain. Be glad to."

"Good. That'll save me a trip across town." He went back in the plane and brought the package. It had no address. Biggs wrote the address on a slip of paper. "Just be sure you give it to this William J. Wheeler. Make him show ID. I'll call and say you're coming."

And that was all there was to it. Addison had run errands and done favors for Army officers for years, and he did not question the contents of packages he was given to deliver. He put it on the back seat of Sarah's car and almost forgot to deliver it. Because when he drove past the street where the delivery was to be made it was dark, and lucky for that, because Sarah's head was in his lap and he was having a hard time keeping his mind on driving. And they had to turn around and drive two miles back to leave off the package.

Now, looking up into Katherine's face in the headquarters building, he was chilled by the thought on that night in Chicago, considering the circumstances, he could so easily have had a car wreck. With ten pounds of heroin riding on the back seat.

Did Katherine know he and Sarah had delivered the package? Did The Bear know? He needed to find out. He asked, "Well, hell, I didn't know there was any dope on that airplane."

"But you were on board, and you were AWOL, and that's not going to be easy to explain to The Bear. Add, this could be a real problem for you, I'm not kidding. The Bear has told Major Burke to get to the bottom of Charley's deals, especially this drug thing. He's told Burke to drop everything and do a thorough investigation. You know well and good your name will come up as at least being on board . . ."

Evidently she didn't know about the delivery, and Addison relaxed a bit. He let Katherine push on, telling him what she knew.

"The Bear's sour on you already, you know," she said. "That fracas of yours in town has brought him some grief, and then when you refused to box on his fight card . . ."

"That was The Bear's deal? I thought Runge was getting that up."

"Runge was just doing the talking, about it being entertainment for the men. But it was The Bear's baby. He was going to fly in some brass for the fights. I don't know for certain but I've got an idea your boxing is the reason you got sent here in the first place. You were going to be his big attraction, his gladiator."

Addison stared at her, puzzled. "How could that be? The Bear hadn't ever heard of me before I got off that bus up yonder at the gate."

Katherine smiled and shook her head slowly in amazement. "I swear, Addison, sometimes you can be so dumb. Listen, there's an unofficial file, this thick, attached to your service record, and it's passed around and read for entertainment. The Bear's read it. Major Burke's read it. I've read it. Hell, I even made a copy of it that The Bear sent to General Boswell, back when he was going to have the fights. All kinds of your little adventures are described in there, in detail. That sailor out in Santa Monica you put in the hospital, that's all in there, and you busting the guy's jaw at The Puma, that's in there. Then those boxing matches in Virginia, that's The Bear's favorite story, where you jumped in the ring in your khakis and your GI shoes and flattened that fellow, that what's-his-name who ended up a title contender?"

94

"But that was just sort of a fluke. I got mad about something."

"And your women, my god. You must be something. A lot of *that's* in your file. I heard The Bear tell somebody on the phone not long ago you were the only enlisted man he knows that ever spent six weeks in bed with a major."

Addison frowned and shook his head. "All right, there you are. It just goes to show you how the record gets messed up. She wasn't but a captain and it wasn't any six weeks. It wasn't but about four, or five . . ."

"And AWOL!" Katherine exclaimed. "I swear, Add, I don't see how you've kept out of the stockade, with your AWOL record. It's a wonder you didn't go off somewhere chasing girls and miss the war. But you've been lucky, Add. I'm telling you, this Charley Biggs thing could be real trouble for you. You may have a hard time walking away from this one."

Addison thought of Sarah, so happy and pregnant in Chicago, smiling in that sweet calm way, playing her piano in the church. He could see the astonishment and the hurt come on that face when his name came out in a narcotics investigation. That record of his, all the womanizing and the street fighting—my god, was Katherine right? Was it all written down that way? He was chilled by the idea that Sarah might hear it all. He couldn't escape the feeling it might cause him to lose her. And then this dark and incredible thought—that Sarah herself might be questioned, about riding in her own car across Chicago with ten pounds of Mexican heroin in the back seat.

"Hey," Katherine was saying, looking at her watch, "I got to get back to my post, and conduct myself in a military manner."

She started to leave but Addison motioned her back. "Wait a second. Listen, how is The Bear getting all this information?"

She shrugged. "I'm not sure but I figure it's got to be from

95

somebody on the inside. One of the crew on that plane, I bet. Somebody's just squealing."

He tap-tap-tapped his pencil on the desk and went ahead and asked her. "When this comes up, maybe you could help me. Talk to The Bear for me. Would you?"

She was grinning again now, chewing that gum. "The day has come. Old Add, asking Katherine for help. Sure, I'll help you, if I can." She struck a silly pose and said, "And then, blinking her false eyelashes, she said, 'Come to my place, tonight, and we'll talk about it. Say around seven?'"

He laughed a little and said, "All right, sure, why not?" But then he said to her, "Look, you might as well know, I'm out of circulation. I don't screw around anymore, I really don't."

"Good grief, you sound like I've propositioned you. I just said we'll talk about it."

"Well, I just wanted you to know."

"I know, I know, you're out of circulation. Come earlier, if you want, and we'll scramble some eggs or something. And stop by Deke Fowler's and bring some of that good scotch he sells you so cheap."

All that afternoon, Addison was so depressed.

# THIRTY-FOUR

UNTIL THE DAY he met Sarah, Addison had been entirely satisfied with being in the Army. He had ten years' service when Sarah walked into his life in her red shoes. He had never given a serious thought to staying in the Army to retirement, yet the longer he stayed, the more comfortable he became.

When there wasn't a war going on that they sent him to, life in the Army was a play-party to Addison. The duties assigned him were so simple, so easy. Yet they fulfilled his demand for a challenge. He found his challenge in carrying out his assignments with more ease and efficiency and speed than anyone else around him. He performed a great assortment of duties, all well.

Most of the regimentation the Army thrust upon him, Addison didn't mind. Some of it he actually loved. He loved to dress up and look sharp. Loved being an example of how to walk and salute and pop to attention. "Look at Addison there. Do the way Addison does." One of his happiest years he spent as a drill instructor in a basic training camp. He enjoyed giving close-order drill. Like the feeling of power and control he got from spitting out an order— *"Leflank!* . . . *Haw!"*—and seeing forty-eight marching bodies pivot precisely and in unison on the ball of the right foot. How beautiful. So orderly. Satisfying.

Addison loved the pageantry of retreat. Bleached khakis and shined shoes and short barked commands. And the flag coming down, and those first three booming notes of "The Star-Spangled Banner" that filled his deep chest with tingles.

When a war needed fighting, it was so exciting to him. Addison was a consummate combat soldier. He fought the way he played football and made love—fiercely and passionately, but always in control. When he had orders he followed them. When he didn't have orders he called on his own judgment, and it had never failed him, not in combat. Lucky, they called him.

Even his wounds were lucky. He came laughing and cussing and limping up to a command post with a sniper's bullet in his thigh. "God dang, those sons uh bitches *shot* me. If that's not a hell of a damn thing to do to a man when he's off so far from home like this." And then six months later, a cluster for his Purple Heart. A little piece of shrapnel went spinning across his scalp, plowing a furrow only a quarter of an inch wide, to send him tumbling and bleeding and unconscious into a shell crater. Then when the medic found him an hour later Addison was sitting up, wiping blood out of his eyes and running his finger along the wound in his scalp and saying, "Those bastards parted my hair on the wrong damn side."

Two months after coming out of high school, he went into the Army. Left home to the accompaniment of a chorus of sobs and objections. From his teachers, from his buddies headed to college, from a considerable covey of girls he had dated. And from his mother and his sisters and everybody in the family—except his father.

"Be quiet and let him go. He's got to go, and there's nothing any of us can do about it."

"Well, Mama, shoot fire, if I don't go to college I'll get drafted anyhow, and I've had enough of school, at least for a while. I want to go see what's out there. I just *got* to."

So he went, and he did see a great deal of what was out there, although seeing it the Army way was a slow trip and included, as he said, "a hell of a lot of it they could have left out."

There were some qualities of the military life that didn't suit Addison. The Army sometimes offended his sense of freedom. When he was struck by a deep yearning to be in another place, usually there was a rule that said he couldn't go, and that bothered him quite a bit.

So he would go anyway, in violation of the rule. Absent without leave. As Katherine said, it was a marvel he had kept out of the stockade with the record he had on being absent without permission.

What saved him was, he never went when he was really needed. He never went off and left a duty unfulfilled. That trip to Chicago, for example. He had been assigned temporarily to The Bear's staff to straighten out a tangle in some records. He was often on temporary duty that way, when a situation had become confused. He was good at troubleshooting, and capable of so many tasks. He was given two weeks to clear up the problem with the records. When he got aboard Captain Biggs' airplane to leave, he had worked on the records five days and completed the assignment. It was against his nature to stay idle in a place where he had done what he went there to do.

Once he even went AWOL in a combat situation, though it wasn't in his record. And here's why it wasn't:

His outfit was dug in in an inactive sector, waiting on artillery and air support, under orders not to move a yard until that support came. Addison learned—simply by going to his company commander and asking—that they would be dug in there at least three days. He learned so much that way, by asking people direct questions. It was the nature of men, he had found, to tell what they knew, and so often they were just sitting around waiting for somebody to ask.

Three days, Addison calculated, should be plenty of time, and so he left. Didn't tell anybody. Just took off, because he hadn't had hold of a woman in three months and three months of fighting without any loving was getting close to unbearable. He went a hundred miles backward, walking, hooking rides in Jeeps and GI trucks and half-tracks, and passing through three towns before he found a woman he wanted to take to bed, and who was willing to go.

He made love to her four times, and left feeling so relieved and pleased with himself. It didn't surprise him when he got back to his outfit that not a shot had been fired or a patrol sent out while he was gone. He went straight to his company commander, a young first lieutenant from Cedar Rapids, Iowa, who had chronic bowel trouble. Addison told him where he'd been and why and for how long.

"We didn't even miss you," the lieutenant said.

Addison brought a present for the lieutenant, a large chamber pot. "A slop jar is what we call 'em at home," he said. He got the pot from the woman he'd made love to four times a hundred miles back. It was a pure luxury for a combat officer with chronic bowel trouble. The pot had a smooth, wide, flanged rim around its top. The lieutenant let his palm move slowly around that wide smooth rim, and he smiled. He was so pleased. Inside the pot, heavily wrapped so it wouldn't break while it traveled, was a bottle of pretty fair brandy. When the lieutenant saw that, that's when he said, "We didn't even miss you."

Addison was walking away. The lieutenant looked up from his new pot and said, "Say, Add, you didn't find any pussy, did you?"

"Oh yes sir, I sure did."

"Really? My god. Was it any good?"

"Yes sir, it was. It was just excellent."

"How many times?"

"Four times, sir."

The lieutenant looked back down into his new chamber pot and pulled out the bottle. He slowly removed the wrapping and pulled the cork and took a great loud swallow and pointed to Addison and said, "Addison, you son of a bitch, if you ever go AWOL from my outfit again without taking me along, I'll bust your ass from here to the state of Iowa."

"Yes sir. I'll remember that, Lieutenant."

So that little adventure didn't get into Addison's record.

But so many of them did. The AWOL's, the fights, the womanizing, which so often involved girl friends or wives or daughters of commissioned officers, and that made it such a sensitive matter.

When his superiors examined Addison's record they were not only entertained and intrigued, but puzzled as well.

"He's a fine soldier, in so many ways. But look here, at all these high jenks."

"If you gave him something big to do, do you think he'd do it if he didn't want to?"

"Probably not. But I think he'd get somebody else to do it. He never has refused to follow an order. At least I don't think he has. It's hard to be certain."

"Do you ever get the feeling he's in this Army because he likes to play with it?"

Inside this cloud of bemused but suspicious curiosity on the part of his superiors, Addison thrived in the Army. But he did not rise in the ranks. Which suited him all right. He had no ambition to rise. He had studied those who wore all the stripes and braid and brass and he saw something he didn't like. There was a tightness around their mouths and a shiftiness about their eyes. They had risen, he decided, above the level where they could stay comfortable and happy. He wanted no part of that.

Until Sarah happened to him, Addison had never concerned himself much about money. If he had cash in his pocket, fine. If he didn't, he still ate and slept and dressed just as well. If he needed extra money, he could usually pick up a few bucks in a crap game. But he seldom needed extra money. He almost always had enough to do whatever he wanted to do.

One sleepy afternoon at Spanish Wells, Major Burke called Addison into his office and had him shut the door and take a chair. "Add, I want to ask you a question. You don't have to answer because it's personal, and I admit I'm just plain curious."

"I understand, sir. Go ahead. Ask anything you want."

"You know that Howell, who tends bar in the officers club?"

"Yes sir. I don't see him much now but I used to, when we were out on the Coast."

Burke nodded. "That's what I wanted to ask you about. Last night Howell told me something he insists he saw you do. I confess I'm fascinated by it. I even took notes, and I want to know if it's true."

"I'll be glad to tell you if it is, Major."

Burke nodded again, and grinned, a little embarrassed. He referred to a slip of paper on his desk. "Howell claims that once out on the Coast he saw you walk out the front gate of the base without a cent in your pocket, and stick up your thumb, and get picked up by a good-looking gal in a convertible. That you got taken into LA, that you saw a UCLA football game, and ate a steak dinner, and slept with that good-looking blonde. And that she delivered you back to the front gate the next morning and you had ten dollars in your pocket. Now I have to know, is that a fact?"

Addison was shaking his head. "No sir, not all of it."

"But some of it is?"

"Well, some of it, yes sir."

"What part of it's not?"

"Well sir, I didn't have ten dollars, really. I think it was just six or eight, and she wasn't a blonde. More of a redhead."

Major Burke crossed his arms and leaned forward and studied Addison's composed face and said, "Addison, does that sort of thing happen to you very often?"

"No sir, not very often. In fact it hasn't happened to me but just a few times."

In those years, when Addison was winging it, free and high and unfettered, he considered the Army to be a lovely organization. Some of its delights did fade, he admitted to himself, when Sarah came along. But she more than made up for them, and Addison had begun looking toward the day that he would go back into the civilian world. He had a year and a half to go on his current three-year hitch when he and Sarah got married. "When that's up," he told her, "I'll come out and go to work. We'll be needing more money, for a house and all." But he hadn't let the matter disturb his peace. Through all his scrapes Addison had managed to live without the burden of a worried mind.

But now—this business about Captain Charley Biggs. This was a worry. It wouldn't have been *much* of one before Sarah, but it was now. There were angles, possibilities, threats in the Captain Biggs thing, and they kept dark thoughts in Addison's head.

He did not feel well at all when he rode to town on the bus, without The Troop, to talk to Katherine.

## THIRTY-FIVE

"IT DON'T TAKE NINE MONTHS EXACTLY. Not every time."

The Troop, discussing Sarah's pregnancy while Addison was gone.

"For hogs," McKavett said, "it takes three months, three

weeks, and three days, every time. Ain't that hell, the way that works?"

"How'n hell would you know that?"

"My grandpaw raised hogs is how I know. Three months, three weeks, and three days."

"Human babies can come quicker'n any nine months. My cousin had a baby in six months one time and they put it in the oven in the hospital in Bisbee and it got all right."

"In the *incubator*."

"Well, shit, Booker, it's a joke, all right? Godamighty, a guy can't even make a joke around here. She just *called* it a oven, OK?"

"They move around in there," McKavett said, "before they're born."

"Pigs do?"

"Naw, man, regular babies do it. I read about it. They kick, and the girl can feel it."

"They do more than that," Booker said, speaking with authority. "Sometimes they turn flips. Just turn a whole damn flip."

"Horseshit," said Trinidad.

"Horseshit," said McKavett.

"No horseshit," Booker said. "Sometimes one will sure as hell turn a flip in there. And sometimes one will be in there with his head down, ready to come out, and he'll just decide to switch ends and put his head up and his butt down and come out ass-first that way."

"You sure about that?"

"Sure I'm sure. Anybody ought to know that."

"How could one turn flips? They wouldn't have room, looks to me like."

"Well, they do."

They fell silent then to dwell a while on that marvel.

McKavett resumed the discussion. "It seemed to make old Add real happy, Sarah gonna have that baby."

"Yeah."

"It's not a hell of a lot to get happy about," Booker said darkly, "if you ask me."

# THIRTY-SIX

BOOKER WAS NOT PLEASED that Sarah was pregnant.

Every night—as all four of them in the tent-shack did—Booker received Sarah in his dreams. Sometimes sleep-dreams, sometimes awake-dreams. When she came to Booker she was wearing so little. She was draped in something flimsy and silky and she came running to him through the yard, past the bedrooms where his mother and his sister slept, to his own room behind the garage. She came in slow motion. He had seen it in a movie, a slow-motion girl running that way, wrapped in flimsiness, and he had made her into Sarah. Beautiful Sarah, who had written him the words, "I would love to see your room at home sometime."

He had told her in one of the letters about The Room. One sundown they were sprawled against the tent-shack, writing to Sarah, The Troop struggling for something to say, and he asked Addison about it.

"Add, you think she'd like to hear about my room, that I built onto the garage?"

"Sure, why not?"

So he wrote her about it. Wrote her how the house had two bedrooms, and his sister Frieda always had the front one. How his father left when he was four. How he had slept in his mother's bedroom until he was ten. How he moved out and slept so long on a cot in that small space off the kitchen where the washing machine was. He stayed there until he was fifteen. Then on Saturdays he would work for Old Man Schroeder, who wrecked houses, and Booker collected scrap lumber and bent nails that the old man would let him have, and he carried them home and built himself a room, a shed-type affair, on the back of the garage.

It had a corrugated tin roof that the rain sounded good on —he told all this to Sarah in his letter—and it had a table he'd found, and a chair with green legs and a red back that he'd painted himself, and it had a wooden bunk he built around a set of springs off an iron cot. He tied into the wiring in the garage—he'd studied electricity some in school— and he brought in an overhead light and one double outlet where he could plug in his radio and an old hot plate that he'd rewired. So he could even cook a little. The overhead light was just a bare 60-watt bulb, with a pull chain, on the end of a wire hanging low over the bunk. He hung it low on purpose because he was short and he hated to strain to reach things that were just the right height for everybody else.

He called it The Room. He'd say to Harvey, his friend, a little older than Booker, "You want to come to The Room?" They'd get in there and smoke and listen to the radio and talk about the pictures he'd ripped out of old magazines and thumbtacked to the walls. Booker loved The Room. It was His Place.

It was where Sarah came to him, when he lay dreaming in his bunk at Spanish Wells. After he wrote her about it The Room became more special still. Because when she answered she said, "I would love to see your room at home sometime." Not knowing what the words could mean to him.

Then one day here was Addison whooping and announcing, "Hey, guess what? Sarah's pregnant! Whattaya think about that? That girl's gone and swallowed a watermelon seed, looks like."

After that day, Sarah would not return to Booker in The Room. Every way he tried failed. He could see her start to come to him, but she wasn't beautiful any longer. She didn't look like Sarah, sexy and slow-motion and beautiful. Instead she was Frieda, his sister, and she would not come running smoothly. She would come fat and waddling and ugly and awkward, and he would open his eyes and she would disappear.

Frieda. Two years old than Booker. She was short and

105

strong and square built. When they were growing up they were often taken for twins. Both had the sunken eyes and the thick overhanging brows. The mirthless grin. The protruding lower jaws. Heavy bodies. Meaty backs. Short arms. Frieda worshiped her mother. She was never happy.

# THIRTY-SEVEN

ONE AFTERNOON after school Harvey said to Booker, "You want to get a little tonight?"

Harvey was always talking about getting a little. It didn't, Booker thought, mean anything. But he said, "Who from?"

"Don't worry about that. You want a little, just come by the house around nine o'clock. We got some lined up. An old gal that'll screw us all. The more the better, is what she says."

A gang bang. Booker went along. It was so exciting to him. Long before they arrived at the place his pulse was racing and his legs were weak and trembly. The gang was beneath the football stadium bleachers. So dark. Up ahead somebody had a flashlight, and now and then it would switch on and Booker could see the head and shoulders of a dozen or more boys in a loose-ordered line. There was little conversation, and it was almost whispered. Occasionally a giggle or a short comment drifted along the line. Harvey and Booker stood at the end.

A tall figure came from under the stadium, walking spraddled, buckling his belt.

"How is it?" somebody asked.

"Well, it ain't the best I ever had."

"Who is she, anyway?"

"I don't know her name. That old fat gal works down at Albert's sometimes."

On weekends Frieda helped behind the counter at Albert's but Booker didn't make the connection immediately. He made it when he heard her voice, strained and tight, calling from beneath the stands in that darkness.

"You son of a bitch, the next time you shine that god-damned light on me, this party's over!"

"My god!" Harvey said.

He turned but Booker was already gone, walking fast, stumbling in the darkness. Harvey ran to catch up.

"Jeez, Book, really, man, I didn't know who it was. I didn't have no idea!"

When they got to his street, Harvey turned off and said to Booker over his shoulder, "See you tomorrow." Never again after that night did he mention to Booker a word about the football stadium incident.

Booker decided to wait for her in the front yard.

Their mother was working. She had worked nights so long, she wasn't able to sleep except in the day. Some of her neighbors argued privately that she worked nights to avoid contact with her children. She was in her fifth year as night clerk in a little dim-lobby hotel on the ragged side of town. Frieda and Booker would go about their work or school for five, six days at a time without seeing their mother. Or at least without talking to her. Booker saw her even less frequently after he built The Room. He had stood in her door and said quietly, "I've finished The Room." She was ready for bed and sleepy but she trudged reluctantly out to the garage and put her head inside the crooked door of that place he was so proud of. And she said, "OK, but just be sure you don't go off and leave that light burning."

Louise Booker was not a bad-looking woman. When she was forty she could still draw two or three traveling men around her at that hotel desk. But they were different men every night, and they didn't hang around long. Because she was neither interested nor interesting. She was a dull woman.

She considered her own children ugly and unrewarding, and was almost never seen with them in public. When she was, it usually generated the comment that it certainly was curious that a good-looking woman like that could produce two such homely children.

Frieda yearned for her mother's attention. Envied her

smooth and trim legs and slender body and pretty face. When she was a schoolgirl, ten, twelve years old, she would sometimes appear unexpectedly at her mother's place of work. After school she would go there and take her younger brother, and this would make Louise Booker so angry.

"Don't come down here anymore. It just means I have to take off and drive you back home. Isn't there plenty to eat in the house?"

Booker had no clear memory of his father. Frieda could tell things about him because she was six when he left. Sometimes Booker pumped her. "What was he like? What was he like?" Until Frieda exploded and screamed at him, "Go look in the fuckin' *mirror*, you ugly little bastard! He was like *us!* Like *us!*"

She came home from the football stadium after midnight.

She was walking, and that offended Booker all over again, Frieda walking home. What'd they do—all twelve or fourteen of them screw her and then the last one pulls up his pants and buckles his belt and walks off and drives away? He had a picture of her, after the last one, sprawled there under the stadium with her legs apart and raising up to look around. Next? Anybody else? Sitting up, then, slow and sore and tired, and finding her underwear there on the ground and pulling it on and starting home. Frieda, Frieda. My god!

"What are *you* doing out here?" she asked him, coming up into the yard.

"Nothing. Where you been?"

"Nowhere. Just walking."

He almost decided not to mention it. But it came out of him anyhow. "I know where you were. At the football field, under the stands."

She turned her back to him quickly, and faced the street awhile. Then she sat down on the step and put her head on her knees. "You mean somebody came by and told you? Announced it, I guess."

"What in hell you want to do that for?" he said. "That's a

hell of a thing to do, take your pants off for every sorry bastard in town. Down there in the dark, and everybody standing around making dirty jokes."

She raised her head to look at him. "Wait a minute. How do *you* know they were making nasty jokes?"

"I heard 'em!"

When she understood, she got to her feet again and laughed that coarse and humorless family laugh of theirs and she said, "Well, well, so you were there, standing in line, hey? That had to be a pretty good little surprise, I guess, when you found out who it was." The laugh again, strained, deep in her throat. "Let me ask you. If it had been somebody else, somebody you didn't know or never saw, that would have been all right, hey? Just another one of them ol' gals likes to screw, and puts out to everybody."

"Do you really like it that way? All those guys?"

"Damn right!" she said, so fiercely. She sat on the step again and turned her head away.

"Is this the first time? You haven't done it before, have you?"

"Yes, I have. I've done it several times."

"Why? My god, Frieda, why?"

She was up again, facing him, and her heavy shoulders were tensed and her stubby legs spread and she said, in a great anguish, "Oh shit, I don't know why. It's because . . . it's just because that's the kind of thing people like me do!"

She went in, but she stopped in the door and put her forehead against the jamb and said, sobbing quietly, "Sometimes . . . I get so . . . lonesome . . ."

Soon after that she took a job working nights. Tried to keep hours similar to her mother's, so she could see more of her. That meant Booker spent more time alone. Harvey had quit coming around to The Room after the night at the football stadium. Booker became almost an eighteen-year-old hermit. He kept more and more to The Room, sometimes for several days. He was a senior that winter, due to graduate in the spring. He had always been able to pass his schoolwork.

Made C's, mostly. But now he missed so many days he was failing every subject and finally he just quit going.

In the month of November that year, Booker's mother spoke to him twice. He marked it on his calendar. And early in December she spoke to him once more, and it was the last time before he left. They met on the street in town. It was dark and she was on her way to work.

"How are you doing in school?"

"OK. All right."

He'd been working two weeks then, full time, for Old Man Schroeder, and hadn't been to school in more than a month.

She said before walking on, "Why don't you count on going up to Granny's for Christmas? I'll have to be working through the holidays."

"OK."

She left him on the sidewalk then and walked on, and he stood with his hands in his pockets and watched her go, and grinned his sad grin.

He didn't go to his grandmother's for Christmas, though. He spent Christmas Eve in a movie, sat through it twice, and went back to The Room about midnight. Frieda was there, in The Room. Something was wrong. She was on his bunk. Her face was sweaty and her eyes said despair, despair.

"You've got to help me." She whispered that, so hoarsely. "I'm having a kid."

"Oh shit!"

She put a forearm across her face. Drew her short legs up. She rolled onto her side. Her brother watched in frightened wonder while she had the pain. When it was over she sat up on the edge of the crude cot that Booker had built and nailed together with Old Man Schroeder's bent nails. The profile of Frieda's body had changed so little. Thicker around the middle. Right up to her time she had worked, and kept the baby a secret beneath her loose clothing.

"I better go get Mama," Booker croaked.

"No," she said. "Mama doesn't know about this and I don't want her to know."

"But you got to go to the doctor, to the hospital."

"No. I'll do it right here. Mama never comes out here and she won't ever know."

"That's crazy! You can't have no baby out here in this garage!"

"I can, too."

"What the hell you think you're gonna do with it when it comes? You can't hide a baby from Mama."

"I'll get rid of it."

She fell back and covered her face again and Booker was just terrified. He folded his arms close in front and squeezed his chest fiercely, a gesture he'd had since childhood, a fierce holding of himself in times of stress.

"I'm gonna get Mama!" He yelled it at her.

When she was able to look at him again she saw his terror, and when she spoke again she talked quietly, in control. "You know Kate Ammers, works at Albert's. They live in that little green house, in back of the fire station. You go there and tell Kate I need her, and to bring her mother. They'll come. Now you go on."

He was almost out the door when she said, even more gently, "Tell Kate to tell her mother there's a problem with this kid. He's turned wrong. A while ago he damn near turned a flip. His head's straight up now, I can feel it, and his little butt's down. Tell her that."

Booker ran. He didn't stop until his pounding heart and heaving chest and shaking legs demanded it. He stood, blowing, and looked ahead and saw the light that burned all night in front of the fire station three blocks away. Two blocks beyond the station, the other side of the highway, was the hotel with the dim lobby where his mother would be. He looked to his right at the square dark outline of the high school. Behind the school, two blocks more, was the hospital. "Tell her there's a problem with this kid."

He ran again. But not toward the fire station. Toward the hospital.

He went to the emergency entrance where there was a light, and pushed in. "Hey!" he called out. A nurse came and he said, "There's a girl havin' a baby. She needs somebody."

"Where is she?"

"At home. At my house. It's my sister."

"Who's her doctor?"

"She hasn't got a doctor. She *needs* somebody!"

The desperation in his voice brought some action, and within a minute he was riding in the nurse's car, showing her the way. Frieda was crying out when they walked up the driveway. It was so awful, hearing her cry out.

He didn't go in with the nurse. Didn't want to. When she came out she said, "That place is filthy. But she's got trouble and I don't think we ought to move her in the car. Show me where the phone is."

"We haven't got a phone."

"You stay here," the nurse told him. "I'll be back quick as I can." She trotted to her car and roared off.

And Frieda in The Room cried out, "I don't want no doctor. I don't want no god . . . dam . . . *doc*tor! Oh Christ but that hurts. That *hurts!* Mama! *Mama!*"

He put his face near the door and called to her, "I'll get Mama, OK?"

"No! You son of a bitch, you do that and I'll kill you!"

So for fifteen minutes Booker stood outside the door, waiting for the ambulance. Afraid to go inside. Afraid of what he would see, afraid he'd be required to do something. Those fifteen minutes were an age to him because of the sounds that came through that crooked door that he had built. Those sounds marked him forever. Hearing her suffer that way, such torment, and knowing he ought at least to go in and sit by her and hold her hand and say, "Somebody's here. Somebody's with you." And not being able even to crack the door and look because, oh, god, there might be blood, and she might be in some awful position, all uncovered, and he didn't want to see.

Why, she might die while he stood there. That thought numbed him. Think of what killed her. Some horny old boy she never had seen pulled down his pants and planted death in her belly, and she let him do it just because she was lonesome. And she never would know which one of them in the line did it, whether it was the first one or the twelfth one. Maybe it was the tall one who'd stalked spraddle-legged from under the stands and said it wasn't the best he'd ever had, and he didn't even know her name. Just knew she was that ol' fat gal that worked down at Albert's. Frieda. Frieda.

When the ambulance came, Booker drifted away from the door, around to the front of the house where he couldn't hear her cry out. They stayed in The Room with her a long time, and gradually her cries and her babbling grew dimmer, and dimmer, until they were just little-girl sounds, high-pitched and petulant. Then nothing. No sound at all.

He asked, when they carried her out, "Is she dead?"

"No, she's sedated."

They drove away and didn't say another word to him. He stayed outside a while before he opened the door and looked in, peeked, as if she might still be there on the bunk.

There *was* blood, a big splotch of it on the dirty crumpled sheet. It looked almost black in the dull glow of the 60-watt bulb that hung low on the end of the wire. He picked up a blanket she had kicked off on the floor and covered the bloody place and sat on the chair with the green legs and the red back.

But he couldn't stay. The awfullest dread enveloped him. It hung in The Room, some kind of depressing mist. He went out in the back yard. It was getting colder, colder. There was a redness in the east. Christmas morning.

He went back in, almost charged in, and jerked open the drawer of the table by the bunk and found the little roll of bills hidden there. His pay for the week, plus ten dollars extra Old Man Schroeder had given him for Christmas. He put on his mackinaw and his woolen cap with the earflaps. He switched off the bulb over the bunk. He went out and walked toward the highway.

113

He hadn't intended just to keep going. But he had stood by the highway only five minutes when a young fellow with a big grin stopped in a battered Jeep and said, "The Lord willing, I'm going to Cleveland, Ohio. If that direction suits you, and if you can stand the wind in your face, I'll be glad to have the company."

Booker took the ride. They couldn't talk much because of the noise of the wind and the engine, and that suited him. When they passed through little towns and slowed down, the young man talked some. He was a minister, a servant of the Lord, as he said, just out of seminary, and he had helped conduct a midnight Christmas service and now he was going home. And if the Good Lord would let the transmission hold up on that old Jeep another four hours he would be eating dinner at his mother's table, and his girl would be there, and they were engaged, and wasn't the weather great, and the world such a beautiful place.

"You going home for Christmas too?" the young preacher shouted, for they were rolling again into that cold wind.

"Yeah, that's right." What the hell, tell him a little lie.

"That's great! Wonderful!" The preacher's spirits were soaring. He couldn't get the wide grin off his face. "Everybody ought to go home for Christmas. Be with people they love, right?"

"Yeah, sure. That's right."

Booker rode all the way to Cleveland, keeping mainly silent, nodding or shaking his head in response to comments and questions, until toward the end of the trip the young minister went silent too.

In Cleveland, Booker might have gotten out and walked to the other side of the highway and thumbed his way back home if it hadn't been for something the preacher said when he let Booker out.

"My friend, whatever your problem is, I'm praying it smooths out for you. And whatever you're searching for, I hope you find it if it's the Good Lord's will."

Booker had never before considered that he was searching for anything, or that what his life lacked could be hunted for and found. Something about that idea appealed to him. It also provided a reason, thin as it was, not to go back and find out about Frieda. If she was dead, if that baby had killed her, he didn't want to know about it. He found a bus station and took out his roll of bills and bought a bus ticket to Des Moines. And spent the next twenty-four hours riding across Ohio, Indiana, Illinois, and Iowa.

## THIRTY-EIGHT

IT TOOK BOOKER less than a week to get enough of riding buses and walking streets and trying to think of something to search for. On the sixth day of January he sat on a concrete bench in a roadside park outside Tucson. With him was a fellow about thirty-five that he knew only as Slim. Slim had been stretched on the back of a flatbed truck that had stopped to pick Booker up at Las Cruces.

Slim was an ex-Army man out of Arkansas who was still wearing the olive drab pants he had on when he was discharged six months before. He was broke, and smelled bad, and didn't tell the truth. But he was friendly.

Booker's money was gone, and his muscles were stiff and aching from the night spent on the concrete bench.

"Well sir, I tell you what," Slim said, "I come to me a decision during the night. I'm gonna walk back into Tucson and do one of two things. I'm gonna find work, or I'm gonna reenlist. It's just too damn cold too sleep outdoors in January, even in the south part of Arizona. Now whatta you think about that?"

"Sounds all right."

"You mean you'd buy that, yourself?"

"Sure, why not?"

Slim laughed. "You're all right, kid. Now then, let's say I flip. I'd flip a coin if I had one but I don't so I'll spit on a rock. If she comes up wet, we look for a job. She comes up dry, we go join that Army. Whatta you say?"

"Flip," Booker said. "Go ahead."

"You'll go with me on it, wet or dry?"

"Sure. Go ahead. Flip."

Slim found a flat rock and spit on it and flipped it and it fell on the dry side, and that's how Booker came to be in the Army. Slim didn't go in with him, though. It developed that he had collected himself a little police record in the six months he'd been out, and the Army wouldn't take him back. So when Booker signed up to be a soldier he was in his same old circumstance—alone, and sad.

# THIRTY-NINE

ADDISON'S SPIRITS were still dragging when he got off the bus in Spanish Wells and walked into the liquor store of his old friend Deke Fowler, to pick up a bottle of that good scotch.

Deke had his customary mask on—a sour face. For about two months after Addison rescued the contents of Fowler's cash register, Deke took the mask off and grinned and waved when Addison walked by. But this time he kept it on, and charged full price for the scotch.

"I've lost my discount, looks like," Addison observed.

"Well, the deal was for cases. You want a case, I give you the discount."

"Sure, sure. Don't worry about it, Deke. I know you have a big overhead here, and giving a guy a discount works a hardship." Addison was feeling ugly. "It's been two or three months now since you stood here shittin' your pants over that toy pistol. I wouldn't expect you to remember it that long."

"Well, hell, you feel that way, I'll give you the discount. How much you want? Ten percent?"

"No, just a nickel. Give me a nickel off."

Fowler shrugged, grinned a little. "OK, whatever you say." He opened the cash register and handed Addison a nickel. Then he said, "What the hell you want a nickel off for? You don't care anything about a damn nickel."

Addison was feeling uglier still. "Damn right I do. When I go around doing my good works, like breaking up robberies and all, I want to be paid, by god. I want to be paid just what they're worth."

Fowler decided to keep quiet.

After he'd picked up the scotch Addison had a fresh ugly thought and he dug into his pocket and found a quarter and flipped it to Fowler. Who said, "What's this for?"

"It's a tip for you," Addison growled. "People like you, serving the public, they need to be tipped."

"What's the matter with you?" asked Fowler, puzzled. "That's crazy."

Addison went on out. It *was* crazy, but it fit his mood to do a crazy thing. He walked to Katherine's, going slow, looking for the number. Maybe the walk would put him in better spirits. He thought of Sarah, tried to feel her walking beside him, close. That was a thing he loved so much, for Sarah to walk close by him, touching, so he could feel her leg move with his, and he could put his arm around her and let his hand ride lightly on that lovely curve, one of his favorite places to touch, there just below her waist, at the side, where she began to flare out. Sometimes even in Spanish Wells he could daydream her into walking with him that way. But this time it wouldn't work, and he had to give up trying.

Katherine was wearing a long and billowy thing, one of those hostess outfits. It was the color of cream of tomato soup. She looked good in it. The fullness of it hid her bad legs, and she filled the top of it very nicely.

She took the scotch and said, "I thought I had some soda but I don't. Will water be all right?"

"I don't really want a drink. You go ahead."

"I've got beer," she said from the kitchen.

"I don't believe . . ." Then suddenly he changed his mind. "Well, wait. I think I will have one. Water's fine." A drink might elevate his mood a little. Just have one, and sip on it slow.

She chattered away from the kitchen and Addison studied

117

the room, as he studied all places he entered for the first time. Katherine's apartment surprised him. Nothing about it reflected the brash and cynical personality she displayed at work. Addison had expected flashy drapes, or loud wallpaper, or big busy pictures. Instead the place was so calm, and orderly, and subdued. It managed to look expensive, too, but surely it wasn't. A civilian secretary working for the U. S. Army didn't figure to live in expensive surroundings.

It's the kind of place, Addison thought, that Sarah would fix up. Reminded him a little of Sarah's room in her folks' home. Done up first-class and yet not loud, so that Sarah Herself was always the Main Thing present. And look here, here was Katherine doing the same, dressing in that tomato-soup getup and overpowering the place she lived in.

Addison breathed shallow and slow, trying to catch what his nose was saying to him. It was faint but finally he got it— cigar smoke, probably from two or three days back, maybe longer. The Bear? Addison wondered if he'd been guessing right, that when The Bear's wife went to Los Angeles on those trips of hers The Bear came to Katherine's place. Interesting if true. Bowlegged Katherine, in the hay with a genuine U. S. Army chicken colonel, regular, purebred, and registered, and the commanding officer of one of Uncle Sam's far-flung outposts in the Great Southwest.

She brought the drinks and they talked for half an hour, about everything except what he'd come to talk about. They talked about the weather, about how it was better to drink scotch than bourbon, about the cost of clothes, and food, and apartments. She even told how she broke her arm falling out of a chinaberry tree at home when she was six, and she fixed another drink.

And she put on some music and said, "Come dance with me."

He hesitated and she said, "I've heard you're a good dancer. Well, so am I. You might enjoy dancing with me." She took his hand and he let her pull him up.

He did enjoy it. She *was* a good dancer, surprisingly light and smooth. They danced through four records, and they stopped talking, and Addison became very much aware of Katherine's pelvis against him, and her large breasts pressing into his chest, and at the end of the fifth record she said, "I'll freshen up the drinks." She went in the kitchen.

When she came back he was standing by the door with his hand on the knob. "Listen, Katherine, I'm sorry. I've got to go. I hope you won't throw a fit about it."

She didn't say or do anything at all. She stood there in the middle of the room holding the drinks.

"I just feel like I ought to go," he said again.

She put down the drinks. "We could talk. No more dancing?"

He shook his head. "No, I need to go. Something's telling me to get out of here. If you can help me, with The Bear and all, well, I'll thank you. If you can't, then you can't and that's it."

She smiled, and nodded. "You want to know, before you go, why I'm not . . . what did you call it? Throwing a fit?"

"All right, why?"

"Because I know you'll be back. You're finally beginning to like me."

"I like you fine," he said, shaking his head, "but I won't come back here."

"Yes, I think you will." She looked soft and vulnerable standing there in her tomato-soup dress. A different person altogether than she was at work, where she wore that armor and stayed tough and chewed gum and talked smart-ass. Here she was now all misty-eyed, saying to him, "But even if you don't come back, I'll help you if I can."

# FORTY

AN EVERLASTING CRAP GAME was held in the locker room of the base gymnasium. Not a big game. A dollar, two dollars, most of the time. Addison walked through late one afternoon and saw McKavett taking part. His skinny shoulders were wedged in among ten players, on hands and knees or squatting, forming a semi-oval around a GI blanket spread on the slick concrete floor.

McKavett had four dirty dollars in his fist when Addison came silently and stood behind him to watch. Here came the shooter, hully-gulling the dice and bouncing them off the wall to get ten for a point.

"Two dollars he makes ten," McKavett said, laying out half his bankroll.

"Two he don't," responded a sergeant the other side of the blanket, and covered McKavett's bet.

On the very next roll the dice came up seven.

"Shit," said McKavett.

New shooter now. Out he came, and got five for a point.

"Two dollars he fives," McKavett bet again.

"Two he don't." The same sergeant across the blanket.

And he didn't. When the dice popped up seven, McKavett stood up, said shit again, and found himself looking at Addison's grin. "These old boys taking your money, Mac?"

"Aw, I can't have no luck in this game. I don't know why I keep playin' it."

"Let's go to chow. You ready?"

Walking to the mess hall, Addison said, "You don't ever do much good, shooting craps?"

McKavett shook his head. "Not much."

"You want a little tip?"

"OK. What?"

"Well, to begin with, you're cheating yourself if you bet even money on a guy making points like ten, and five, like you did back there in the gym. That's just not an even-money bet."

MacKavett shrugged. "Well, I don't know, I just always figure either he's gonna make it or he ain't gonna make it."

Addison said gently, "No, see, that's where you're screwing up. Look, say a guy's got ten for a point and you're betting *with* him, like you were back yonder a while ago, betting he makes it. So he's got to roll that ten before he rolls a seven, right?"

McKavett nodded. "OK, sure."

"But the odds are against him. Because those dice have got more sevens on them than they've got tens. So he's a lot more apt to roll seven and lose than he is to roll ten and win. In fact, there's exactly twice as many sevens on those dice as tens, and that makes the odds two to one against him. Two to one odds, on ten, two to one. You can take that rule and put it in the bank, because it's true on every pair of honest dice in the whole damn kingdom, whether you're at Spanish Wells or Las Vegas.

"To get a fair shake, when you bet a guy two bucks that the shooter's going to make ten, you need to make him put up *four* bucks, to give you the odds. Just put your two bucks out and say, 'I'll take the odds on that ten,' and that means whoever fades you has got to lay out four. Of course it works the other way around, too. If you want to bet against the ten, you got to put up four bucks to try to win two.

"But that buck sergeant back yonder, what's his name, I guarantee you he'll flat love you, as long as you sit there and bet him even money on a ten. He'll bet with you all day and ask you to come back after supper and tell you what a nice fellow you are.

"Now then, the same odds go on the point of four, two to one. On five and nine, odds are three to two. On six and eight, odds are six to five. A lot of guys bet six and eight even, but it ought to be six to five. Unless you play the odds, you're screwing yourself." Grinning down at McKavett then. "Unless, of course, you can find yourself a pigeon, like that buck sergeant in the gym did, who wants to bet you even money that a guy will make ten."

"I'll be damn," McKavett said, and nothing more.

Until after chow. They were strolling toward the tent-shack, and he said, "Add, would you write that stuff down for me? About all them odds and all?"

"Sure."

Then a week later Addison was going through the locker room again, and when he passed the everlasting crap game he recognized McKavett's high and whiny Georgia voice:

"Why hell no I ain't gonna bet even money I'll make four." Usually McKavett's tone was apologetic but here he was speaking loud and strong. "I ain't gonna bet four even, not when there's twice't as many sevens on these dice as fours. Still I've got two dollars here says I can make it, and if you want to bet I can't, you can put out four to my two because the odds on four are two to one, and it's that way on ever pair of honest dice in Las Vegas or Spanish Wells or anyplace else in the whole damn world . . ."

Addison walked on, grinning. What the hell, shoot fire, if he's gonna shoot dice he might as well know enough to get a fair shot at it.

## FORTY-ONE

"YOU EVER BEEN IN LOVE, TRINIDAD?"

It was almost time to go out and write to Sarah. Addison was reading the paper. The Troop was waiting for him, making loud talk, trying to draw him into their conversation, get him talking. Because lately he had seemed withdrawn and didn't talk so much, and they did love to listen to him.

He had brought them a long way. Before they walked into that tent-shack and met him, not one of them would have talked to the other about love. Screwing, sure. Whores, fine. But love? That was an embarrassment. It was pantywaist. Girl stuff.

But here was their hero who talked about love more than anything else. Their hero who could break a man's jaw with his bare hand. Who was entitled to wear a Purple Heart with a cluster. Who could boot a football seventy yards. And he was in love, and glad to be, so it was all right, at last, for them to talk about love.

Trinidad answered the question. "I *guess* I was in love. I chased that black-headed little gal in Bisbee around for a year and half, nearly every night."

"Trying to get into her pants?" asked Booker.

"Damn right."

"Well, then you weren't in love. You were just trying to screw her."

"Can't I be in love and want to get in her pants at the same time?"

"Well, sure, but it's not the same thing. Is it, Add?"

"What?" Addison lowered his paper.

"Trinidad says being in love with a gal and wanting to screw her is the same thing."

"I didn't say that, either. That's not what I said."

Addison laid the paper aside. "Well, whatever you said, you're into a deep subject, I guarantee you. There's been millions and millions of people mess up their lives just because they couldn't tell whether they were in love or in heat. It's not always easy to know the difference, at least not on short notice."

Here was Booker asking then, "What does it mean, Add, to be in love? How do you tell if you are?"

Addison rolled out of his bunk. He was wearing only his shorts. He sat on his footlocker, so he could see all their faces. He was quiet and thoughtful a little while, and The Troop could tell by that he was about to deliver them a Message. They leaned a little closer.

"All my life," he began, "I've heard people say, 'When you meet the right person, you'll know, right away, and you won't have to ask yourself whether you're in love or not.' Well, bullshit, is what I say to that. I didn't believe it when I heard it and I haven't seen anything in thirty years on this earth to make me think it's so. How could anything that important come bulging and flashing to you in a second, and decide your entire life for you? You know what I think is one of the biggest troubles in the world today?"

"No, what?"

"It's people getting married when they're not really in love, but just horny, or lonesome, or afraid, afraid they're gonna be left out. You know the first time I ever suspected I might be in love?"

"No, when?"

"When I was eighteen, and a senior in high school. I got to sniffing around a little old yellow-headed girl named Tina Marie Wilson. Cute? God but she was cute. Twisty little old walk. Best damn dancer in school. Man, that girl could squeeze my hand in the hall and I'd pretty near bust the zipper out of my pants. I worked on her so hard. I thought if I didn't get that girl's pants off I was just gonna crawl under the porch and die. But she wouldn't let me. What she *would* do is make a maniac out of me by talking about it all the time. Oh, they know. They know how. She'd say, 'No, now you just keep your zipper zipped because I'm saving this stuff for my husband.' Then she'd say, 'But whoever he is, he's going to be one well-screwed man. He's going to be screwed six different ways a dozen times a day.' Well, hell, you know what that did to me."

"No, what?"

"My god, it drove me up trees. I'd get out of the car, I'd swing from limbs, I'd holler shit, I'd kick tires, throw rocks, beat on the hood. Sometimes I'd just cry, just really cry about it. So that was the first time I thought about getting married. I had to do *some*thing. Finally I went and talked to the Old Man about it. He listened and nodded and kept calm and then he told me, 'Add, don't ever get married just for a piece of pussy. It's the worst reason there is to get married. It's not necessary. Hell, that stuff's on the market. You can go out and buy it, if you can't get it any other way.' Well, it kind of shocked me for the Old Man to talk that way but it sort of straightened me out. The next night I took that little gal out to the lake, and parked on the bank, and I told her. Told her I wanted to make love to her mighty bad but if I had to marry her to do it was no deal, because I wasn't ready to get married and I'd make her a poor husband. She got all swelled up and made me take her home and said she didn't ever want to have anything more to do with me. Well sir, you know what that little old gal did?"

"No, what?"

"It wasn't two months later she married an old boy named Al Stanton, friend of mine, that I played ball with. Then here's something else, the damnedest thing. The last time I was home before I met Sarah, I saw that Tina Marie. Ran into her in the drugstore and bought her a cup of coffee. She's thirty now and she's put on about twenty-five pounds and she's got about four kids and she's got a damn *tooth* missing, right here in front, my god, and old Al's working for the City, in street maintenance. You wouldn't believe what she told me."

"What! What'd she tell you?"

"Said she'd been saving up for a whole year to get her teeth fixed, and old Al found the money and took it and bought himself a new shotgun. I told her—I felt kind of sorry for her and figured she could use a little boost—I told her when I was out knocking around and thinking about home and pretty girls and all, I always thought about how she looked in the moonlight, out there on the lake road where we used to park. She said well, if she had it to do over again she'd do it different. But that was sad to me, and it scared me a little, too, because I came so close to marrying that gal, just so I could get her pants off. If I had, maybe I'd be there in Pandoval right today, working for the City, or something worse, and I never would have seen Chicago, or met Sarah."

All four considered that tragic thought a few moments, and their faces grew so dark.

"But talking about how you know whether you're in love or not, somebody's always got a simple test to tell you about. The trouble is, there's not anything simple about being in love. It's a mighty complicated matter, and no simple test of it is any count. I've heard guys say, 'Man, if you meet a gal and want to take her home and introduce her to your folks,

125

look out, it means you're in love.' Well, hell, I've taken a *lot* of girls home with me to meet the folks but I wasn't in love with 'em and didn't even think I was. What am I talking about, one time I took a gal home with me on a ten-day furlough from Louisville, and she spent the Christmas holidays with us. Name was Pamela, and god *dog* but she was a good old gal."

He laughed aloud, remembering her. The Troop laughed as well, as if they had known her and were pleased to think of her again.

"She was a *big* gal," Addison said, grinning still. "And smart. And funny. And tits? God-oh-mighty General Lee! That gal was made up about forty percent of tits, and I don't mind saying I had myself a good time with 'em. But you want to know why I took her home with me?"

"Why? Why? Why?" they said, leaning toward him.

"I wanted the Old Man to see her," Addison said, spreading his hands, a gesture that seemed to say he'd given the most obvious of all reasons. "The Old Man got the biggest charge out of looking at girls. What am I talking about, he still does. And I just wanted him to see that Pamela. Hell, I wasn't in love with her, or she with me, either. But the folks liked her. Victoria and Kat liked her. The Old Man thought she ought to have been the first woman President. When she'd walk through the house wearing one of those fuzzy sweaters and all that meat and potatoes bouncing in front of her the Old Man would sit and shake his head and grin and he'd nudge me and whisper. He'd say, 'I bet that sure is fun, Add.' And I'd tell him it sure was.

"Listen, we even gave a party for that gal. Had a big bowl of punch, and Henny Chappell came. He was a history teacher at the school, and loved Mexico. Used to go down there all the time and bring home Mexican booze. At the party he spiked the punch with two quarts of Oso Negro gin, and everybody got to feeling pretty good. Victoria must have hit the punch bowl a good lick because she collared me in the kitchen and she told me that when I was playing around on those mountains—talking about Pamela, you know—when I was playing around on those mountains I better be careful and not fall down between 'em because I'd smother and they wouldn't ever see me again. I guess what she was trying to say was, I ought not to get married to a pair of tits. Seemed like every time I brought a gal home, somebody took a notion I was fixing to marry her when hell, I just liked her, maybe, or wanted the Old Man to see her.

"But I can't give you any one test that's gonna tell you you're in love. I tried a bunch of them, up there in Chicago when I'd met Sarah and was roaming around trying to figure out what had happened to me. I'd play games with myself. I'd ask who, of all the people in the world, I'd rather be with. Say I had my choice of anybody. Say I was going to Switzerland, which is where I've always wanted to go, and I could take a movie star with me if I wanted to. I could take the world's most beautiful woman. I even made a rule I could revive dead ones and take Cleopatra, or that Delilah girl of Sampson's. Well, I never could even *imagine* anybody else I'd rather have with me than Sarah, and I still can't.

"But look at your poets. They've been sitting under trees for hundreds of years writing verses about love, and every damn one of them has a different notion of what it is. Your song writers, same way. And your book authors, my god, you could stock a public library with the stuff that's been written about love, and the reason for that is, it's so hard to explain. And it's so personal. Far as I'm concerned, love is what happened to me with Sarah that never had happened with anybody else. *Funny* things, some of them. Like for instance the effect that a touch can have. About a month after I met Sarah I'd be walking around during the day and something would feel wrong with me. I couldn't tell what it was exactly. I was . . . well, I'd feel empty some way. It kept me uncomfortable, and I couldn't get rid of it. Then I discovered how I could make it go away."

He paused, and looked at them as if they would know the explanation and finish giving it, like students in a classroom.

But their faces were blank, and they asked, "What made it go away?"

He put out a hand, and stopped it in midair. "All I had to do was touch her."

"Touch her where?"

"Why, *any*where. Hand. Arm. Hair. Face. Shoulder." The Troop nodding as he named the places, expecting the next place to be more interesting. "Knee. Hell, even her foot. It didn't matter where. I could take hold of one finger, and whoosh, the empty feeling was gone. It was that simple. When I was touching her, I felt good. When I wasn't, I felt wrong.

"Well, after I discovered that, I kept connected to her as much as I could. I guess probably it bothered her, at first anyway. I didn't want to be separated from her. I didn't even like to sit across the table from her if we went somewhere to eat. I wanted at least to have a finger on her. We'd be out in public and she'd get up and go to the restroom and stay gone five minutes, and damn if I wouldn't miss her, while she'd gone to pee." He laughed. "Reminded me of old Art Clifton."

"Who?"

"Art Clifton. Art and Beulah Clifton. They lived next door to us when I was about thirteen or fourteen. Old Beulah was the ugliest woman I think I ever met. Had warts, even, and a big old mouth full of crooked teeth. That woman could scare a spook. Well, when she was nearly forty she surprised hell out of everybody by marrying Art Clifton. Art about forty-five, I guess, and the best old boy. And really a pretty nice-looking guy, too. Old maids all over town been after him for years, and here he married Beulah, and he was just absolutely crazy about that woman. The Old Man used to watch 'em out in the yard, working in the flower beds, and he'd tell Mama that Art couldn't keep his hands out of Beulah's drawers even when they were pulling nut grass.

"One night they came over to see us, and while they were there Beulah remembered she wanted to show the folks some pictures they'd taken, so she went back to the house to find 'em. Gone ten minutes, I guess, and when she came back and sat down close beside Art he reached over and patted her on the knee and he said, 'I missed you, sweetie.' God dog, I nearly laughed out loud. Later on, at supper, I said I didn't see how anybody could miss an old lady ugly as Beulah and Mama almost sent me away from the table. 'They're in *love*,' she said, just like that would explain any mystery there was. I didn't understand what she meant till I found that Sarah girl, and then there I was doing the same thing Art did—telling Sarah I missed her while she was gone to the toilet.

"I miss her right now. I'm feeling awful empty. You know what I can do? I can stand up close to that girl, and hold her against me, and there's a special something that passes out of her and into me, and it's something I need, to keep me going. I can't say exactly what it is but I can feel it. No, wait now. It hasn't got anything to do with screwing. It's a warm feeling, and a tingling, and it goes into me here [touching his chest with both hands], and here [touching his belly], and here [his pelvis], and here [his thighs], all up and down me, and makes me feel good. It's not even what you'd call a romantic thing. I tell Sarah it's a damn necessity, like a transfusion, or getting my tank filled with fuel. How long I could go without it I'm not sure, but I'm getting pretty low right now, I tell you that.

"A good many other strange things have happened to me since Sarah. I'm not as selfish as I used to be. I even enjoy doing without something I really want so I can get something for her. And I want to share everything with her. Good food. Pretty music. Nice scenery. None of that is as good to me as it used to be unless Sarah is sharing it. Why, I can walk out here on this damn desert and find one of those big yellow blooms on a cactus and I'll think, Well, that'd be a real pretty flower if Sarah was here to see it. Like it wasn't pretty at all just because she couldn't see it.

"Then there's pride, too. I don't see how a guy could really be in love with a woman unless he's proud of her. Proud of the way she looks, of what she can do, of the kind of person she is. Up there in the church when I would sit and watch Sarah play that piano while those little old girls sang, she looked so good to me, just fantastic. One time I brought a couple of guys from the base with me. I told 'em, 'Come on, I want to show you the damnedest sight you ever saw.' So I took 'em into the church when the choir was practicing and I said, 'That's her, that's Sarah at the piano. Now watch.' Then after we'd been there a while I said to 'em, 'Did you ever see anything like that in your whole life?' And they didn't seem to understand what I meant. And it took me a while to see that they *didn't* know what I meant. Because to them, Sarah didn't look the same as she did to me. They said, 'Well, she's a pretty girl, all right.' But they didn't think she was the most beautiful thing that ever pulled a skirt on."

"Why?" demanded McKavett. "Why didn't they think she was beautiful?" He seemed offended.

"Because, man, they weren't in love with her. It's something that happens to a woman that gets fallen in love with. She gets beautiful, just a pure-dee knockout of a beauty, to the guy that loves her."

"But Sarah *is* beautiful," Booker challenged. "I mean she already was, before you met her."

"There's no way, though, she could be as beautiful as she looks to me. If she was she'd have movie scouts following her around. But the thing is, even if she was ugly as Beulah Clifton, still I'd *think* she was beautiful."

Booker wasn't satisfied. "But if she was ugly, you never would have fallen in love with her."

"I don't know," Addison said, "I might. Look at old Art Clifton. He fell in love with Beulah."

The Troop nodded, and went thoughtful, and left him sitting there in his drawers on the footlocker.

Presently Trinidad said, "Add, does it work the other way around, too? I mean if a girl fell in love with a guy, is the guy going to look real good to the girl? Will he even look . . . you know . . . handsome?"

"Damn right he will," Addison said, and laughed. "Look here at this face of mine. I've been through forty states and six foreign countries and a packing plant in Kansas City and I never have met but one person who told me I was handsome. I'll give you a hint who it was. It wasn't my mother or the Old Man or either one of my sisters."

"It was Sarah," they guessed.

"Right. Sarah was the only one."

For a minute they studied his face, looking close, in a way they didn't normally look at him. He was a long way from handsome. His face was good and friendly, but it had that peculiar look of age because of the curious slant of the wrinkles at the outer corners of his eyes. And his nose was crooked, from being broken three times in the ring and on the football field. And his teeth weren't quite straight.

He pulled on his coveralls and got his kit and went outside to write to Sarah. Before they followed him, The Troop lay in their bunks a while and thought about all the things he had said.

# FORTY-TWO

THE DEAL that The Bear offered to Addison did not, of course, come directly. It came down through Major Burke and Sergeant Runge.

The Major first: "Captain Biggs has come clean. He's admitted flying the heroin to Chicago, and he has said you delivered it." Burke took a deep breath. "You and your wife. Is that true?"

Addison nodded. "We delivered a package. But we were just doing the Captain a favor, saving him a trip across town. We didn't know what was in the package. Didn't have any way to know. You know, Major, sometimes I'm not too smart but I'm just not dumb enough to do that, put a pack-

131

age of dope on the back seat of the car and go peddling across Chicago. Put my wife and myself into that kind of risk without getting a penny of pay? I wouldn't do that, Major."

Burke looked so tired. "No, but you have to recognize that you're in a bad spot here, Add. The Bear is down on you, and he's in a position to make you a lot of grief on the dope thing. A lot of embarrassment, at the least."

"I don't know why he'd be so down on me."

The Major watched Addison's face a few seconds to make sure he was serious. He drew in another great breath and let it out slowly and he said, "Well, I can make you a pretty good little list of why he's down on you. One, you jump on his airplane without a pass and ride to Chicago and stay four days. Two, your record shows that sort of thing, AWOL, is a habit with you. Three, while you're in Chicago you deliver a ten-pound package of illegal narcotics. Whether you knew you were doing it or not, you did it. If you hadn't been AWOL in Chicago you wouldn't have delivered the stuff. Four, The Bear wanted you on the fight card and you refused, even after you'd fought in the parking lot of a damn beer joint in town and messed up The Bear's PR. That adventure of yours at The Puma took place the very night of the day that The Bear had addressed the Spanish Wells Civic Association. In that little address he assured the leaders of the community that his soldiers were gentlemen and he would personally see to it that they behaved themselves when they came to town to spend their pay . . ."

"Oh boy. I didn't know that. Bad timing."

"Bad timing," agreed the Major. "Then your latest sin may be even more serious than the heroin thing. You have poked that tool of yours into The Bear's personal life, and he is plenty unhappy about it, and he intends that you'll be punished for it. I am talking about what you did last week."

Addison spread his hands, his gesture of innocence. "What'd I do last week?"

"That visit to Katherine's apartment. That was sure bad judgment, Addison."

Addison got mad. His face flushed. His voice trembled. "Major, just what in the cornbread hell is going on around here? Has he got detectives tailing around after GI's? I went to Katherine's on my own free time, just to . . ."

"OK, OK, now settle down," Burke said. "I'm not sure you're aware that the territory between those fine bowed legs of Miss Katherine's is The Bear's private playground, or anyway that's what he thought. Either she told him you were there, or somebody else saw you, I don't know, but he found it out."

"I went to Katherine's to talk to her about something personal," Addison pled. "I was there maybe an hour, an hour and a half at the outside."

Burke's patient smile. "Addison, The Bear imagines things. Right now one of the most important things in your life is what he imagines. As much as he's heard about your conquests in bed, I expect he imagines that in an hour and a half you could lay the queen. But now listen, let me explain the danger to you in this. The Bear is capable of some really dirty doings. Like seeing to it that a man's wife gets the word that he's screwing around on her."

That was the threat that got Addison's attention. Suddenly he could see Sarah's pretty face contorted by pain. "He would do that? Even if he wasn't sure it was true?"

Burke nodded.

Addison sounded weak now, and hoarse. "What do you think I ought to do?"

"Take the offer. It's the best way."

"He wants me to fight that Grover?"

Burke nodded again.

"And what do I get out of it if I do?"

"The flight to Chicago will go off the record. You simply will not have gone, so you'll be clear. That's his promise."

"What'll happen to Captain Biggs? Court-martial?"

"Oh hell no," Burke said, short and quick. "Bear doesn't want Washington knowing one of his officers put anything over on him. But don't worry about Biggs. Bear made a deal with him. He'll keep his mouth shut and be reassigned, and no formal charges will be made. The same deal's been made with the crew, including the one that squealed. You'll be clear."

"It's blackmail, in a way," Addison said.

"Well, you don't think for a second that outside rules apply here. The Army is not a democratic institution, you know that."

"You think I can depend on him? Will he keep his word?"

"Yes. He delivers, just like he says. He delivers on benign promises the same as he does on dark threats."

"Tell me what to do."

"First of all, keep quiet about all this. Report to Runge and tell him you've changed your mind, that you'd like to fight if they're still going to have the matches."

Addison frowned. "That won't be pleasant. Taking Runge's shit."

"No, but you can do it. But wait a minute before you go. How about this Grover? Is he any good?"

"I can't see he amounts to much. He's a big swinger, strong. But he can't box. I've watched him in the gym."

"You can whip him then?"

"Yeah, sure."

Here came Major Burke's deep sigh again. "In that case, don't waste any time on him. Don't fool around with him. I've got a rumor that The Bear may spring a little surprise on you. I think when you finish with Grover he's going to send out another one for you to fight."

"My god!"

"Yeah, my god. The Bear's a strange man. He would have been happier in Ancient Rome. But to protect yourself, if Runge says fight two men, fight them. Remember when Runge says something, it's The Bear talking."

Addison stood with his hand on the doorknob, and looked at Burke and grinned.

"What's funny?" the Major asked.

"I was just thinking, it hasn't been long since you sat there behind that desk and told me to run away from anything that looked like a fight."

## FORTY-THREE

"TWO WEEKS!" Addison objected. "I need more than any two weeks to get ready for a fight. Man, I haven't been in a ring in more than a year."

"The date's been set," Runge said, "and it ain't gonna be changed."

Running, pounding the bag in the gym, trying to get in shape, Addison was not happy. The Troop, though, was elated. When Addison told them he had changed his mind and decided to fight, all three of them marched directly to Sergeant Runge and volunteered to fight on the card. "We been takin' lessons from Addison," they said. Runge had a place for one flyweight. He picked Trinidad. Booker and McKavett grieved. To fight on the same program with Addison, what a glory that would be.

## FORTY-FOUR

THE BOXING MATCHES in the gym were promoted as being for the entertainment of The Men, meaning the enlisted personnel. That didn't mislead The Men. They understood that the best seats ringside would be occupied by officers.

Much of the brass seated up close on all four sides of the ring was from other installations. General Boswell flew in, with a flock of colonels and majors and captains buzzing around him. A big night for The Bear. He sat next to General Boswell and laughed a lot and produced great clouds of cigar smoke.

The preliminaries seemed endless to Addison. He helped speed the time by acting as second in Trinidad's match. Runge put Trinidad in with a boy who couldn't box much better than the Comanche Slasher, as Addison sometimes called his smallest student. They went a harmless three rounds and Trinidad lost on a split decision. He was devastated.

"He never touched me," Trinidad told Addison.

"Yeah, I know."

"Then why did I lose?"

"I guess because you didn't touch him more times than he didn't touch you."

Trinidad hid his small dark head in the great gloves. He wanted to win so bad, for Addison.

"Hey, come on, man," Addison said, "for the first time out you did all right. Now get your head up."

During Trinidad's little fight, Addison got to look over the crowd. Scattered civilians sat among the officers. These were mainly the key people of the Spanish Wells business community, the group The Bear was courting in his PR program. Addison was surprised to see a woman in the audience. She sat directly behind The Bear. She was small and dirty-blond and stiff-mouthed and hollow-cheeked.

The seat beside her was empty. It was filled while Addison watched. Filled by a large gent in a white shirt. Addison finally recognized him as Bates, the pipeliner he had whipped at The Puma. So the woman had to be Bates' wife. The Bear was being careful to pay attention to her, turning away frequently from General Boswell to twist in his seat and take his cigar out of his mouth and talk to her. Bates, Addison decided, still looked a little sore-jawed.

It was past ten o'clock when Addison got into the ring and shed his robe. The big Okie, Grover, looked so good. He looked ever so much more impressive than Addison, who had never looked dangerous in boxing trunks. With those thin calves and ankles and the too-wide butt, he just didn't seem tough.

And tonight his face was different. It was calm, flat. It didn't show its customary frown-grin that seemed to say, "I'm not real sure how all this is going to come out but I'm glad I came anyhow." His face wasn't saying anything, which meant he was worried. Major Burke's hint about a surprise, that bothered him. And now Bates being there, that somehow had to be connected.

Two hours later he would understand why he'd been concerned: he was about to take the only really serious, bloody beating he'd ever taken in a boxing ring.

No, not from Grover. He stretched Grover flat, thirty seconds into the third round. But even that much boxing tired him. His legs were shaking, his arms a bit heavy. Out of shape. Two rounds, and tired. Ducking and dancing away from Grover's roundhouse rights had burned a lot of his fuel.

Addison had walked over to see if Grover was all right when Runge climbed into the ring and drew down the mike to make his announcement. Don't go away, folks, he said, because the show's not over and you ain't seen nothin' yet.

Here it comes, Addison thought. The surprise.

In view of the obvious fact, Runge was saying, that the main ee-vent was so brief, and the fighter who ee-merged victorious hadn't much more than got warmed up, he had volunteered, for the entertainment of The Men, to take on any other heavyweights present, as long as he could last.

A great explosion of applause and yells from The Men. Calm smiles from the officers at ringside.

And so, Runge said, from San Antonio, Texas, coming along the aisle right now and weighing two-oh-six in red trunks, was the first volunteer, by the name of Red Culhane, so hang on a minute for some more action.

Addison locked onto Runge's face. The sergeant stared back, his features entirely blank. "Remember when Runge

137

says something, it's The Bear talking." Addison looked out into the crowd for The Bear. He was turned around, talking to Mrs. Bates.

The red-haired fellow from San Antonio looked a little long in the tooth. But he was wise. He could box, and until he began tiring he moved well. Addison conserved, thinking of what might come next. He managed to coast for a couple of easy rounds, and began to feel a little better. But the redhead had a troublesome jab that got through a time or two to Addison's eye and blurred his vision some. It took him six rounds to win. The referee wouldn't let the redhead come out for the seventh, when his corner couldn't stop the bleeding from a cut high on his cheek.

By then Addison was so tired. He collapsed on the stool, laid back, and fought for breath to ease the awful burning in his chest. For a minute or two he drifted away from that place, away from the buzzing and the shouting and the lights and the smoke and the hurting. Sarah. Sarah. And Runge came, and made another announcement, and Addison was aware of a new kind of noise sweeping over the audience. A high-pitched buzzing. He watched another fighter climb into the ring. Big. Dark-haired. And young. With the longest arms.

Then here was Runge squatting in front of Addison. Leaning in close to talk. He had the smallest, roundest eyes. Almost black. He said, "You ready to quit?"

See how those little round black eyes gleam. Addison said, "Fuck you, and the mule you rode in on." He felt renewed.

Addison had never seen this third fighter. He was a man of such great size. And he could fight. Maybe Addison could have made a fair show of the match if he'd been in shape, and fresh. But there was no way, now, for the fight to be anything but a beating, a punishment. Addison understood that, and took it.

Even The Men seemed to sense it. Once in the third round, when Addison had already been knocked down twice, the big man got careless and Addison somehow revived his right and staggered the big fellow and The Men rose from their seats and screamed and hoped for the impossible. It happened again in the fourth, and some of The Men pushed forward and began calling his name in a curious, low-pitched chant.

"*Addison! Addison! Addison!* . . ."

He lasted six and a half rounds. He went down seven times and got up six. The last time he hit the canvas, The Men had pushed down the aisles, into the officers' section, chanting, chanting his name.

"*Addison! Addison! Addison!* . . ."

He felt he was dying. He no longer hurt but an awful, wrenching sadness enveloped him. It had to do with Sarah. Sarah . . . Sarah . . .

He was helped out of the ring, and toward the locker rooms. The officers stood. The Men, almost all of them now, hundreds of them, were in a great crush around him, letting him move but ever so slowly, wanting him to see them, to hear them shouting his name. There was something almost terrible in that great sound. Guttural, and pulsing, like the roar of some large animal that makes a trembling in a person's intestines.

"*Addison! Addison! Addison!* . . ."

The officers left the gymnasium quietly, looking back at that strange scene.

Two MP's on the fringe of the little mob looked at Major Burke, standing beneath the basketball goal. They raised their brows to ask the silent question, "Should we break it up?" The major shook his head in response. He was saying, "No, let them alone."

"*Addison! Addison! Addison!* . . ."

# FORTY-FIVE

"CHRIST," said Colonel Brookfield, M.D., when Addison crept carefully into the emergency room of The Bear's hospital. He had come directly from the gym, on orders from Major Burke.

"We'll need to patch on you some, all right," the colonel said. He chuckled, and Addison smelled scotch. "You look like you been gang-busted. How many of the enemy did all this?"

"Three," Addison said.

The colonel gave him a thorough going-over. He took stitches here and there, and painted him up with antiseptic, and put on patches in various places. He then delivered the aromatic opinion that Addison had taken a pretty good whipping but he ought to survive, given time and proper rest and balanced meals. "Now git."

So they were walking out of the hospital, Addison and The Troop, all of them so quiet and tired and deflated. They cut across the parking lot. Here came a set of headlights. And tires swishing on the asphalt. A car stopped in front of them, beneath a light pole, blocking their path. A big man rose out from under the wheel. Not a military man. It was Bates.

Addison and The Troop stood alongside the front fender and waited. Bates came around the car slowly, studying Addison's face. "I was at the fights tonight," he said.

"Yeah, me too," Addison said.

The woman got out and stood close to Addison, to see him better in the light from the parking lot lamp. She had the stiffest face.

"I just wanted to get a good look at you," she said. "How does it feel?"

"Not too good," Addison said.

Bates let go a kind of laugh-growl. "I want you to know I enjoyed every lick you took."

Addison moved to the fender, looking so whipped. He faced away from the car, leaning his buttocks against the fender and folding his arms. He wasn't able to speak normally, because of the swollen lips and the cut mouth. Both his eyes were puffed, and would be brown and purple and blue by morning. "You waited all this time to see my wounds? You want me to bleed for you a little?"

"I thought maybe you wouldn't be such a goddamned smart-ass after you got your butt whipped so bad," Bates said.

The Troop, all three in perfect unison, sucked in a loud breath. And held it, and held it, waiting for Addison to do whatever he would do about Bates' cursing him. What *could* he do?

When he spoke it was low, so that they all had trouble hearing. He said, "Well, if you've come out here to get me to fight you, why you picked yourself a good time. I had me a busy night already, and I don't feel any too tough. But I expect that would suit you just about right, wouldn't it, Bates?"

Bates had worked himself into a state, almost slobbering. "Why, I wouldn't dirty my hands on you. I don't have to. I can get somebody else to do it for me, just like tonight."

"You bastard!" hissed Mrs. Bates.

Addison evidently was about to faint. He slumped. He bowed his head. He put a hand to his eyes. Then both his hands went to the fender of the car, close beside him, as if he needed support. But he was getting leverage. Getting into position to brace himself. Now he took a great painful breath, and gathered up all the strength left in him. He raised his head, and leaned back, and with astonishing speed and force he buried his great right foot deep in the belly of that Bates, who released the most awful noise, and went down on the asphalt.

It was such a terrible blow. The effort almost put Addison down with Bates. The Troop stood frozen. Mrs. Bates made curious high-pitched noises. Her husband was doubled up, trying for breath but not getting much. Producing dry, raspy, whooping sounds.

When it began to look as if Bates might recover, Addison said to The Troop. "Help her get him in the car." They got him in, enough to close the door. Mrs. Bates took the driver's seat and Addison leaned in the window and said to her, "You ought to tell your husband to stay out of parking lots. He's always getting hurt in parking lots. At The Puma. Here. Parking lots are bad luck for him. Now go on."

Addison had to admire her. That Mrs. Bates was a tough one. She said before she drove off, "I'm going straight to your commanding officer with this, first thing in the morning."

Addison nodded. "I know."

He told The Troop when the car was gone, "Fellows, I'm gonna have to have me some help, getting to the tent. Prop me up a little, will you?"

McKavett and Trinidad ducked under his arms to support him, and Booker waddled along close, wanting to help but not knowing what to grab hold of.

They walked crooked and stumbling, because he was really leaning on them, he was so exhausted. But he wouldn't quit talking. "I tell you what, Troop, old Add screwed it up again. I had it settled and I let it get away. I had it pretty well paid, when I left the gym. But that frigging Bates, he couldn't go on off and call it square."

The Troop didn't talk. Didn't know what to say. Just get him in the sack, get him to the tent, get him home.

"I can't find a single place on me," Addison panted, "that doesn't hurt."

He put back his head, and squinted his eyes so tight, and tried to hold it back. But he wasn't able to. So he cried. They took him by the latrine, and held him up before the urinal while he cried quietly, about the aching in his body, and about everything that had happened that night. Sarah . . . Sarah . . .

# FORTY-SIX

HE DIDN'T REPORT for duty the next morning.

He stayed in his bunk all day. He rose up only to write a short letter to Sarah, and go to the latrine, and inspect his bruises and cuts in the shaving mirror.

He slept, but not well. The Troop kept quiet, watched him turn and hurt, listened to him groan in his sleep. Wanting so bad to help, to ease his pain.

He didn't report the second morning, either. At noon, Trinidad came. "You want us to cover for you? Tell anybody anything? Go see Burke? Tell us what to do."

Addison shook his head. "Naw, don't worry about it. I'm just gonna lay here on my butt and let 'em come get me. What's the word on it?"

"That's just it," Trinidad said, offering his Latin shrug of the shoulders, "there *ain't* no word."

"Nobody is asking where I am?"

"No. Nothin'."

"I'll be damn. That *is* funny."

# FORTY-SEVEN

"I FIGURE I may as well come on in," he told Major Burke, "and give myself up."

On the fifth day he felt better, physically at least. His eyes were still beautiful—so many colors, red and green and blue and brown and purple—but the swelling had gone down some. And he could shave again, except in certain places. So he rose out of his blankets, and cleaned up, and walked across The Bear's Base to the office of Major Burke. He was still sore.

"Give yourself up?" Major Burke said. "What for?"

Don't answer that, Addison's judgment said.

Burke shuffled papers on his desk. "Are you giving yourself up for not winning all those fights?"

Don't answer that one, either.

"I'm just trying to establish what you're feeling so guilty about," Burke said, grinning a little now. "Would it be because of what happened on the hospital parking lot?"

Addison tried to figure out what Burke's grin meant. Then the grin graduated into a laugh and the major said, "Sit down, Add, and relax. Listen, you're all clear. You're a hero around here."

"You mean Bates didn't come to see The Bear about the parking lot?"

"Mrs. Bates did," said Burke. He laughed some more. Addison had never heard the major laugh out loud, and it was strange. "But you know what? The Bear wouldn't believe her. She tried to tell him you attacked her husband right here on the base, after the fights. Bear said bullshit, that he saw you practically get carried out of the gym about midnight and he didn't believe you could have hurt Orphan Annie in the hospital parking lot two hours later. Besides that he had the word of Colonel Brookfield that when you left the hospital emergency room your physical condition was such that you needed help getting to your quarters.

"Well, Mrs. Bates, she kept saying there were witnesses, that you had three small soldiers with you. I figured they had to be your little buddies in the tent. So this morning I called them in here. McKavett. Booker. And that Latin one. What's his name?"

"Trinidad."

"Trinidad. I'll say this, you damn sure coached those boys well. They sure said the right thing. I . . ."

"Pardon me, Major. I didn't coach those boys on this. I didn't tell 'em to say a word."

"Well, anyway, I talked to each of them separately and not a one could remember seeing anything whatever happen on any hospital parking lot at any two o'clock in the morning."

Addison grinned. "Son of a gun."

"I did scare up one witness that saw you after you left the hospital. His name is Stephens, that New Jersey boy that's such a hot softball pitcher. He said he saw you about a quarter to three in one of the latrines, and you were so beat up your little buddies had to hold you up to the pee trough."

"He's right about that."

"He said you were hurting so bad that you . . . well, he said you were crying."

Addison nodded. "He's right about that, too."

"The Bear has told Mrs. Bates to stay off the base and quit bothering him, that he's done everything he can to appease her and he's tired screwing with it. She's getting the same song from the prosecuting attorney in town, too. Hell, he was here, at the fights. Sat down there ringside, with The Bear and General Boswell, and saw what you went through. Mrs. Bates couldn't get him interested at all in any aggravated assault charge against you, not on *that* night. So it looks like you're all clean, Addison. Now, do you still want to surrender?"

Addison grinned. "Major, that beating The Bear gave me, that wasn't just to satisfy those Bateses."

"Naw, that was just a small part of it. In fact, it was an afterthought on The Bear's part to ask Bates out here to watch you get sacrificed. The Bear is hell on killing several birds with one stone. It's a big part of his philosophy and his style to do something and accomplish several ends. That's going to make a brigadier out of him, too, and soon, and get him the hell out of this awful place he's in.

"No, your part in all this was a little hand-slapping, from The Bear, telling you to straighten up. Telling you especially to stay away from his secretary. Telling you don't even go by her apartment for a drink. I hope you got that message clear.

"But everything's cream around here, right now. The Bear's happy. You know who that fighter was, that tore you up so bad?"

Addison shook his head. "I haven't even heard his name. I tell you this, though, that bastard can hit." He put a hand to his jaw.

"Addison, that boy's name is Paul Chavez. He's nineteen, and one of the best damn heavyweight prospects in the country. In another year, soon as General Boswell thinks he's ready, he'll go out of the Army and turn pro, and the general will own him. Some guys with money own horses, some own boats, some own ranches, General Boswell owns boxers. Finds 'em in the ranks, trains 'em, brings 'em along,

145

then turns 'em out to make money. He's been bragging to The Bear about Chavez for a year."

"You mean," Addison said, "General Boswell brought this fighter down here just to whip me?"

"Sure," the major said. "The Bear asked him to bring Chavez as a personal favor. Then he bet him two thousand dollars you could last three rounds. When the general saw you with the other boys, saw you weren't in shape, he offered to up the bet to whatever The Bear wanted to lay out.

"Then by god you lasted six rounds, and took the best punches Chavez could throw, and kept getting up, and damned if you didn't break the bastard's *nose!*" Burke put his head back and giggled like a schoolboy.

"I don't even remember hitting the guy," Addison said.

"And to top it off, you won five grand for The Bear. To win even two bucks off Boswell is a great treat for The Bear. But five grand! Man, he's in a good humor."

That night Addison wrote a long, long letter to Sarah. He said seven times that he loved her. And then, because he couldn't keep from it, he went to The Garden and called and made love to her over the phone.

# FORTY-EIGHT

THEY WOULD ASK HIM, "Is it better, sometimes, than other times? Is it always the same good? Is it ever bad?"

He would tell them, "It's never bad. With Sarah it wouldn't be possible for it to be bad. Sometimes it's extra special, though, better than the time before. And sometimes it's so good it makes you sad when you finish, because you think it's not possible for it ever to be that good again. You think you've just had the best that ever was, or ever will be, and it's over and done with, and can't ever be felt again. Then pretty soon, *bam!*—there it is again, even better than what you thought was the best there ever was . . ."

For long, quiet weeks after the fights, life in the tent-shack was smooth. Addison was back to his old self. Happy, good-natured. Lecturing them, teaching, leading, and showing. Their best times were spent with Sarah—writing to her, making love to her over those long and lonely miles, talking about her.

They would ask, "What makes a time extra-special? Do you know, before it happens, that a time will be extra-special?"

"No," he would say, "you *don't* know, for sure. You don't know so you have to keep trying. You try different places, different times, different ways . . ."

"What kind of ways?"

"Why, *every* kind of way. The regular ways, and the *ir*-regular ways. Sarah and me, we've done it straight, and we've done it crooked. We've done it backwards, forwards, upside down, and hind part before. Crossways, sideways, tilted, slanted, lying down, sitting up, bent over, twisted around. We've done it wet and we've done it dry. Done it naked as picked chickens and completely dressed, or almost. We've done it on beds, sofas, back seats, stairs, grass, benches, sheets, quilts, blankets. Done it on grass, sand, solid concrete . . ."

"Second base! Second base!"

". . . second base, and once in a hayloft in the state of Wisconsin . . ."

He would pace, there in the tent-shack, wearing only his shorts, waving his arms, shaking his fists. All worked up about Sarah.


# FORTY-NINE

THERE WOULD BE TIMES of low voices and solemn eyes. He would talk about death, and defeat, and tears.

"What's it feel like to get shot?"

"I don't much remember," he said. "When I got hit here

147

in the leg that time, all I remember is just getting jolted and spun around, like some old boy had blind-side blocked me playing football. It didn't even hurt, at least not for a while.

"Then the other time," putting his hand into his hair, "when that little old piece of shrapnel cut me up here, I can't tell you how it felt when it hit because I don't remember it at all. I was just walking along, thinking about chocolate pie, or pussy, or something good like that, and the next I know I wake up in a shell crater and I've got blood running down my face like I've stuck my head in a bucket of it."

"And it didn't hurt?"

"Not right then. There was a kind of numb feeling for a good while. I felt like maybe the top of my head was gone, and I was afraid to put my hand up there to see, afraid of what I'd touch. There was a minute there I argued whether I might be dead or not, because maybe I was, and that's why it didn't hurt for half my head to be gone. But then I decided I couldn't be dead and still be sitting up and looking around and all, so little by little I worked my fingers up the side of my head, like this, feeling along, so if I hit anything real horrible I wouldn't get my hands all in it. I'd go up higher, and a little higher, and keep on feeling hair and head, and by the time I worked on up to where the blood was coming from that medic came along. He looked at me and said I wasn't going to have anything but a Purple Heart and a bad headache.

"Well, he was damn sure right about the headache. I mean to tell you, Mildred, I *had* a headache, several days. I stayed laid out in a field hospital about a week, and sometimes I hurt so bad I'd just bawl about it. Cry, damn right.

"One day there was a little old pee wee colonel walked through there, the kind that there's not much to him but bark and bite, with stubble hair and a bullet head. Wouldn't weigh a hundred and twenty-five with his medals on. He saw me blubbering and snapped at me about it. Wanted to know what the hell I was crying about. I told him by god I was crying because my head hurt so bad. He asked what the matter was with my head. I told him I got my scalp split by shrapnel. He said there's a soldier over yonder across the aisle with his leg blown off, and he's in bad pain, and you don't hear *him* crying. I said by god maybe it would help him if he did. That little old colonel looked down at me a minute, and finally he said, "You may be right, at that," and he went on.

"But I never have been afraid to cry. It's not too popular, in public, for men to do it. But I learned from the Old Man, and from Victoria, about crying. It's got a value . . ."

He was about twelve when he learned that. He had walked past the open door of his sisters' room and saw Victoria lying across the bed, sobbing, and he went in to ask her why. She said Beverly's little dog got run over and killed. Beverly was her friend. She had that little old ugly dog she led around everywhere, and it gnawed pillows, and peed on rugs, and was always yapping.

"Well, it's just a little old ugly dog," Addison said.

And Victoria said, "But it was like a person to Beverly, and she's so sad. Besides, this is just a sad day. There's so much sadness everywhere today." And she went on crying. But that night at supper she was entirely repaired. Eyes weren't even red, and she was happy and seemed improved somehow.

That was of deep interest to Addison. Because at that time he had lately discovered he had a tendency to cry that way himself, and it worried him. When he got hurt, when he failed, when he felt frustration, he would feel tears pushing at his eyes, wanting to come, and it was so hard to keep them back. But here was Victoria crying and evidently getting some kind of benefit from it.

Not long afterward Addison came home carrying a note for his father. It was from the principal of his school.

"Tell me about the trouble," his father said.

"I cried at school," Addison said.

"Why?"

"Because I wanted to win the race. I came in second, and I cried. I couldn't help it."

"But what caused the trouble?"

"James Simpson."

"What did James Simpson do?"

"He called me a fucking crybaby."

Addison's father swallowed hard. Coughed. "What did you do?"

"I whipped his butt."

Addison's father took his hand and they walked to the garage and got in the car and drove around.

They talked to each other about crying. Addison's father said it was a ridiculous notion that it is all right for women to cry and a disgrace for men to cry. That men came equipped to cry the same as women, boys the same as girls. He said crying wasn't only a way of expressing grief and pain, that it was also a release, a way of getting rid of things inside a person that bothered, and gnawed, and wrenched the spirit. He said girls came into the world knowing this by instinct, and most of them used it freely, and the result was that they lived longer and happier lives than men. The men have made a mistake, Addison's father said, about crying. They don't know how to use it.

"But you don't cry," Addison argued. "I've never seen you cry, ever."

"I do, just the same. I'm going to show you something. A place."

He turned off the road outside town and went to a grove of low, brushy trees on the bank of a little creek. He stopped there.

"When I get more inside me than I can hold," Addison's father said, "I drive out here alone, and I cry it out of me. I can't afford the luxury of crying every time I feel like it. If I did, the school board would consider me emotionally unstable and find a way to get rid of me. So I store it all up, and when I get full I come here to cry."

"What do you cry about?" Addison wondered.

"About everything that pains my spirit. About all the little

150

tragedies that parade through school every day. About your mother, and everything I want to do for her that I can't do. About my own parents, and the things I could have done for them but didn't. I cry for you, and Victoria, and Kat, because you'll leave us someday and I won't be able to do anything to help you when you need it. Mostly, I'm afraid, I cry for myself, because of my shortcomings. Because of everything that needs changing that I can't change, or won't try to change."

Hearing his father say that was a great event for Addison. He was proud to be told such private things, and yet embarassed a little. It was almost as if his father were making a confession to him.

"I don't know," he said, "if I can hold it back that way. The crying, I mean. How do you hold it back till you get out here?"

His father nodded, and grinned. "It took practice."

Addison was near to crying just then, mainly because of the circumstance, because of the moment, the emotional high. So he put his head down and cried, about so many things he had been needing to shed tears about. He cried quite a long time, feeling the weight and warmth of his father's great hand on his shoulder. And when he raised up he saw that his father, too, had been crying.

When they drove away Addison felt so good. Elevated, somehow. He told his father about Victoria, about how she seemed to feel strangely elated after she'd cried.

"Maybe this is how she felt," Addison said, grinning.

"Yes. Of course it is." And they both laughed.

That was a peak, in Addison's time. The day he cried with his father . . .

He told all that to The Troop, the best he could, and it had such an effect on them. They kept silent and thoughtful when he finished.

McKavett thought about the day he had come home from school crying, after being in a fight. His father whipped him. Not for fighting. For crying about it.

Booker thought about the time there in the tent-shack

that he sat sobbing before Addison, after he'd taken Sarah's picture beneath his blankets. He had been so ashamed for crying that way. But now . . .

Trinidad thought of the day, when he was ten, that he had looked in the mirror and studied the scars and the pocks on his narrow face and realized, for the first time, that for all his life he would be ugly. His sister had caught him crying into the mirror and she let go one of her vicious laughs and said, "You silly little shit."

Oh, they dealt in deep things there in the tent-shack.

They dealt with life on other heavenly bodies, and whether it existed. They even took to reading something other than the sports sections in the newspapers that came by bus to Spanish Wells, out of El Paso and San Antonio and San Angelo. They read, and read, to get information for questions they could introduce, to hear his answers. He always had an answer.

"Life in outer space? Well I *guess!* How could there *not* be? Now that's a better question. Come out here a minute, outside. Come on, and look at the sky. The by god universe is so frigging big it scares me to think about it. Now, look up at these stars. God oh mighty General Lee, what a night, look at that. I wish Sarah could see it. All right, you see the Milky Way streaking across there. Everybody knows the Milky Way. Now the Milky Way is what they call a galaxy. A galaxy is just a big bunch of stars. Millions and millions of stars. This earth we're standing on is a part of the Milky Way, but it's not a star, oh hell no. It's just a little old half-assed planet. Our sun is a star but it doesn't amount to anything. They've got stars in the Milky Way make a thousand of our sun. Now then, pick out a star and call it the closest star there is to this earth. Just *say* it's the closest. Then say you've got a spaceship, and you've left out of here going a thousand miles a second. Not an hour, now. A thousand miles a *second,* all right? So how long do you think it would take you, going that fast, to land on the closest star there is to the earth?"

"How long? How long?"

"It would take you seven by god hundred and ninety frigging years!"

"Oh, horseshit!" exclaimed Booker.

"You just made that up, I bet," McKavett said.

"How the hell," challenged Trinidad, "do you *know* it would take that long?"

"It's in books," Addison told them. "It's in that big old atlas that stays on the table just outside The Bear's Den. I'm not making it up, Troop."

"Well, so what about it?"

"I'm just trying to show you how big a galaxy is, OK? And how far apart stars are, and planets, and moons and things. Now get this. The Milky Way isn't the only galaxy. Oh hell no. There are hundreds, thousands, millions of the damn things out there, wheeling and grinding and sizzling and flashing and entertaining the Lord Godamighty that made them all. Now then, yonder's God, sitting up there somewhere at the end of time, and one day he decides he's gonna put some life in the universe, some living things. Maybe he's tired of blinking lights, I don't know. But here's the question. Do you think he'd put life on just one little old speck of dirt in his entire *u*-niverse? A little old fourth-rate planet not as big as a freckle on a microbe? Why, even God would need a telescope to *find* this place. You think he'd come stumbling down in here in the ragged end of the Milky Way, in the damn *slums* and make it the only place in everlasting space that he's gonna have trees, and grass, and bugs, and fish, and deer, and . . . ?"

"Girls? Pretty girls?"

Addison laughed. "Pretty girls, damn right, Book, good thinking. Anyhow, can you figure God doing that?"

McKavett shook his head slowly. And said, "It wouldn't make no sense."

Addison put his long arm around McKavett's skinny shoulders and turned back to the tent-shack. He said, "That's the best damn argument I've heard. It wouldn't make no sense."

# FIFTY

WHILE THEY WERE TOGETHER at Spanish Wells, Addison spoke of death only once.

The subject came up one night when they had led him into telling about his combat times. And somebody asked, "Weren't you afraid of getting killed?"

"Oh, I don't know. I can't say I ever worried about it much. I guess it was because I didn't really have what you'd call any unfinished business to take care of, unless you want to count a couple of gals I thought I needed to screw. But there wasn't anybody there waiting for me, like now. I figured if I checked out it really wouldn't leave much of a space. The folks, they'd do a good deal of wailing, but not for long. Pretty soon I'd be just a picture on the piano, and when they looked at it they'd remember good things, not sad ones. Because we had good times always. Oh, we got kicked around some but it didn't really hurt us.

"But why would they grieve much over me? Hell, they did everything they could possibly do for me, when I was home. They damn sure didn't owe me anything they didn't pay. The Old Man, he used to talk about the things he wanted to do for the family that he couldn't do, but he was talking about Mama, not about me or Victoria or Kat.

"Now if anybody owed, it was me owing them. But then they wouldn't ever think of that. So my notion was, when I was in all that shooting, if I got hit in a bad place, OK, don't worry about it.

"I guess it was in the back of my head maybe that one of these times I'd strike something that would settle me down. But I thought it'd be something I wanted to *do*. I never did imagine it would be a girl, a woman, that changed everything this way."

He was on his footlocker again, wearing nothing but those GI shorts. Leaning forward, staring blankly at the screen door but not seeing it. Not seeing anything. Not even talking to The Troop now. Just talking.

"The truth is I never have been afraid to die until just lately, until right now. If I farted around here doing dumb things and got myself killed now, it sure would make me mad. Because of Sarah, and that little old baby growing up there in her stomach. But not just because I'd be leaving them behind. Also because I never have *done* a damn thing. What have I got to show for my thirty years? Couple little old medals. Thousands of guys got the same ones. It doesn't take half a cup of brains to go out and get shot in a damn war. But I tell you what, Mildred, I'm straightening out from here on. No more of that fighting for old Add. You know a guy can get killed in the ring? Sure can, especially if he's out of shape and he's in there with a man that can hit. When that Chavez put me down that last time, that scared me. I thought I was dying. I thought, Well, I've lost. But not the fight. The hell with the fight. I meant I'd lost Sarah, and my life, and I'd lost the chance to do whatever I was put here to do."

# FIFTY-ONE

WHEN TRINIDAD WAS FOUR, skinny and undernourished and so small for his age, he came near dying from a neglected case of chicken pox. His smooth brown skin erupted into large dark sores. Some took months to heal, and left his forehead and cheeks and chin deeply pocked.

Neighbors said, "Look at the size of those scars. That kid had *small*pox, wouldn't you say?" They kept their own children away from him long after he was well.

When he was five, still so small, he climbed onto a chair to get a box of dry cereal out of a kitchen cabinet. He dropped the box. Spilled some cereal. He got the broom and dustpan to sweep it up. Bending, he grasped the broom handle down near the straw. The top of the handle hit a small saucepan on the cookstove. The pan came down. It contained soup, bubbling-hot, left too long to heat by Trinidad's sister Gloria. The scalding soup splashed along the left side of his face. He would carry the burn scar always. Angry red with whitish spots. It took a crooked path down his jaw, from just below his ear almost to the point of his chin. It was continued then on his lower neck and along his collarbone.

When he was six, he took a bread knife into the back yard. He attacked a scrawny ash sapling with that knife. The knife was a dagger. He had a dagger fight with the sapling, which was a pirate with a black scarf on its head and a patch over one eye. He saw an opening, and lurched forward to make the kill.

He stumbled. His hands went before him to break the fall. The blade of the knife sheared a narrow sliver of skin and cartilage off the outer rim of his right ear. Cut it off so cleanly. When he raised up, there it was, lying almost on the blade. If the knife had turned inward rather than outward it would have cut into his face. The ear sliver was about a quarter inch wide and almost an inch long. He picked it up and flung it over the back fence. Into the weeds.

He went in. Nobody was home. He buried his cut ear in a bath towel and sat two hours on the little front porch until his mother came home from work. She unwrapped the towel from the ear and the bleeding had stopped. But from then on, to go with the pocks and the scars, Trinidad had the trimmed-off ear.

"You little fart," his father said that night. "Careful you don't cut anything else off you. There's not much left now. Pass the butter."

Trinidad was his mother's last baby. To have him, she was obliged to enter a hospital with what she would forever describe as Complications. The doctor stood over her afterward and said, "No more babies for you, Maria. I've gone in and tied off everything you've got. If you get pregnant again, face the east and look for a large star."

That day she was thirty-three. At home she had a daughter, Juanita, who was eighteen. She also had Gloria, sixteen. And Teresa, fourteen. She had Alonzo, thirteen. Pedro, eleven. She had Margarita, ten. And Consuela, eight.

A string of barren years had followed Consuela. Crop failures, the doctor called them. Maria decided that she was safe at last, and so did the doctor. After all, eight years without issue. Maria had gone to work and accumulated six years' seniority at her grocery store job.

Then here came Trinidad. A tiny, wiggling, dark-eyed, coarse-haired inconvenience.

He was left at home to be raised by his brothers and sisters, who were already tired of raising each other. His brother Alonzo pronounced him to be, when he was three, "a little old pain in the ass to everybody." They handed him around and traded him off like a dishwashing chore. Some of his keepers, Pedro and Alonzo in particular, weren't faithful about serving their sentences. Before he was old enough for school, Trinidad had learned to survive entire days in the house alone.

When he did enter school, he was not happy there. He was stared at. Pointed out. Talked about. "Look at his face. Look at his ear. Part of his ear is gone, see there?"

Without realizing it, he developed a way of hiding in a crowd. When teachers, when anybody looked directly at him, he sunk—actually, physically, inside himself. He lowered his head and brought his shoulders up, as if that hid his pockmarks and his scars and his bad ear. He was hump-shouldered by the time he came out of the sixth grade.

But he was so quick. How he zipped about. "He's a scared little rabbit," his father said, watching him and laughing. "Look how he goes, so fast. Ducking and hiding all the time. Crazy little fart. Pass the potatoes."

When he got into high school, Trinidad appeared to go through a personality change. He tried to quit being a scared rabbit. He was no longer shy, retiring, quiet. He became talkative, challenging, often critical, sometimes defiant.

He made a desperate attempt to stop seeing himself as

ugly and insignificant and inferior. He avoided his reflection in mirrors. When he combed his hair he squinted his eyes to blur his vision and hide the truth that the mirror held. He loved to shave. He shaved so many times when he had almost no whiskers to shave. He would work up handfuls of lather and spread it thickly over his face, over his pockmarks, over his scars where no beard would ever grow. He liked his face pretty well when it was half hidden beneath that great white mask of soap.

His attempts to be outgoing did not succeed. Even at times when he felt the least confident he would go charging into situations where almost certain failure lurked, waiting for him. In the classroom, if a teacher presented a difficult question that no one could answer, Trinidad would rise up impulsively and take a shot at it. He would do that when he hadn't the vaguest idea of what the right answer was. He would sometimes push himself into a little circle of girls and try to talk to them in a jaunty and clever style. The result: disaster.

He discovered alcohol. He discovered that two bottles of his father's beer, forced into his small stomach with much gagging and belching, made him ever so confident and courageous. He would show up at school dances literally beer-bloated, eager to ask the prettiest girls onto the floor. Ready to talk smart-ass even to the athletes. So full of self-assurance and poise. As such times he even felt large and smooth-skinned and not scarred or pockmarked at all.

He learned he could gain attention by telling small lies. Small ones that kept growing, getting better. His brother Alonzo was in the Marines—now listen to this—and on weekends he went to Tiajuana, where the whores would put on private shows. They would screw one another with great cucumbers, and with Carta Blanca Beer bottles, and two big fat ones, Alonzo knew their names, had a burro with a dong this long, and they would do it to that burro at parties and all. It's true. It's no lie.

He let the lying get away from him entirely. In the locker room after gym class he told about going to see Sally Randermann, last Sunday night. Her folks were gone, out to play cards somewhere, and he and Sally got to fooling around—you know how you'll do—and one thing led to another—you know?—and they ended up getting it, twice, on the living room rug. You talk about nervous! With her folks likely to walk in any old time? Man!

That story traveled. It reached Douglas Randermann, who was Sally Randermann's brother. Sally Randermann's *big* brother. Douglas worked at the auto store and rode a great shiny motorcycle. He came and took two handsful of Trinidad's shirt and lifted him off the floor and said he was a dirty little lying son of a Mexican bitch and if ever he mentioned Sally's name again he would get his guts scattered along the border from here to Nogales. Then Douglas Randermann held Trinidad out, almost at arm's length, and dropped him in a corner where he stayed a while, in a small limp heap.

He was a senior that year.

After Douglas Randermann said those impressive words to him, Trinidad reverted for a while to scared-rabbit status. Darting and hiding again, keeping silent. For almost a month. Then one dusk, on his way home, he passed the Randermann house. Alongside a hedge Douglas' big shiny motorcycle was parked.

He walked on home. No one was there. He got a bottle of his father's beer and drank it. He opened another, and thought about Douglas Randermann's motorcycle. A person could slip up to that motorcycle, and because of the hedge he could stay around there a while without being seen. He finished the second beer.

He opened a third. That goddamned Douglas Randermann. That loudmouthed bastard. Thinks just because he's so big he can go around making threats, mistreating people. Thinks everybody's afraid of him.

Trinidad sauntered through the house. Swaggering a little now. No more scared rabbit. He stood in the middle of the kitchen floor and took gulps of the third beer. The pantry door was cracked. On the bottom shelf was a full gallon can of the ribbon cane syrup his father ate every day of his life.

Trinidad went to the toilet. Then to his bed. He took from under his mattress the hunting knife, with scabbard, he had ordered a month before. Back to the kitchen. Finished the beer. Picked up the gallon of syrup. He walked straight up the middle of the street in the darkness to Douglas Randermann's house.

He squatted behind the hedge, by the side of Douglas' big shiny motorcycle. He pried the lid off the syrup can with the hunting knife. He poured about a quart of the syrup in the great wide seat of the motorcycle. The best he could in the dark, he poured the remainder of the syrup in the gas tank. Still it was not full. He scooped up dirt and leaves and twigs from around the hedge and poured and stuffed them into the tank. He let the air out of the tires, and carefully carved them up with the knife.

Then he walked back home, so slow and brave, in the middle of the street again.

He put the empty syrup can in the garbage behind the garage. And washed his knife and shined the blade.

The scared rabbit gradually returned. It was not yet nine o'clock but Trinidad went to bed. He tried to enjoy seeing Douglas Randermann go out to sit in his sticky motorcycle seat, and start up the motor fueled with syrup and dirt, and drive away on slashed tires. But there was no satisfaction in the scene.

Because now the effect of the three beers had faded and this was clear to him—that Douglas would know, and would come again to find him, and scatter his guts along the border from here to Nogales. Trinidad rolled out of bed and dressed. He took twenty dollars from the face powder box his mother kept her money in. He left in the night. Still, nobody was home.

His father laughed and said, after Trinidad had been gone a week, "I bet he's joined the Marines, to look for Alonzo. He was always chasing after Alonzo. Crazy little fart. Pass the syrup."

## FIFTY-TWO

THE MARINE CORPS didn't want him. Trinidad tried the Navy. It didn't want him either. The Army welcomed him, evidently on the ground that a scar on the face and a slice off the ear were no handicap to a soldier who would spend his military career emptying trash cans and sweeping offices and mowing grass and digging holes and planting shrubs.

But in the Army, Trinidad had such a hard time doing things right. His life was never level and smooth. He lived on the tops of mountains or in the depths of dark canyons. Fighting the awful inferiority that his size and physical imperfections had given him, he continued making the same mistakes he made in school. He would charge in, defiantly, against overwhelming odds. His charges came when he was on one of his mountaintops, soaring at the peak of one of his highs, inspired by a bellyful of beer, or by his volatile Latin spirit, or both.

Then when his attacks failed, he plummeted into the depths of self-contempt and pity.

Before he was sent to Spanish Wells, to sweep and to dig holes and plant shrubs in The Bear's Base Beautification Program, he had been at the brink of physical disaster a number of times. On every occasion girls were involved.

Trinidad suffered so for the company of girls. Such a deep yearning he had—for sex, for hand-holding, for dancing, for whispering, for conversation, for a girl who would sit and talk to him about the weather, the movies, the Army, about anything.

But he had been rejected, refused, ignored, or scorned so

161

many times, he had gotten afraid to approach a girl unless he was on one of his highs. Then he bulled ahead and practically demanded that one go to the movies with him, or dance with him, or go outside for fresh air with him. And he had a great talent for picking the wrong girls. Girls that were out of his class, or else snobby ones who were sensitive about being approached in a bold way by a little brown guy with a funny face and a bad ear. Or girls who were already attached, either married or escorted, like the one in The Puma with Bates that night.

After all his time in the Army, he had not experienced one satisfactory association with a girl.

Unless he counted Sarah. He saved, and worshiped, the short one-paragraph notes to him that she included in her daily letter to Addison. They were so beautiful. He read them all every day. The shape of her written words, the loops and the crossed t's and the very apostrophes, they were exquisite to him.

". . . so we've had so much rain I haven't been able to . . ."

After that, rain in Chicago was of immense importance to Trinidad. If he found out that it rained in Chicago, it meant something special, because it affected Sarah.

" . . . the White Sox lost again to the Indians, so it looks as if . . ."

She had assumed he would be interested in baseball. He didn't even know who the White Sox or the Indians were. That mattered nothing to him, though. What mattered was the way those names looked, in Sarah's handwriting, speaking to him.

But he wasn't able to do everything right, even by mail, in dealing with Sarah. There was the matter of the gift. He bought it on one of his famous impulses. It was on a slender mannequin in the window of Schiller's Department Store, two doors down the main drag of Spanish Wells from the The Puma.

That Saturday afternoon he had sat at the bar in The

162

Puma and taken on such a load of beer he was almost foaming at the ears. He walked out and floated along the sidewalk a little way, bubbling and sloshing and grinning and giving off fumes, and he saw the black bra and panties, trimmed in lace, on the mannequin. They were sprinkled, sort of, with some silver stuff that flickered in the sunlight. Trinidad stood a minute as steady as he could and declared that set of underwear was made in heaven by angels, especially for Sarah Allen of Chicago, Illinois. He pushed into the store and bought the bra and panties right off the mannequin, and left it naked to the stares and snickers of Spanish Wells schoolboys on Main Street. He paid ten dollars for the set, and two dollars for packaging and mailing, and it was the wrong thing to do.

Wrong! He had gone in and made that purchase in an absolute explosion of love and high esteem and thoughtfulness for the only woman in the Milky Way that cared anything about him, and it was wrong.

Addison explained it, later on, after Sarah had received the package and written the soft little thank-you note. Don't worry about it, he told Trinidad, not this time. Because Sarah understood and she appreciated the present and all. It's just that some girls, he said, would take it the wrong way if you were to go mailing them underwear that way, OK? OK.

"Now come on," Addison laughed, "let's go up to The Garden and see if the beer's cold. You got any money? Hey, look, Slasher, get your chin off your shirt and stand up straight. I don't like to see my partner going around feeling droopy."

When he had done another wrong thing, and sunk from high to low, a few warm words from Addison could bring his spirit flying out of the depths. He suddenly darted out in front, and turned, and grinned, and walked one of his funny little tight circles, so eager to go. To be a friend, a partner, to this large person was intoxicating to Trinidad, who had known so little of friendship. Walking to The Garden, he had to control the urge to grab onto Addison's great right arm, and suspend part of his weight there, and match the long strides. The way he had done with his brother Alonzo when he was a child.

## FIFTY-THREE

"IT MOVED! Hey, Troop! It moved! It moved!"

Here was Addison, half-running, half-trotting toward the tent-shack, waving the daily letter from Sarah. "By god it moved already and it's not even five months old yet!"

They gathered close around him in a tight semicircle on the floor. He took his place on the footlocker and read them parts of the letter, about the baby moving for the first time.

"Let's see, she says here, 'I was in the living room reading the paper and I felt a little movement, right in the middle of my stomach. At first I thought it was gas . . . '"

Addison looked up. "She gets gas, all right. I'm telling you when that girl gets gas she can outbelch a bullfrog. Right after we got married she shut herself in the bathroom one night and let loose one of those explosions, god oh mighty General Lee, you never *heard* the like of it. I yelled and asked her what in eternal creation was *that,* and she said it wasn't anything but a burp. I told her burp my behind, it sounded to me like a thunderclap, and . . ."

A trio of sudden laughter from The Troop. The smallest humorous exchange between Sarah and Addison, even heard second hand that way, was enormous entertainment for them. What a perfect audience they were for Addison.

He read on. "Anyway she says, 'At first I thought it was gas but then I put my hand on my stomach, and waited, and after a while I felt it again. Not exactly a kick. Just a stirring inside me, a gentle movement. So it's the baby, moving already. I am in bed now, sitting up, and I just now felt it again. It's moving early. Maybe that means it's a boy . . . '"

"I *hope* it's a boy," McKavett interrupted.

"Shut up, Mac," Trinidad snapped.

McKavett wouldn't shut up. "Don't you want it to be a boy, Add?"

"I don't care. I just want it to be a human being, with one head and a couple of arms and legs and the standard deal on toes and fingers. A girl would be fine with me. Maybe it'd look like Sarah. I'd rather have a girl that looked like Sarah than a boy that looked like me."

"What else does she say?"

He skipped along, reading silently, looking for parts that were all right to read aloud. "Oh, I guess that's about it. She's mostly just talking here about her clothes, and the way the baby's riding. Says right now it's in a nice round shape and pooching right straight out. Says she's gonna be one of these pregnant women that look like they've got a beach ball in their britches."

"Some of 'em don't show much at all." That was Booker, putting in his contribution. "Even right up to the last. Don't even look pregnant."

"You know so damn much," Trinidad said.

"Well, it's a fact. An old gal that's kind of fat, and built thick through the middle, she can go right up to her time and nobody will know. I've seen it happen." Booker thought of Frieda. Was she alive? That football stadium baby, unless it had died, it would be about four years old now.

Addison was reading the letter over again, silently, from the first. Then in an instant he had left them. Departed, as he often did, and went off to be with Sarah. The Troop knew the signs so well. To talk to him, get anything out of him, was impossible while he was gone. The only thing to do was sit and wait until he returned.

It was customary for him to return slowly, gradually, never with a sudden jerk. During the returning there was a stage where he talked. Not to Sarah. Not to The Troop. To himself, they supposed. He did that now. He said quietly, looking down at the letter:

"She says here at the end that when she felt the baby

move inside her, the feeling came to her that she would never again be alone as long as she lives." He looked up at them then. "That's good."

McKavett, recognizing the end of the discussion, went outside. A soldier from the tent across the way asked him, "What was Add so excited about a while ago?"

"The baby moved," McKavett said, "for the first time."

"What baby?"

"Our baby in Chicago," McKavett said.

# FIFTY-FOUR

AT ONE of the letter-writing sessions, McKavett piped up in his high-pitched, complaining whine and said, "Add, I just be damn if I can think of anything else to write about. I've told Sarah twice everything I've got to say."

Booker said, "That goes for me, too. I'm about written dry."

"Well, you don't have to write to her every day," Addison said. "Just let it rest a while."

"But if we did that," Trinidad argued, "she'd quit writing to us."

"Why don't you write to your folks?" Addison suggested. "For all they know, you've grown a beard and moved to Mobile since you wrote home."

"Who would I write to?"

"Well, shoot fire, write to your mother, your sisters, your dad. My god, haven't you ever written home?"

"Sure. I wrote home when I got shipped to Hawaii that time."

Addison poked a little sarcasm at him. "What'd you do, send 'em a picture postcard?"

"Yeah, that's right."

Addison turned to stare in astonishment. "You mean to say you were stationed in the Hawaiian damn Islands for a year and a half and you wrote your folks one frigging postcard?"

"That's right."

"Did you get an answer?" McKavett wanted to know.

"Naw," Trinidad said. "When I got back home on furlough they said I forgot to put my address on it."

"I guess I could write my mother at the hotel," Booker said. "Even if she's moved, she ought to get it at the hotel."

"Say, Book," challenged Trinidad, "whatever happened to that big-titted blonde in Pennsylvania you were always writing letters to? You were gonna get her to send you a picture for us to see."

Booker had not confessed to Trinidad and McKavett, as he had to Addison, that the girl was a fiction. "Aw, I don't know. I think she got married, or something."

"What would I tell 'em," Trinidad asked Addison, "if I wrote home?"

"Tell 'em where you are, to begin with. Tell 'em you're all right, that you're well. Say you miss 'em. Hell, say you love 'em, it won't hurt you to say that. Ask how everybody is at home. Tell 'em to send you snapshots, and put in one of those pictures of yourself that we took. Just write whatever you're interested in, whatever you'd talk to 'em about if you saw 'em face to face. Think about all the stuff we talk about around here, a thousand different subjects. Write about that, as long as it's not nasty. You guys like to get mail, well, if you want to get mail, you got to put mail out."

Trinidad said, low and wistful, "Alonzo would answer me if I knew where to write him."

McKavett said, "I don't know what my mother's address is, or my sisters', either."

"Just write to 'em general delivery then," Addison told him. "Or if you've got kinfolks, or friends, that you know where they are, write to them."

"I know a lady there, runs a place on the river."

So that evening, urged on by Addison, instead of writing to Sarah they wrote home.

Trinidad wrote to his sister Consuela, mainly because she was the only one of his sisters whose married name he could remember.

Booker wrote to his mother, at the dim-lobby hotel on the ragged side of town.

And McKavett wrote to Flora Ward, gas station operator, beer-joint owner, small-dog lover, and part-time prostitute.

On the outside of the envelope he scrawled directions on where Flora Ward's place of business was from the post office. In the letter he said he was at Spanish Wells and he was all right. He asked how Flora was doing, how business was going. He put in a snapshot of himself and asked Flora to send him one of her. He said the weather at Spanish Wells was still warm in the day but very chilly at night.

All that he wrote, and still not half the page was filled. So he wrote that there is life in outer space. He wrote that the earth is a member of the Milky Way. That Sarah's baby moved in Chicago on the twenty-third of October. That on the third of September, Addison went six and a half rounds with Paul Chavez but was healing up pretty well.

He wrote that he could buy three toothbrushes for a dollar at the base PX. That the trouble with people was that they went around getting married to each other when they weren't really in love but only lonesome and horny. He considered a minute and erased the word horny and let the sentence end with lonesome. He wrote that for a dollar at the tailor shop, Jonsey would take up your khaki shirts to where they weren't so baggy around the waist. And he wrote that when shooting craps, the odds against the point of ten are two to one, because there are twice as many sevens on a pair of honest dice as there are tens. Yours very truely, Melvin S. McKavett.

# FIFTY-FIVE

WITHOUT MEANING TO, Addison caught Trinidad alone in the tent-shack, examining the scarred side of his face in a hand-held shaving mirror. His eyes so solemn.

"You know something, Add?"

"What?"

"I think this old scar skin on my face is changing. It's not as red as it was. I don't think it's as big as it used to be, either. Do you think?"

He turned to Addison, presenting his face. An awkward moment. He had never before mentioned the scars or the pockmarks to Addison or McKavett or Booker.

Addison had brought a newspaper. He fell into his bunk and stretched out. "Aw, I don't know. You want to know the truth, I never do pay any attention to you having any scars, or whether they're redder or smaller or what."

For a few seconds Trinidad was struck silent by that. What could it mean? "How come you don't pay any attention to it?"

"I just mean," Addison said, opening the paper, "that I don't ever think about you having any scars."

"Why?" Trinidad demanded. He was standing close beside Addison's bunk now, the shaving mirror still in his hand. "I got scars all over. This burn thing. All these old pocks. How could you not think about me having scars?"

"All I'm telling you is, when I look at you I don't see scars. I just see you. Ol' Trinidad."

But Trinidad wouldn't let it rest. "I don't understand that."

Addison put his paper down. "Well, the thing is, people don't see what you think they see. Let me think a minute, about somebody you think you look at a lot. All right, take old Jackson, behind the bar at The Puma. You see him at least once a week, right?"

"All right, yeah."

Addison laughed a little. "Hadn't been long since you sat in there, so he tells me, and looked at him all the way from sober to drunk. All right, now tell me, does Jackson wear glasses?"

"No," said Trinidad. Then, "Well, wait a minute, I think . . ." He tried to bring Jackson's face into focus. "By damn I don't know, whether he does or not. I can't remember."

"Well, I can tell you he sure does. Wears great big old black horn-rims, cover almost half his face. You don't ever see him without them so you don't even know they're there."

Addison fell back onto his pillow and raised his paper and began reading again. Just as if his example had settled the matter forever and any further discussion was pointless.

Trinidad sat on his bunk and considered. Could it be? Could it really be that when people looked at him they didn't see him all scarred and gruesome? Didn't Addison just say it was so? Could it be, then, that somewhere there was a person, a girl, who would look at him and like him, and not see his scars and pocks but think he was good-looking, and even *love* him? Hadn't Addison said, before, that when a woman loved a guy she would think he was handsome, no matter what he looked like?

Trinidad raised the shaving mirror and faced himself again. Now look, is that so bad? He smiled at the face in a composed and confident way. See there? Really now, this is not a bad face at all, taken as a whole.

From that moment forward, the tempest that had raged inside Trinidad for so long was not as fierce.

# FIFTY-SIX

ALMOST A MONTH to the day that Addison had promised himself to stop taking risks and pulling stupid stunts, he pulled one of the stupidest of his career. What inspired him to do it was a fifth of sour mash bourbon.

He had not been drunk since the memorable night in Chicago, at the company Christmas party where he met Sarah. Following that performance he had told Sarah, the first time he ever spoke to her on the phone, "I don't get along too well with liquor. I don't even drink it, as a rule. Listen, that's the truth."

And it was. Just a single social drink was rare for him. He didn't like the taste and smell of liquor and he didn't like what happened to him when he drank it. So his rule was to keep away from the stuff. He rarely violated the rule, but when he did he violated it in a spectacular fashion.

If he had ever carefully reviewed his drinking history, which he had not, Addison would have revealed unto himself a set of impressive facts:

That he had been drunk exactly a dozen times in his life.

That all twelve drunks had led him into disaster, sometimes minor but mostly major.

That each of those drunks, and their associated calamities and misfortunes, were visited upon him when he was engaged in the desperate pursuit of sex.

The beginning of it was when he was fifteen. Burton Sheffield, who was seventeen and therefore knew all things, convinced Addison that one cheap bottle of champagne would get him into the pants of Nadine Compton. "She really loves that champagne," Burton said, winking and grinning. He further stated that when a bottle of champagne was waved at her, Nadine would follow the waver into garages, barns, forests, fields of tall grass, vacant lots, back seats, houses where parents were not at home, and so on and so forth.

Addison thought what a good thing that would be, to lure Nadine to a secret place. Nadine was dull and giggly and had funny teeth and bad posture. But she was good about sitting around in school with her thighs showing, and a number of excellent stories were circulated regarding what she enjoyed doing.

Getting his hands on a bottle of champagne turned out to be harder than Addison thought. He had the idea to substitute dewberry wine. His father made dewberry wine annually and kept it on the floor of the pantry. True, dewberry wine wasn't champagne, so Addison decided to compensate by waving two bottles instead of one.

Nadine was delighted. "I'm baby-sitting at my sister's house Friday night. Bring the stuff and come by." So he went on by, and they sat on the back steps and listened for the baby to cry. Nadine provided two glasses. She wanted to make toasts, and clink glasses and everything. The wine was dreadful. It was sour and burned Addison's throat. Nadine liked it. "Come on, drink up," she said, and giggled. Addison drank up, because maybe when the wine was all gone, that's when they'd do it. But the wine lasted a very long time.

He remembered her putting a hand on the inside of his thigh and squeezing, and that seemed all right but then that earthquake came and messed everything up. The entire back yard began to spin, and waver, and tilt. He shut his eyes and opened them again and the garage passed by.

He stood and stepped out on the grass to get a better look at the earthquake. God oh mighty General Lee, what an earthquake! It caused the back yard to rise up and whap Addison a severe blow to the side of his face. Talk about your earthquakes! It caused the ground to stand at a vertical position. Here was Addison, flat-footed and erect, and the lawn was standing up just beside him, so close the grass was against his cheek. And look there at the garage, it's hovering now, up in the air, directly above him. *Look* at that thing!

So on account of that great natural cataclysm, Addison didn't get to do anything whatever to Nadine. In fact, his father had to come and fetch him home. He came after Nadine's sister called about ten o'clock and said somebody better do something about this kid or he's gonna lay out there in the back yard and puke his damn head off.

After that, Nadine went off to live with an aunt, they said, in Dallas or someplace. For days and days Addison was a juvenile villain around his own home. He thought they would never run out of things to say about what happened in the back yard of Nadine Compton's sister.

And so Addison, remembering, did not take another drink until he was gone from home and safely in the Army. He was nineteen, and already taller than six feet, and a pretty tough boxer, too. In the city of Baltimore, Maryland, a young woman with the blackest hair introduced him to martinis. She believed him to be twenty-three years old, because that was what he told her. He was afraid she wouldn't want to have her bra unhooked by a nineteen-year-old amateur boxer who never had tasted a martini. He had already dealt with those funny little buttons on the back of her blouse, and was exploring around to see what sort of hookup he would have to unhook, and it would be such a shame to fail now, being so far along and all. So when she made the martinis he drank three, and said they were good. They were made about six to one, and his stomach was empty, and here came another one of those damn earthquakes. Everything was lost.

So that's the way it went, with Addison and booze. Yet, in that mysterious way that men court disaster, he was drawn at times into those bouts of outrageous drinking.

Liquor was poison to him. He would get the heaving sicks, or he would do nutty things, and the next day he would remember them only vaguely, or not at all.

Look what he did to Father Frank, that time in Los Angeles. Father Frank, the best, the most lovable, the most understanding and valuable chaplain the U. S. Army ever had. Who slept in the barracks with the men, because that's where he was needed. Who went along with them when they marched forth at night in search of trouble.

For three consecutive nights Addison had sat in one of those drinking places, a lounge, with soft lights and thick carpets and slow music, and each evening he had let a couple of beers get hot in front of him while he tried to hustle the singer. She was tall and blond and had the prettiest mouth and the whitest arms, and Addison had decided that if he didn't make love to her he would just pass away. She wouldn't even come to the table for a drink.

The third night Father Frank was sitting with him. When she finished, Addison went up and said, "Look, I've got a priest with me tonight. A purebred Catholic priest, roped, branded, and registered by the Pope in Rome. What could happen to you bad, sitting at a table with a priest?" She laughed and said she could think of two things. One, she could lose her job, and two, her husband. So she didn't come, and Addison was so frustrated he astonished the waitress by ordering a series of double scotches when he had sat there nursing hot beer for three evenings.

Father Frank stayed, and observed the poisoning. When it was complete and Addison went out, he went with him. On the street he grabbed Addison's arm, to keep him from stepping off the curb into a taxi's path. Somehow the gesture annoyed Addison and he turned and knocked Father Frank down. A short right to the ribs, and down went Padre Paco, one of God's most blessed children, onto the sidewalks of Los Angeles.

The next day Addison didn't remember the incident. Father Frank told him about it, forgave him for the blow, and showed the purple bruise on his ribs. "Did you ever think of giving up liquor, forever?" he asked. Addison said, "I do. I quit, forever."

And he did, for more than a year, until something else came along that made him want to poison himself again.

## FIFTY-SEVEN

ADDISON'S FALL FROM GRACE at Spanish Wells came when he finally ran entirely out of fuel. He had been gone from Sarah seven months, and a great emptiness was inside him. He needed to touch her, to renew himself, to get from her, as he sometimes referred to it, a transfusion. He had never been gone from her this long, and his time had run out.

He fought his need by writing her a series of remarkable letters. All of them pure love letters. Love*making* letters. No I-went-to-town-Friday stuff. None of the log of their daily lives that they usually wrote. He produced long, paragraphless pages of fantasies in which Sarah became the most-made-love-to woman in creation. In the fantasies he was a lover of exquisite artistry and astonishing control and incredible endurance. He could maintain a magnificent erection for hours, to send her soaring to such joyful heights. She would reach peaks of delight never before attained. Not even by nymphs and satyrs in palaces of pleasure hidden away in unknown misty forests.

Then he would reconstruct in the letters, in every intimate detail, their actual love scenes that were extra-special. The first time they did it, on the blanket in the back yard beside her mother's flowers. The time they did it in the park, on second base. The time they spent the hundred dollars his father gave them at their wedding reception and told them to use it for something extravagant and unforgettable. (They rented for one night a spacious hotel room with a great round bed.) Then the time they went to Wisconsin to meet her relatives on the farm, and they climbed the loft ladder and did it in the hay. And the *last* time, on the moonlit bed.

Sarah, pregnant in Chicago, read the letters with trembling hands and racing heart and sweating brow, and with such astonishment. Addison . . . Addison . . . How long, she wondered, would she spend discovering all the wonders inside this strange large person she had married?

Writing the letters failed to calm the awful restlessness in Addison. One Saturday afternoon he called her and said abruptly:

"I want you to come down here."

"Addison! When?"

"Now. As soon as you can. I need you."

His manner disturbed her. He was blunt, demanding. "Addison, are you all right? Is anything wrong?"

The tone of concern in her voice caused him to soften. Don't get her worrying, now. "No, I'm all right. I just need to touch you. I need to take you to bed."

She tried to lighten the moment. And laughed, and said, "Listen, lover, didn't you get that picture I sent, showing my beautiful trim figure in profile? I'm seven months', love. I'd be like making love to a Halloween pumpkin. I'm sticking out to here."

"I don't care how far out you're sticking."

175

"But you wouldn't believe it. I can almost see this baby growing. And move? I think it's got somebody else in there, and they're playing leapfrog. I just don't see how it can last two more months. Dad says if I really go the full time I'm going to need wheels in front."

He didn't say anything. There was a brief silence.

Then she said, "Addison, are you unhappy with me?"

"No-no. I just had this wild notion. I've just been missing you so bad. I know I haven't ever wanted you down here in this awful damn place but then the last few days . . ."

"I'll come," she said, "if you say so."

"I know. I don't guess it was a very good idea, though, with the baby so far along and all."

"Is there a possibility you could come up here?"

"No. There isn't any way right now. I can't even get a three-day pass. I need to save all my time, so I can come up there when the baby's due."

"Listen, maybe I better come on. I think I ought to."

"No, it's all right. I'll be OK. I feel better now, talking to you."

And so they let it go at that. He hung up feeling so low. Somebody was standing behind him, waiting. It was Grover, the big Okie he'd knocked out at the fights.

Addison told him, "I hope to hell you didn't come to fight again. If you have, I give up."

Grover grinned, and stuck out his big hand. "Naw, man, I just stopped to thank you for that boxing lesson you gave me. I thought I was a fighter till I got in there with you. You about took all the fight out of me. I've decided to take early retirement from the ring."

"Wasn't anything personal."

"I know. Listen, I watched you against Chavez. I just wanted to tell you I thought you were great. Damn if I don't think you might have whipped him if you'd been in condition."

"Well, we'll never know, because I've retired too."

They were at The Garden, in front of the phone booths.

Grover carried a sack from the PX. But what he had in it wasn't from the PX. He showed Addison. Four fifths of sour mash sippin' whiskey. The best.

"I'm fixin' to crack one of these sweethearts," Grover said, "and I thought maybe you'd have a little snort with me. The last time I saw you you cold-cocked me. Well, this time you can drink with me, OK?"

Addison nodded. "OK, but let me get a beer. I'm not much of a whiskey drinker."

"Naw, man, try this. This doesn't even *taste* like whiskey, it's so smooth. I sent all the way to San Antone to get this stuff."

So they went to sit in Whiskey Corner. Liquor in The Garden was against regulations but it was there every night. Some paper sacks and cartons were kept in a back corner, for hiding whiskey bottles. It was generally drunk straight, out of beer cups.

Grover turned out to be pretty good company. Addison eased down two modest drinks, and when Grover left he gave Addison one of the bottles, the seal intact. "Just for friendship, all right?" He had a big date in town and went on, leaving Addison alone in the corner.

He thought of how Sarah sounded on the phone. Recalled her every word and how she said it and what it meant. The whiskey was smooth, like Grover said. Pretty decent of him, leaving the bottle. Expect it cost him a lot. Did Sarah sound sort of cool? Different? Just a tiny bit eager to get off the phone, maybe? Crack the seal on the bottle. Take another little one. Stuff's all right. Nice and warm in the old belly.

Within ten minutes Addison was able to see that he had made a mistake on the telephone. Look what he'd done. He'd called up there and told her he needed her, told her to come, and then he'd backed down, told her *not* to come. Why, shoot fire, didn't she say, right out, that she'd come? She said, "I'll come if you say so." No, wait, she said more than that. She said, "Maybe I better come on. I think I *ought* to." She *did* say that. Why in the cornbread hell did

177

he want to tell her not to come then? My god, she's gonna think he doesn't *want* her to come.

He got up and walked fast to the phone booths. And called her again.

Her mother answered. Sarah wasn't at home. "She's gone to a movie," her mother said.

"Gone to a movie? By herself?"

"No, she went with Phyllis Bradley. She'll be crushed that she missed your call. I know she wouldn't have gone out if she'd known you were going to call back. Are you all right, Addison? Is anything wrong?" The same questions Sarah had asked.

"No, nothing's wrong. I just . . . well, I wanted to tell her something I forgot to say. But it doesn't matter. Tell her I'll put it in a letter."

But he walked away with a set of hurt feelings. Couldn't help himself. There he'd been, not an hour before, calling her all lonely and desperate and missing her so bad he was pretty nearly in a state of despair. And quick as he hangs up, she goes traipsing off to a damn movie, with that silly Phyllis. Sort of teed him off.

He shoved his hands in his pockets and walked out of The Garden toward the tent-shack. Then he remembered the bottle, and went back.

# FIFTY-EIGHT

STEPHENS, the softball pitcher from New Jersey who bunked across the way, stopped at the tent-shack after they had waited for Addison two hours. He told them, "Your big buddy is up at The Garden, just drunk as hell. Did you know that?"

"Bullshit. Addison don't get drunk," McKavett said. "He don't even like to drink."

"Well, then he's putting on one hell of an act. He sat up

there and killed a fifth, almost, in less than two hours. He was getting loud and acting sort of mean when I left."

Trinidad rolled out of his bunk. "We better go check."

They went double-time together to The Garden, but he was gone. He had finished the bottle and gotten on the bus and gone to town. One of the beer drinkers said, "Drunk as he is he'll be lucky if the MP's don't pick him up soon as he gets off the bus."

The Troop was wearing fatigues. They couldn't board the bus for town dressed that way. They trotted back to the tent-shack and got into khakis and hurried back to the gate. Then they had to wait more than forty minutes on a bus, and so they were an hour or more behind him. The ride into town took another half an hour. It was after nine o'clock when they found somebody who had seen him. He had gotten off the bus at Deke Fowler's liquor store.

"Yeah, he was in here," Fowler told them. "Bought a bottle of bourbon. Didn't look to me like he needed it. But I hear that bird can get mean, when he wants to. So I sold it to him."

"How long ago?"

Fowler shrugged, looked at his clock. It said a quarter to ten. "Hour and a half ago, I guess. He went on toward town, from here."

They stayed behind him that way, searching, trailing, for so long. He was hard to catch up with but easy to track. They just walked along the main drag and asked any uniform they met. Almost every GI on the base knew him since the fights.

"He was outside The Puma a couple of hours ago. Really skunked, too. Said he was going to The Shacks. Said he couldn't steal any so he was going over there and see if he could buy him some."

They trudged across town to the whorehouse, to The Shacks. It was Saturday night. The Shacks would be crowded. Maybe there would be a line, all the way around the inside of the little parlor and reaching even outside. Guys standing stiff and grim-faced, waiting their turn on slippery decks.

The idea of Addison going there, doing that, standing in that line, that was so hateful to them.

One Saturday night he had led them over there, to see the line and to make his little speech.

"All right, Troop, just ahead of us and a little to your right, is a gen-yew-wine North American den of iniquity. You've seen 'em before but you don't know the facts, I bet, about cathouses. The thing to remember about 'em is that in a whorehouse you'll hear the truth but not the *whole* truth. Now Madame Ella, that runs The Shacks here, she'll tell you you can sweat her line on Saturday night, and put your money down, and get anything you want. And that's sure true, as far as it goes. What Ella doesn't tell you about is what you get that you *don't* want. Like the bullhead clap, that crosses your eyes, and shrivels your kidneys, and rots your peter off. Ella will say, 'Don't you worry, boys, every one of my girls goes once a month to the doctor and gets checked inside and out, so poke it right on in.' And I tell you what, she's right, too, about all her girls getting checked once a month. But look here, say one of those old gals checks out clean on the first. Then on the second she turns a trick with an old boy just back from a three-day pass on the border. He doesn't know it yet but he has imported the clap. He got it from Senorita Josefina in Boys Town at Piedras Negras, and he pulls up his pants and walks away from The Shacks here and he's left you a little present, in a nice warm incubator. It's in there wigglin' and lurkin' and waitin' for you. So here you come, and you're doing things smart. You make the old gal show that piece of paper from the doctor, and you go right on in bareheaded and confident because the piece of paper says she was clean on the first. Well, hell, this is the *third*, Troop, and you collect that little present from Piedras Negras and by the twentieth there you are, clawing walls in the latrine and peeing flames. No, I don't say there's no such thing as a clean whorehouse. I'm saying they're a mighty poor risk. You'll be better off lopin' your mule. If it's too tight you can loosen up and if it's too loose you can tighten up and you damn sure ain't gonna catch anything . . ."

It was such an impressive speech, and they took it straight into their hearts, and admired him so for knowing such things, and loved him for caring and sharing that way.

Then this. To see him standing in line, with Sarah pregnant in Chicago and all, how could they bear that? How they hoped he wouldn't be standing in that terrible line. They marched on to The Shacks, silent and stone-faced.

He wasn't in the line. "He was here, though," Hatfield said. Hatfield was Ella's man of all work. During business hours he stayed out front and discouraged loud noises and line crashing. "But Miss Ella wouldn't let him in. He was too drunk. She don't want no drunks. They take too long."

They walked back to The Puma, where they had missed him again. He had been there while they were at The Shacks. "He's sure loaded," Jackson told them from behind the bar. "I ain't never seen Addison drunk and it's kind of scary. But he's still on his feet pretty good. He still knows how to stand up and take a cussing out."

"Who cussed him out? When?"

"That Bates woman, just about half an hour ago, right here at the bar. He came in and stood right there and she came up from the back. Bates had a table back yonder in the corner, four or five couples. They're gone now. She came up and I swan I never heard a better cussing out, from male or female. You could dang near see the fire coming out of her mouth."

"What'd he do?"

"Just stood and took it. When she ran down he sort of leaned over to her, kind of polite like, and told her if she was through cussing she could go on home and fuck herself."

"Oh my god! What'd she do?"

"Went back yonder and told Bates, I expect. Addison waited around here a good while but nobody came up. I guess Bates has had just about all of Addison he wants."

"Is Add by himself?"

"Yeah. Seems like everybody's walking around him, real wide."

"We need to find him, get him off the street before he gets picked up. Did he say where he was going?"

Two customers at the far end of the bar were calling Jackson. "Wait a second," he said, and went to pull beer. When he got back he told The Troop, "He said something that didn't mean doodley-squat to me. Maybe it does to you. He said he couldn't think of anything else to do so he thought he'd go screw old Katherine. Maybe that was just his whiskey talking. You know anybody named Katherine?"

## FIFTY-NINE

THEY DID NOT, in fact, know Katherine's last name. They went to the pay phones in the bus station. The Spanish Wells telephone directory was thin, and they went all the way through it looking at first names. Not one Katherine was there.

They huddled in the waiting room, and decided the thing to do was call the base and try to get Katherine's last name or address or phone number.

"You want me to call?" Trinidad asked.

"Yes," Booker and McKavett said, almost together. "You do it."

Without realizing it Trinidad stepped, or was forced, into a position of leadership over the others. Booker and McKavett were shy about things like calling the base and asking sensitive questions.

The base would give out no addresses or phone numbers. The Troop sat close together on the waiting room bench, as if closeness would help them know what to do.

"You reckon he's really at Katherine's?" asked McKavett. His tone said he hoped with a deep passion that it wasn't so. "He wouldn't do that. Would he?" Pleading, to be agreed with.

"He might, drunk," Trinidad said. "He went to The Shacks."

"But he didn't go in," McKavett argued. "Anyhow, even if he is at Katherine's it don't mean anything. It don't have to mean he's *screwin'* her. Does it?"

No response to that came forth. But doubt showed so clearly on those faces, McKavett's included.

"I guess we could just leave him be," Booker said darkly. "If he's at Katherine's he's off the street. I mean the MP's won't get him."

"No, now wait," Trinidad said. "The thing is, we don't know if he's at her place or not. If he's drunk as everybody says, for all we know he's in a ditch somewhere. The least we got to do is find out if he's at Katherine's. If he is, well, he is. If he's not, I think we ought to start walking the streets and looking. If it was you or me drunk somewhere, you know *he'd* look till he found us."

They both nodded. "He damn sure would."

Trinidad's face was so intense. Tiny furrows danced across his narrow forehead. He leaned forward, being the leader, gesturing, counting off points on his fingers:

"OK, it's a quarter after twelve now. Means there'll be two more buses, at one o'clock and then the last one at two. I say one of us ought to stay here at least till the one o'clock bus leaves. Lots of guys from the base will be drifting in here. Maybe we could spot one that works in The Bear's building and knows Katherine. Might even know where she lives. How about it if the other two split? One go back to The Puma. One back to The Shacks. Ask everywhere. Remember him talking about how he'd get so sick, and that's why he didn't drink booze? Hell, he could be sick behind a building somewhere, or in somebody's yard. Look everywhere you can. And get on back here by one-thirty at least."

183

Which meant that he would be the one to stay at the bus station, and Booker and McKavett didn't dispute him. They hurried off. And Trinidad took up the watch, for GI faces that seemed familiar to him from the days he had spent sweeping in the headquarters building.

He didn't see a face he knew until almost time for the one o'clock bus to pull out. And it wasn't on a GI. It was on Major Burke. He was sitting at the counter of the bus station coffee shop, reading a newspaper. He was alone. And he knew what Trinidad needed to know. Katherine's desk was less than ten feet from Burke's office door. He had to know what her last name was, at least.

But was it safe to ask him? That was so hard for Trinidad to decide.

There were things about Addison's affairs that The Troop didn't know. They didn't know he'd been in trouble with The Bear about the trip to Chicago with Captain Biggs, or about going to Katherine's apartment. They didn't know he'd *been* to Katherine's apartment. They didn't know he had fought three men in the gym that night to get out of trouble with The Bear.

But they did know that The Bear slept with Katherine. At least they thought they knew it. It was talked about all over the base. Therefore it had to be a most sensitive matter if, at this moment, Addison was in the sheets with Katherine. Major Burke was a good man, and he liked Addison, but . . .

Trinidad decided to ask anyway. It was getting late. He would try to tell Burke as little as possible.

"Sir? Major Burke?"

Burke remembered him. He looked tired but not irritated. Go ahead, ask.

"Sir, I need to ask a question."

"All right."

"The colonel's secretary. Katherine? Do you happen to know her last name? Or where she lives?"

He tried the hardest he could to look the major in the face

but he couldn't manage it, and with great relief dropped his eyes and studied the floor of the coffee shop. Burke was a man whose very job was trouble, dealing with it, and he could read it so easily on the narrow brown face before him now. It was there in neon lights.

"Why do you want Katherine's address?"

Trinidad shook his head. "I just need it, sir."

"Where's Addison tonight?"

Shake of the head again. "I don't know, sir." Well, he hadn't told a lie yet.

"Does this have anything to do with Addison?"

Trinidad knotted every muscle in his small face and chewed on his lip and looked so miserable, and Burke said:

"That damn fool's not at Katherine's, is he?"

The response to that was a great swell of anguish in Trinidad's eyes, and Burke then saw he was making a mistake and he said:

"Wait a minute. Let's do it this way." He tore two coffee checks off the bottom of a pad of blanks on the counter. On one he sketched a quick map and he said:

"It's easy to find. Go back east on Main and turn left at the little bakery. That's Mulberry Street, I think. Look for the first two-story house on your right. Her apartment is upstairs on the left. Her last name is Russell. Katherine Russell."

Trinidad decided to say, "He's drunk, Major. And maybe sick."

"Jesus!" Burke muttered. He turned to look at the phone booths, but frowned and said, "Her number's unlisted and I don't have it." He scribbled a note on the other check blank and folded it and handed it over, and he said:

"Give this to Katherine. Now listen, I'm not going to ask you any more questions, but if Addison is there get him the hell out, drunk, sick, or what, and get him back to the base. Do you have anybody to help you?"

"Yes, sir."

Burke checked his watch and said, "You're going to miss

the late bus. Do you have enough money for a taxi?" Even before he got the question out he was reaching for his wallet. How could this little GI have money for a seventeen-mile taxi ride? He folded several bills and handed them over, and he wrote again on another blank and he said:

"I'm going on to the base. If you have any trouble, call me at that number. But don't call me unless you just have to. Now go on."

## SIXTY

THEY MISSED THE LAST BUS, all right. By the time Trinidad had rounded up Booker and McKavett and they had found Mulberry Street, it was almost two o'clock. Turning at the bakery, Trinidad was talking so fast, explaining the strange interview with Major Burke, telling them about the instructions, and the taxi money, and the note for Katherine.

"What's the note say?"

"I don't know. I haven't read it."

"Did he tell you not to read it?"

Trinidad stopped under a street light and said, "No, he didn't tell me not to read it, but it's not for us, it's for Katherine, so we ought not to read it." Booker and McKavett gave him blank stares and he said, "Let's read it."

So they did, and it said, "Katherine, Bear's driving in tonight from SA. Departed about 11 P. Mrs. staying in SA. Expect company early Sun., by 4 A. GWB."

"What's it mean?"

"Sounds like The Bear's coming to Katherine's is what it sounds like to me."

"By four o'clock. That's this morning, too. My god. That's not but about two hours from now. Come on."

They trotted along Mulberry, looking for the first two-story house on the right. McKavett said, his voice quivering from the trot, "I never saw so damn many strange things happenin'. A while ago on Main, I run into that Sergeant what's-his-name, that Italian? Said he talked to Addison about ten o'clock and Addison said somebody tried to run him down tonight in a car. Run right up on the sidewalk, he said, just like in a damn gangster show, and tried to hit him. You reckon that could really be?"

"That sounds crazy. Just drunk talk, I guess. Hey, here it is. Upstairs, on the left. There's a light on."

## SIXTY-ONE

OH YES, HE WAS THERE.

She came to the door in a long pink robe and she said he was there. Then when she read the note her hand went to her mouth and she turned quickly to look at the clock.

"Come on in. I hope you can get him up. He's dead to the world now. He's been sick."

They entered in little shuffly half steps and stood in a close bunch, caps in their hands, their shoulders touching, looking at Katherine with round eyes, not knowing what to say in that place.

She was nervous, wanting them to hurry. "He's in the bedroom," she said, impatience in her tone, as if she wanted to follow with, "Where in hell did you expect he'd be, in the kitchen?"

She did say, when they had started to move across the soft carpet to the bedroom door, "He's naked. Hasn't got on a stitch."

They all three turned back to her and stared again, and blinked some, and seemed to nod just a tiny bit.

"He was sick all over himself," she said. "Even into his damn socks. I cleaned him up and washed his things. I'll get them. Let's hurry."

Trinidad found his tongue enough to tell her, "We need a taxi." She called about the taxi and The Troop went to work on Addison. He looked seven feet tall, stretched out in that pretty soft bed. They never did get him entirely conscious. They worried his pants on, and his shirt, both not yet dry. They stuffed his great feet into clammy shoes, and crammed his damp socks and underwear into their pockets.

It took all four of them to get under him and get him up and out in the hall and down the stairs. When they were halfway down he let go the awfullest, most ominous gagging noise that seemed to originate in hell itself, and Katherine was able to see him vomiting again all up and down the stairway and she wailed, "Oh, *shit!*" But there was nothing left in him to throw up so he just heaved that way, and got heavy as a house, and they all came ever so close to ending up at the foot of the stairs in a great pile of arms and legs and torsos and damp khaki and pink housecoat. When they won the front door, Katherine was sobbing quietly and not really holding up her end too well.

But after they tumbled him into the taxi, she seemed to recover. She checked her watch and saw that Addison's resurrection and translocation had required only fifteen minutes, instead of the hour she imagined. She leaned into the window and said to The Troop and a yawning taxi driver, "Listen, this man is so full of nightmares and trouble. And whiskey, too, I know, so I can't really tell how much to believe of everything he said. But he told me, soon after he came tonight, that somebody took a shot at him, just a few minutes before, right here on this street."

Trinidad told her, "Well, he talks funny a lot. Stretches things, you know, even when he's sober. I don't know."

"Who is Sarah?" she asked. "Is that his wife?"

"Yeah, that's his wife."

She went in then, and they rattled and smoked and burned oil to the base in one of the six taxis in Spanish Wells. The Troop did not speak one word, all the way. They sat and listened to him groan and snore. And hoped that he'd been too drunk and too sick all night to do anything with Katherine. If he did do it with her, it was going to be so hard to forgive him. Two-timing Sarah, the woman they loved.

# SIXTY-TWO

THE WEEK following the great drunk was an awkward time around the tent-shack. Not much conversation. The Troop was removed from Addison now, even when they were all together under that little canvas roof. They didn't sit with him at letter-writing time. They would walk with him to the mess hall, but not close, the way they did before. They didn't go with him to pick up the daily letter from Sarah.

There was a great deal of joshing from the men about Addison's doings in town Saturday night. Half the population of the base must have been on the street to watch him participate in that great debauchery, that swaggering, wobbling, yelling, walking-around-town, bottle-waving binge. Something about that was a great amusement to the men, coming so soon after Addison had made a hero of himself at the fights. "Hey, Add? Man, last time I saw you Saturday night you sure wasn't feelin' no pain!" And they'd shake their heads and laugh. Or they'd ask, "Hey, Addison? Did you have a good time Saturday night?" And he'd say, "I don't know. You're gonna have to tell *me*, because I was absent." Laughter, laughter.

But The Troop didn't take part in that. They were struggling with the feeling that Addison had betrayed them, and Sarah too. All those months of love talk and then this, finding him in Katherine's bed, naked. So he was drunk, and sick. Well, he ought not to have *been* drunk. He knew what liquor did to him. Hadn't he told them several times? It was a deep wound on them that he had done this thing, that would hurt Sarah so, if she knew. All right, she *didn't* know. But they did, and it was almost the same thing.

They kept expecting him to explain it all, to clap his big hands and say, "All right, Troop, front and center. Let's talk about the big drunk, OK?" Then he'd tell them, grinning and fist-pounding, sitting in his shorts on the footlocker,

how it sort of slipped up on him . . . that expensive sippin'
whiskey, that stuff's *sneaky*, Mildred . . . drunk before he
knew it, and roamin' around, kind of out of control . . . but
going to Katherine's that way, shoot fire, Troop, didn't anything happen there except he just got sick and . . .

But he didn't call them together to talk about it. Sunday
before noon when he woke up he stared miserably down at
his underwear on the floor and asked how the hell he got to
the base. They told him they'd found him in town and
brought him home in a taxi. He mumbled, "That's one I owe
you, Troop." And fell back and pulled the sheet over his
head.

For several days, most of what they learned came to them
in dribbles and bits, from offhand comments he'd make. Or
from what he would say to others, who didn't mind asking
him questions.

Sergeant Bagnoli, a casual acquaintance of Addison's,
came to the tent-shack and said, "I've been wanting to ask,
do you remember what you told me in town, Saturday night
when you were howling at the moon?"

"What'd I tell you?"

"You said a car tried to run you down on the street. Said
you had to climb the side of a damn building to keep from
getting hit. Remember telling me that? You were pretty well
sluiced."

The Troop watched his face. It went deep-thoughtful and
frowning. He told Bagnoli, shaking his head, "I don't know,
I'm not sure. That whole night is just sort of a haze."

# SIXTY-THREE

TO HAVE LOST the accurate record of an entire night of
his life was a source of deep concern to Addison. Keeping
track, knowing what was happening, that had always been
his strong suit. Now he felt that a part of himself was missing and he didn't know what it was. To have lost it on a
drunk—now that was just plain dumb-ass.

190

He had been dumb-ass before, but this time there was a gnawing inside him, an awareness that the missing what-ever-it-was could be of the gravest consequence. He lay awake nights, trying to retrieve it.

His duties now were so simple. Colonel Brookfield had asked for him, and he was stuck away in the back of the base hospital, doing in half a day what a couple of paper-shufflers hadn't been able to do in two. But there were things he liked about it. One was, three and four times a week he got to take a Jeep or the colonel's staff car and drive into Spanish Wells to meet the bus from San Antonio or El Paso. To hustle back with special-ordered medical supplies, or blood test results. Or to pick up a case of scotch at whole-sale from Deke Fowler. He didn't care about spending any time in town, because the great drunk had taken care of that. But he enjoyed the driving, being outside, being alone to think and look at the country.

He spent hours trying to reconstruct the big drunk. There were brief periods of the highest recall, when remarks and colors and shapes and sounds and odors were so clear. But long dark blanks in between. He made mental lists of what he remembered.

Calling Sarah. Drinking, so cautiously, with Grover in The Garden. Calling Sarah again, and getting his feelings hurt because she'd gone to a movie while he was missing her so bad. Talk about *dumb*-ass! Going back to the bottle in The Garden.

Being in town. Walking, looking down. Studying the pattern of cracks in the sidewalk. Seeing a pair of red shoes and nice ankles. Suddenly looking up. Sarah? No. Standing outside The Shacks. Seeing Mrs. Bates there. Telling her to go fuck herself. No, wait, wasn't that at The Puma? Jackson's broad face. Deke Fowler counting change out of a ten, saying "Watch out for the MP's." Isn't that out of sequence? Wasn't that earlier? Headlights, harsh and glaring. Roaring engine. Tires screaming. What in the cornbread hell was *that?* Meeting a short little guy in khaki, bobbing and weaving. "Come on, Add, get 'em up. Protect yourself or I'll murder you. Add? Whatcha been drinkin', Add?" Answering, "Chocolate malts, little friend." Laughter, laughter.

A street sign. Black letters on a white background. Mulberry. Some of the white flaked away. Walking, one foot in the gutter, one on the curb. Nausea. Stop, be sick. Heave. Hey, a goddamn *earth*quake! Sidewalk rising up to smite him. One of Nadine Compton's earthquakes. Cars passing. Headlights. Backfires. Backfires? Falling again. Shoulder hurts.

Then sitting on the curb across the street from the two-story apartment house, calling her. Calling loud, between being sick. "S-a-a-r-a-a-h! S-a-a-r-a-a-h!" Watching for the red shoes. Feet, at last. But not red shoes. Fuzzy pink bedroom slippers. And a voice. "Addison? My god but you're a mess. Phew! Can you walk?"

After that, nothing.

But he knew well enough whose feet were in the fuzzy pink slippers, and whose voice asked him if he could walk. So The Troop had found him at Katherine's, and that's why they had their daubers down so low. He needed to talk to them about it. But not just now. He had to think about what he was going to say, and how.

Maybe do it bullshit style, tell 'em, "Well, what the hell, Troop, I just got drunk and did something I wouldn't do sober. But I tell you what, you can hold my feet to the flames and you can't make me say for sure that I even touched that gal, because I don't know. I don't think I did. I damn sure don't *feel* like I've screwed anything lately . . ."

Do it like that, all jaunty and smart-ass? Or do it humble and tail-tucked, asking forgiveness, sort of the way he'd have to say it to Sarah, if she knew about the great drunk: "You're just going to have to forgive me. I haven't got any excuses. I was drunk and . . ."

Oh Lord no, both ways sounded weak. So let it slide right now. See what happens. They'll come around, won't they?

And they did, sooner than he thought. Booker came around first.

# SIXTY-FOUR

WHEN ADDISON got the word that Major Burke wanted to see him, his spirit crashed. It meant, surely, that Burke had found out about Addison going to Katherine's again. He picked a time when Katherine was not at her desk. He hadn't seen her since the great drunk and didn't want to.

Burke was snowed in by stacks of The Bear's paperwork and he was blunt and brief. "We've located the father of your little buddy, Booker," the major said. "He's in Houston. Wants to drive out here and visit." Burke was looking at a letter. "But he's not sure Booker will want to see him, after so long. He wants Booker to call him collect, if he will. Why don't you work with them on this?"

He handed over a phone number and an address and that was all there was to the meeting. Not a word about Katherine. Big relief.

And a big surprise, to Booker, when he learned his father was in Houston. That evening Booker was restless. While Addison was writing his letter Booker went in and out of the tent-shack several times, slamming the door, clearing his throat, walking to the latrine and back, flopping on his bunk, rising back up.

"Add?" he said at last. "Would you go with me to make that call? Man, I just don't know what to say."

They walked up to The Garden. Booker said, "He wants to come and visit? To Spanish Wells?"

"He's probably seen a hundred little old half-ass Texas towns like Spanish Wells," Addison said. "Why don't you see if he'd like to come out here to the base? If he could come on Saturday or Sunday you could show him around, let him see where you sleep and eat and all. That's what parents want to see, generally."

So that's the way they did it. Booker's father came the next Saturday. This was quite an event. Booker wanted ev-

erybody in the tent-shack to stay with him, the entire afternoon. He was tense. Here was a guy who hadn't seen his father since he was four, and he needed support. They all got
up early and scrubbed and shaved and shined and brushed
and combed, and walked in a military manner to the front
gate to greet Booker's father.

It worked out so nice. Booker's father was a surprise to
Addison. He looked—well, tidy, almost fashionable. Stocky
but not paunchy. Strong straight back and heavy shoulders
and a round face with a fine bushy mustache in the middle
of it. And on his arm he had Genevieve, who was maybe
forty and smiled about something all the time and didn't
have a flat place anywhere on her. She consisted entirely of
soft circles and pleasant bulges, and practiced the habit of
fixing her eyes just below the belt buckle on every pair of
trousers that went by. Noticing this, Addison decided it
was probably the source of her smile.

He also noticed, studying the face of Booker's father, why
that dapper gent cultivated the bushy mustache. He used it
to camouflage the ugly, loose-hinged protruding lower jaw
that he had passed along to his son. It worked beautifully.

They had such a time. They went to the tent-shack, and
said funny things, and laughed at themselves. They visited
the motor pool, where Booker did his daily duty, the mess
hall, and The Garden, where they drank beer and reviewed
personal history and family information. Booker's mother
had moved to Scranton. His sister Frieda had two babies
now, and was married to a truck driver and living in Buffalo.
They ended up writing phone numbers and addresses on little slips of paper and making promises about Christmas. At
departure Genevieve put a kiss on Booker's cheek. It didn't
appear, on delivery, to be much of a kiss, but it must have
been because it had the curious effect of causing Booker's
face to flash in different colors, mostly red.

For so long after they left, Booker wasn't able to keep his
grin controlled. He grinned even when he said, "You know,
Add, until today I didn't know if my sister was alive or

not?" Then the grin spread when he said, "He looks pretty good, don't you think?" Meaning his father.

"What are you talking about, man?" Addison said. "That little gent looks sharp as knives. Book, you know if you grew a mustache, you'd look exactly like him, except about twenty-five years younger?"

"Bullshit," Booker said, his grin running wild now, entirely out of control.

"I'm telling you."

Booker rubbed the back of his hand across his mouth and said, "Well, I might try it. Just for the hell of it."


## SIXTY-FIVE

UNEVENTFUL DAYS NOW for The Troop and Addison. They stayed mainly on the base, even on weekends. Addison didn't care about going to town. Said his trips for Colonel Brookfield gave him all the town he wanted now.

He spent a lot of time over his writing kit, looking thoughtful, studying the little calendar card in his billfold. Looking at December. He had Dec. 15 circled. He had chosen that as the baby's birthday. He liked the look of it, when he wrote it. Dec. 15. December 15th. December the Fifteenth. Looked classy any way he put it down. Hell of a good birthday date.

A good bet, too, because Dec. 15 lacked only two or three days' being exactly nine calendar months from the night he and Sarah had made such delicious love in Chicago, while the moonlight flooded the bed. Sarah thought that was the time she got pregnant, that one particular lovemaking time, even though it was preceded by another time on that same day and followed by still another the next morning. But Addison, too, wanted it to be that time in the moonlight. Because it was one of their most extra-special times, maybe the best ever.

At night in Spanish Wells he grieved for that time.

Mourned it, as he would mourn the death of a person he loved. Because that beautiful hour in the moonlight would never again be. Other ones could be—better ones? was it possible?—but that exquisite love-time? Never again.

Sometimes that phrase—never again—pounded at his spirit, and waves of the deepest sadness washed over him. It was like a heartbeat—*never again, never again, never again.* When these spells of sorrow were on him he would sit up in his bunk and stare into the darkness. Sarah . . . Sarah . . .

November now. Too cold at sundown to sit outside and write the letters. They wrote in their bunks. The Troop rejoined him for the letter-writing soon after the visit of Booker's father.

Addison felt he had been on trial that day, at least by McKavett and Trinidad. They watched him so closely. And he had been a giant again during the visit of Booker's father. Doing everything right, helping, but letting it be Booker's day, staying in the background, not stealing it away. No matter what he had or hadn't done at Katherine's, he had not changed, and they needed him.

He was studying a book about childbirth and fatherhood and postnatal care. On cold nights when November's winds blustered off the foothills of the Rockies and popped the tent-shack canvas, he read or lectured to them. About contractions and cervixes. Dilations and vaginas. Placentas and uteruses. About umbilical cords and bellybands and bowel movements and breastfeeding. He would astonish them with frequent commentary on the subject matter:

"That Sarah girl wants to *nurse* this baby. I told her I might let the little fart have Tuesdays and Thursdays but even if she had Siamese twins they weren't gonna root me out of *my* place."

The study of the baby, of the private parts of women, of Sarah's pregnancy, sent them off at times on long and happy discussions and debates. Addison passed around the snapshots Sarah sent, showing her in maternity clothes, demonstrating week by week the growth of the great bulge in her middle. Booker didn't like to look at the pictures. To see

Sarah's beautiful body distorted that way was distasteful to him.

"I don't see why it's got to be such a mess," he said.

"What's got to be such a mess?"

"The way babies are born. Why do they have to grow inside that way, and make the woman pooch out so bad, and cause all that pain and blood and everything? Why can't babies just come, without all that trouble?"

"Well, Book, you've got me there," Addison said. "You'd have to go up and talk to God about that."

"What you want 'em to do, Book," Trinidad asked, "squat and lay an egg?"

"That wouldn't be a bad idea," Booker decided. "Just break the shell, and there's your kid."

Discussions of that sort kept them occupied for entire evenings. They once invested a full hour trying to get McKavett to retreat from a position he held that he once went to school back in Georgia with a girl named Vagina.

McKavett was a dedicated student of the Sarah pictures. He could lie and look at one for so long, and find something new he hadn't seen before. "Hey, Add, who takes all these pictures, anyhow?"

"Her mother and dad, mostly. And Phyllis Bradley sometimes."

McKavett felt the time was right. He went ahead and asked the question that had bothered him for months. "Well, when she sent that picture where she didn't have anything on—you know—on her top? Who took that?"

Addison laughed. "Who you think took it? I took it myself. That was the last shutter I clicked before I got sent down here."

During those long nights of thought and reading and conversation, so much of it about the baby, Addison dwelt on the matter of childbirth in ways that were new to him. What marvels these were. He would roll out of his bunk and pace the floor, waving his arms, trying to make them see the great wonder of it.

"I'm telling you, Troop, it's a flat miracle. These folks that run around looking for miracles all the time, they're not looking in the right places. Something will happen over in France, maybe, and the judges will meet and think about it, and they'll decide, well, now that was a miracle, it qualifies. Then something may happen in Mexico, say, and they'll study it and decide that's *not* a miracle. Like miracles were scarce. When miracles are popping out of women every day by the thousands. Isn't that a fact? Look, here's a little old wiggle-tail sperm, that you could stack a zillion of 'em on the head of a pin, and yonder he goes, swimming upstream, and he meets an egg coming down, an egg so little you can't even see it, and they hook up, and they do to each other whatever it is they do, and looka here, what happens—that egg grows, fast, man!, and makes a human damn *being,* and it comes out wigglin' and yellin' and wantin', and it can eat, and pretty soon walk, and think, and make things, and have fist fights, and do favors, and laugh, and cry, and grow six feet tall, and get this: nobody knows why, or how. Now if that's not a miracle, where you gonna look for one? I say it's a miracle or General Lee's alive in Virginia."

## SIXTY-SIX

HE WENT TO TOWN with them because they wanted to buy presents and didn't know what to get. The baby was due in less than a month. He had been cleared for leave early in December so he could go to be with Sarah when the baby came. The Troop wanted him to be carrying their presents for Sarah and the baby.

In town he didn't talk much, and seemed removed from them. After they bought the gifts The Troop wanted to go to Lupe's for Mexican food, to The Puma for a beer. It was Saturday, midafternoon. Jackson at The Puma kidded Addison about the great drunk, asked how long it took him to cure the hangover. Addison told him it wasn't cured yet. "I promise you one thing, Mildred," Addison said, and didn't even grin, "that was my last drunk." And about that, he was right.

He was ready to go back to the base before they were. He led them east, away from the bus station. "We can catch the bus at Fowler's corner," he said. For several blocks, between The Puma and Deke Fowler's liquor store, Addison walked slow, examined the sidewalks and the curbs and the windows and walls of the shabby low brick buildings along the street.

"What you lookin' for?" they asked.

"Aw, nothing, really, I was just checking something. That night I was drunk I know I went to Fowler's, and I figure I must have walked along here when I left. You remember what Bagnoli said in the tent? Said I told him a car tried to run me down? Well, I don't think that really happened, but somehow or other I keep thinking I did have some kind of a run-in with a car, right along in here. I don't see any tire marks or anything, though."

Since the great drunk Katherine's name was, by unspoken agreement, prohibited around Addison, but now here came Trinidad charging in with, "Old Katherine told us that night you said somebody took a shot at you."

He looked a long way off then, and rubbed his chin, and made a laugh sound that had no humor in it, and he said, "Well, hell, that just shows you, I was dreaming things up that night. I been going to too many of those horse operas and gangster shows with old Mac. Hey, here comes the bus."

## SIXTY-SEVEN

THE LAST THING he enjoyed with them was McKavett getting a letter from Flora Ward.

Trinidad did not get an answer from his sister Consuela,

and Booker had not heard from his mother after writing to her at the dim-lobby hotel on the ragged side of town, but McKavett got an answer from Flora Ward on the bank of the Altasillo in Georgia.

"Flora Ward," Trinidad laughed. "Sounds like a school-teacher. I had a schoolteacher once named Miz Ward. Is she a schoolteacher, Mac?"

"Naw, she ain't no schoolteacher. She's a pretty nice lady. She give me the first piece of tail I ever had."

"Oh horseshit," said Trinidad.

"Oh horseshit," said Booker.

"Well, read it yourself, you want to." He flipped the letter to Addison, as if the others couldn't read, as if nothing would be officially read around there if Addison didn't read it.

Flora Ward said in the letter that she did, indeed, re-member Melvin. She remembered the day she took him into her bedroom behind the filling station. ("Now, by god, *see there?*" McKavett interrupted in delicious triumph.) She remembered the day his father drowned in the river. She was glad to hear from Melvin. She had found Spanish Wells on the map and it did not look so far from San Antonio. Did he ever go there? She had an older sister in San Antonio who was crippled up with arthritis and didn't answer letters any longer. In San Antonio, would he check on her, Mrs. Bella Savage? Yours very truly, Flora Ward.

"Find out if she's got a good-looking daughter not but five feet tall, Mac," Trinidad said. "I might go to San Antonio with you."

"Aw, I ain't goin' to San Antonio to check on *nobody.*" But he was so pleased to get Flora's letter. Nobody had ever asked him to go check on a person that way. It seemed im-portant. He liked it.

That night he caught Addison alone and asked him how far it was to San Antonio.

"Farther than your friend thinks, I expect. Around three hundred miles. Make a pretty long bus ride. It's a great town, though. Be a good place to go for Christmas."

# SIXTY-EIGHT

A BEAUTIFUL DAY. One of those gleaming-jewel kinds of days that can come to the Trans-Pecos country of Texas in winter. Such days follow cold fronts that blow clouds out and raise skies and broaden horizons and purify air. And by midafternoon the temperature can climb up into the high seventies after a frosty night and the atmosphere is so dry and clean you can stand in the front yard of a ranch house and watch a windmill turning five miles away. That's the kind of day it was when they found him in the Jeep at the side of the road. Almost exactly halfway between the base and Spanish Wells.

He had gone into town to meet the bus for Colonel Brookfield. He had made the trip four consecutive days, at about the same time in the afternoon. Except this trip he took the Jeep instead of the staff car. The choice was his, and he wanted to be in the open vehicle, to breathe in the clean crisp air and feel the warmth of the winter sun.

When he got the radio report, Major Burke went directly to the scene. Two young state highway patrolmen and a deputy sheriff were there, pacing around the Jeep. They said so many things to the major, and some of them registered. "Sure, deer season's on, and the weapon was damn sure a high-powered rifle, judging from the damage . . . Look, this wasn't any accident. This wasn't any stray bullet from any deer gun . . . An ambush, looks to me like. These salt cedars along here are the only heavy cover between the base and town . . . I think he was flagged down and already stopped before the shot was fired. Look how nice that Jeep's parked by the side of the road that way . . ."

The ambulance came and took him away. Major Burke said to the officers, "Let's go to the base and see the C.O. . . . We have a couple of names we could give you, I think."

And that's how it ended for Addison. In a Jeep, eight miles south of Spanish Wells. On such a beautiful day.

# SIXTY-NINE

TRINIDAD was digging another hole, for a young tree to be planted in The Bear's Beautification Program. Booker was changing the oil in a GI truck at the motor pool. McKavett was pushing a broom in the projection room of the base theater. Major Burke sent for them.

They went in the headquarters building all together, in their dirty fatigues, and stood outside the major's office near Katherine's desk and waited to be called in. Katherine was at the desk but she didn't speak and tried not to look at them directly. Her face was so stiff and white.

Even Major Burke didn't face them. When they stood before him with their faces so solemn he left his desk and turned his back and walked to a window. He looked out at the close-clipped grass turned yellow-tan by frost, and he told them. He told them all he knew about where and when and how it happened. He told them what was being done about it, said it would be taken care of, the proper way, that it was important that they not try to do anything about it themselves. He said that this sort of trouble, with those Bates people, had a way of building, and building, and one day erupting into a tragedy, and he wished he could say why it had to be that way. Major Burke said he couldn't tell them why.

When he didn't talk any longer and stayed turned to the window they went out, without asking a question, without making a sound.

They walked to the tent-shack. A lieutenant they didn't know was there with two men who were gathering up Addison's things. His uniforms. His sheets and blankets. They carried out his footlocker that held his socks and underwear and his writing kit with the cardboard flap and the brown lace to tie it down. They folded the head of his mattress down to the foot of his bunk. And so, in those few minutes, everything of his in that place was taken away.

At sundown, at letter-writing time, they went out and sat in the gray dirt and the cold, and cried.

For the next two days they didn't report for duty, but they were not sent for. They wandered. They didn't want to stay in the tent-shack with his mattress folded down on his bunk. They moved about in that curious close formation, in quick short little nervous steps. And not very military, with heads down and hands shoved in pockets. They circulated on the base to places he had so often led them. To the gym, the theater, The Garden, where they would sit apart, letting nothing show on their faces. They went to town, and walked by Deke Fowler's, Lupe's, The Puma, The Shacks, where he made them the speech that night. They even walked along Mulberry Street, past the first two-story house on the right.

Back at the base they stood at the flight line, outside the chain link fence, and watched his casket slide out of the hearse from Spanish Wells. Watched it carried across the ramp to the airplane. Watched Major Burke walk along beside the big, big man who would ride with the casket to wherever it would go. To Sarah? To Pandoval? They didn't know. Didn't ask. Weren't told.

"He walks just like Addison," McKavett said about the big man climbing on the airplane. It was the same great airplane Captain Charley Biggs once flew to Chicago with Addison in the back, on his way to make Sarah pregnant.

"It's his dad, all right. It's got to be."

They watched the airplane take off and shrink to a speck in the north. A basketball game was going on nearby, on an asphalt court, one of The Bear's Outdoor Recreational Facilities. The Troop stayed a while. The men on the court were laughing, yelling, trading loud good-natured insults, having great fun. They were the same men who not so long ago crowded so close around him in the gym and chanted his name. "Addison! Addison!" Now they laughed and played, while he grew smaller and smaller inside the speck of the airplane.

# SEVENTY

SO THAT WAS ABOUT IT.

They did hear from Sarah, in January, almost six weeks after he was buried. She wanted them to know how much she regretted that arrangements had not been made for them to attend the services. She was especially sorry that they hadn't met Addison's father when he came to Spanish Wells for the body. But she was sure they understood that at the time everyone was so consumed by shock and grief, many things that should have been done were not done. Then, in her own case, there was the baby that came along just afterward. It was born on December 15, and it was a girl. She had received the nice gifts from them, and that was so thoughtful. She wrote that she knew how fond Addison was of them, and she wanted to thank them for being his friends, for helping him through that long and difficult year at Spanish Wells. She asked them to continue writing. She said they should keep in touch, always.

But they weren't able to write her. Now, without Addison, it was like writing to a stranger, not Sarah at all. So they didn't answer. She did not write again.

They read her last letter many times. For so long afterward the phrase that would stick in their minds was, "that long and difficult year." Because to them it had been so short, and so good.

In February a clerk sat down at a typewriter in the headquarters building and cut a set of orders that began the breakup of The Troop. Trinidad first. McKavett a month later. Booker soon after. Trinidad was shipped to California. McKavett to Virginia. Booker to Germany.

# BOOKER

"HEY, MAN, you're not bad at all with those gloves. Guy like you, so short and all, you're tough to hit, too, way you move around."

"Well, I took a few lessons one time."

"Really? That seems strange, for some reason. You just don't look like the kind who'd go in for boxing lessons."

"I didn't take them so I could go around picking fights, if that's what you mean."

"Why did you?"

"To learn how to defend myself. That's the main reason for learning how to fight. Then, well, the time can come when a guy just has to fight, because he's a man, and has to live with himself. But there's a responsibility to knowing how to fight, especially if you can hit hard. People get hurt fighting, and it can lead to bad things. You go to getting mad, or drunk, and hitting on people, bad things can happen."

"Where'd you take lessons?"

"From a guy I knew in the Army. A hell of a fighter. Hell of a man."

"That right? What was his name?"

"Addison."

# McKAVETT

"ALL RIGHT, TROOP, now listen here, you guys are just not keepin' clean. Half of you in the bunch is smellin' like ten feet downwind of a billy goat. We're gonna be stuck here in close quarters this way, all of us together, for a long time. Six more weeks, at least, before they ship you out. Well, I want you ever one to start scrubbin' your tails and washin' under your arms, and quit gassin' up the barracks. Check yourself ever day to see if you smell bad. You know what my old mama used to tell me? She'd say, 'Melvin, if you can smell yourself, it means you been stinkin' already for three days.' Listen, before long they're gonna let you out into town on Saturday nights where you can chase girls. Well, if you want to catch one, the best thing you can be is *clean*, I guarantee you General Lee! . . ."

# TRINIDAD

"HAVE YOU EVER BEEN IN TEXAS?"

"Yes, I spent almost a year at Spanish Wells, in the Army."

"Where in hell is Spanish Wells?"

"About halfway between San Antonio and El Paso, in that rough country."

"In the desert."

"Well, some people call it desert."

"There's a military installation there?"

"Used to be. Seventeen miles out in the boondocks from Spanish Wells. We lived in tent-shacks. At least that's what we called them. A canvas tent, fitted over the screened-in frame of a small shack, big enough to house four men. The frame was set on a concrete slab, and walled up with boards about two and a half feet high, where it met the canvas. I expect if you went there now you'd just find rows and rows of those little concrete slabs."

"Pretty tough, huh?"

"Well, the men bitched, of course. Too hot in summer, too cold in winter. The Army would leave a man there only about a year, then ship him on out. Figuring he'd served his sentence, I guess."

"You were glad to get out of there, then."

"The fact is, I wouldn't trade what I learned in eleven months at Spanish Wells for one of those degrees of yours. I was educated there."

"By the Army, in Texas?"

"No, by a man. A man I lived with in a tent-shack."

"Who was he?"

"His name was Addison."